SHADOW ON HER GRAVE

BOOKS BY B.R. SPANGLER

Detective Casey White Series

Where Lost Girls Go

The Innocent Girls

Saltwater Graves

The Crying House

The Memory Bones

The Lighthouse Girls

Taken Before Dawn

Their Resting Place

Two Little Souls

Our Sister's Grave

Her Last Hour

Gone in the Storm

Dark skies Apocalypse

When the Sky Falls

When the Dawn Breaks

B.R. SPANGLER

SHADOW ON HER GRAVE

bookouture

Published by Bookouture in 2025

An imprint of Storyfire Ltd.
Carmelite House
50 Victoria Embankment
London EC4Y 0DZ

www.bookouture.com

The authorised representative in the EEA is Hachette Ireland
8 Castlecourt Centre
Dublin 15 D15 XTP3
Ireland
(email: info@hbgi.ie)

ISBN: 978-1-83618-514-7
eBook ISBN: 978-1-83618-513-0

ONE

A drop of seawater struck her lips, cold and sharp. Violet Jones blinked her eyes open with a start, her heart fluttering like a trapped bird. Moonlight shimmered above her; a silver thread against a black sky. It felt distant, as though mocking her with its delicate beauty. The ground beneath her was gritty and wet, the dampness seeping into her bones. The air was cool and biting and clung to her skin like the touch of a corpse. It was too cold for summer, and this wasn't autumn either.

Where am I? Violet blinked again, her mind sluggish while trying to catch up with reality as though waking from a bad dream. *Spring. It was springtime.* The thought urged her awake, the thoughts brighter now. The leaves had unfurled, and the flowers were blooming. Wasn't it just yesterday, she had knelt in her garden, coaxing the vegetables to life with tender care? *I'm not supposed to be here.*

Her eyelids snapped wide as she registered her surroundings—a graying shoreline, the beach stretching endlessly beneath the night's sky. The stars above glinted like eyes, watching her predicament. The scent of salt and brine mingled with something darker, something metallic and sour rising in the back of her throat. She wasn't in the market's parking lot anymore. But... when had that changed? Her last memory was of dusk, of standing beside her car as the sky turned pink and lavender, the sun dipping below the horizon. *How did I get to the beach?*

Wet sand and broken seashells scraped across her arms and legs, her clothes sticking to her like a second skin. Her head grated against the sand, hair tangling with bits of seaweed. She grunted, the sound muffled by the roar of crashing waves. Someone was pulling her, dragging her across the shore. The thought pierced through her mind like a blade.

"I'm not alone?" Her thoughts screamed the words, but her voice barely made it past her cracked lips. Panic surged through her, sharp and electric. *I can't move!*

Another tug, harder this time, legs lifted as if she were nothing more than a sack of grain. Her body flopped forward, her ankles held like the handles of a wheelbarrow. She could feel the sand digging into her back, her skin burning from the salty friction.

"Oh goody! Look who woke up." The voice was soft, low, a purr of satisfaction that sent a jolt of terror racing down Violet's spine. Her left leg was dropped, landing with a wet, sloshing thud into the sand. The right leg followed with a splash into icy water lapping the shore.

"Who—" Violet grunted.

"I guess it wore off," the voice continued, a hint of disappointment coloring the words.

Violet tried to move, tried to push herself away, but her limbs were heavy, unresponsive. A wave of nausea rolled through her. Drugged. The realization struck her like a hammer, the taste in her mouth and the dull throb in her head now making sense.

"Help me," she croaked, but the words came out broken, her

throat raw. Her lungs burned with every shallow breath she managed to take.

A figure appeared above her, silhouetted by the pale moonlight. The face was hidden, just a shadow against the night, but the eyes... they were watching her, a soft gray light gleaming with something dark and predatory. The figure crouched beside her, and for the first time, she felt the cool sting of a needle pressing into her neck. The bite of the drug was instant, a liquid fire injected straight into her veins. It was hot and sharp and turned her stomach inside out.

"I was afraid I'd used too much before," the figure murmured, almost thoughtfully. "But this time, I want you awake."

"What... what do you want?" Violet's voice trembled, her heart racing painfully in her chest. She could barely manage to lift her head, her body refusing to cooperate.

"Silly girl. You don't know?" The figure leaned closer, and Violet caught a glimpse of lips curving into a smile, cold and humorless. "I want you dead."

The words echoed in Violet's ears, each one landing with the weight of a stone. Dead. A scream boiled deep down and rose through her like a geyser. She tried to scream but her jaw stayed locked, the sound trapped in her throat. Her chest heaved as she struggled to breathe, the world tilting sideways beneath her.

"Aww," the voice cooed mockingly. "Don't worry. I used just enough. It'll be better this way."

Fear shot through her like an explosion, a wild, uncontrollable terror that consumed every inch of her being. She tried to move her arms, tried to claw at her throat, but nothing happened. Her body was a prison, each muscle locked in place, betraying her in the most vital moment of her life. She could feel the drug seeping deeper into her veins, numbing her from the outside in.

The figure stood, moving like a predator before taking hold of her feet again. She needed to wince at the vice-like power but couldn't. Violet's heart pounded in her ears, the roar of the ocean growing louder with each step, each second. The dark, crashing waves beckoned, licking hungrily at the shore as if she were a sacrifice. She could see the moon's light tipping the edge of the sea now, the dark abyss waiting for her.

I'm going to drown, she realized, the thought wild and frantic. The sea was a looming monster, rising higher and higher with every tug, every pull that dragged her closer to its frothy mouth.

Another wave crashed over her, the cold water rushing across her body, soaking her hair and face. Goosebumps sprouted and her skin tightened with the cold. Her veins turned to ice with a bitter realization of what was going to happen. The thought striking her like a lightning bolt. She was going to die here.

Violet's fingers twitched then, just barely. It was a faint, almost imperceptible movement, but it was enough to ignite a small spark of hope. She flexed her hand again, this time feeling the grains of sand slipping between her fingers. It wasn't much, but it was something. What started with her pinky finger, continued with her index, each moving slowly, painfully, but regaining some feeling.

The figure continued to drag her, oblivious to the slight movements she managed. Another wave struck her, nearly tumbling her captor off balance. There was a sharp laugh, dark and twisted, as her killer steadied themselves, and for a brief second, Violet felt her body roll, her face pressing into the wet sand. Grit filled her mouth, her nose, choking her.

The next wave rolled over her back, the sting of saltwater biting into the scrapes and cuts she hadn't realized were there. Her ears filled with the rush of the ocean, the bubbles rising around her like whispered promises of death. But then, she felt it—her captor's hands were gone.

Violet felt herself floating, drifting away, the gentle pull of the retreating tide carrying her. For a fleeting moment, she wondered if this was it—if the sea had finally claimed her, if she was slipping into its cold embrace for the last time. Her body stopped abruptly then, her ankle leashed by the metal chain, the touch a fierce reminder of her situation.

No. Not yet. I can fight.

She tried to turn herself over, muscles straining against the numbness, but her body was nearly motionless, her movements slow and disjointed.

I need air.

The urge to breathe was suddenly overwhelming, her lungs burning with the desperate need for oxygen. But her face was pressed into the sand, the wet grit blocking her mouth and nose. She couldn't move her head, couldn't lift herself. The panic surged again, hotter this time. She needed to breathe, but there was no air, only water.

Her feet hit the ocean floor, the soft sand beneath her heels. For a moment, she thought about standing, that she could rise and fight back. But then her killer's hands returned with a biting grip that was fierce and unrelenting.

"Now is good," the voice murmured, cold and final. "This is the spot!"

Without warning, Violet was shoved beneath the water again. The moon's sliver disappeared, replaced by the endless black of the ocean and sting of saltwater in her eyes. The pressure was immediate, crushing. Her chest heaved, the need to breathe stronger than ever. She could feel her heart racing, each beat harder than the last, pounding in her ears.

Tom's face appeared before her, his green eyes soft, his blond hair tousled the way it had been the first time they'd met. He was just as she remembered him from that day in the park, floppy hair caught in a breeze, his eyes locked on hers with that playful grin. But now, his expression was grave, shadowed, as if knowing what was to come—what had already come.

Violet wanted to scream, but the icy water filled her throat, silencing her as it poured into her lungs. She gagged, her insides convulsing, every cell screaming for air. But there was no sound. Only the cold. Only the sea. Her vision blurred, the edges of her world fraying, becoming more like a terrifying dream. A nightmare.

Tom, she thought desperately. *Help me, Tom.*

But he was dead. Tom was only a memory she'd brought to life in her dying mind. He couldn't help her now. The last time she had seen him, he had been lying in a hospital bed, frail and thin, his once-strong body consumed by sickness. His skin had been pale, almost translucent, the life already draining from him even before his heart stopped. She'd tried to close his mouth after he passed, but it had been locked open, his face frozen in a grimace. A nurse had told her that sometimes happened, that there was nothing they could do.

That was the last time she had touched him. The last time she had felt the warmth of his skin, the warmth that was now gone forever.

But here he was, in her mind, his image flickering in and out of the blackness. He seemed closer now, his hand outstretched, reaching for her. His lips moved, but she couldn't hear his voice. It was drowned out by the ocean, by the relentless muffled roars of the waves above, each pulling her under.

I can't hold on, she thought, her chest aching as the water continued to fill her lungs. *I can't...*

"Violet," Tom whispered, his voice cutting through the water, so soft she almost didn't hear it. "I'm here."

She blinked, her eyes stinging from the salt, her vision warping as the current dragged her in every direction at once. Was she still fighting? Was her body still thrashing, trying to escape? She couldn't tell anymore. The world was becoming distant, her limbs floating uselessly in the dark water, the cold numbness spreading to every part of her.

"I'm here for you," Tom said again, his voice stronger now, clearer. He was close, just inches from her, his green eyes searching her face, his hand still reaching out.

"I know you're not real," Violet tried to say, her lips moving without sound. "You're in my head."

But it didn't matter. His presence, real or imagined, was enough. Enough to calm the storms inside her, even as her killer's storm raged around her. The pressure in her chest eased, the fire in her lungs fading to a dull ache. The need to breathe was still there, but it was becoming quieter, less urgent, as if her body had finally given up the fight.

Tom smiled gently, his fingers brushing her cheek. "You can let go now," he said softly, his voice filled with love. "I'm waiting for you."

She wanted to hold on. She wanted to fight. But there was nothing left. No strength, no will, no air. Only the darkness. Only Tom.

Violet's insides convulsed once, twice, and then went still. Her mouth opened wide, the last of her air bubbling to the surface, rising toward the distant moonlight. She felt the water rush in, filling her completely, as if the sea was claiming her at last. Her captor's laughter echoed in the distance, growing faint as her senses dulled. She was sinking, sinking into the depths, the weight of the water pressing down on her.

But Tom was there, his hand still holding hers, his face serene and peaceful. "I'm always here for you," he whispered.

"I'm afraid," she admitted, though her voice was only in her mind now. The words didn't matter, nothing mattered. She was too far gone.

Tom's hand tightened around hers, a comforting warmth

that seemed to cut through the cold. "I know," he said softly. "But you don't have to be."

The pain was fading. The struggle was over. Violet's body floated gently beneath the surface, her limbs limp, her mind quiet. The world around her was dark, but it was a peaceful darkness. The waves no longer seemed menacing; they were cradling her like a quiet lullaby in the middle of the night.

"I love you, Tom," she whispered in the silence of her mind.

"I love you too," his voice echoed, soft and distant, but still there, still with her.

And then, there was nothing. Only the ocean, vast and endless, swallowing her whole.

The night sky above was serene, the crescent moon remerged, hanging low as the waves lapped lazily at the shore. The wind whispered through the dunes, carrying the scent of salt and seaweed. And somewhere, in the depths of the dark waters, Violet Jones drifted, lost to the sea's eternal embrace.

TWO

Is this the last dead body I'll ever see? That is, through the eyes of a detective. The ocean and breeze were masking the odor, but I knew it might be there and applied the salve diligently knowing the smell was apt to strike while we processed the remains. The crime scene was a short distance from the path over the tops of the beach's sand dunes, the shallow hill made up of soil and sand with beach grass and sea oats to anchor them. When we reached the dune's apex, the crime scene came into view, early light casting long shadows that were a stark contrast to the bright sands.

In my career, I'd never considered an end. It was here now. It was close. My name is Detective Casey White and in a few weeks' time, the residents of the Outer Banks in North Carolina will only know me as Casey. I stopped at the edge of the sands, a thin strip of crime-scene tape twisting and flapping haphazardly as a wind picked up. Inside the crime scene, the body of a young woman lay face down, a chain attached to one of her legs.

"This has to be the last one," I mumbled and slipped on a pair of latex gloves.

"What's that?" Emanuel Wilson asked, grunting when he

ducked beneath the tape. He blocked most of the sun, standing, his broad shoulders and height casting a long shadow over me to turn the day cold. "Casey?"

I stepped aside to return to the sun's heat, the early spring weather leaving our mornings cold. "Are you ready to be lead detective?" I'd asked that question before when Emanuel was first considered as my replacement. A former basketball star, he'd retired from the sport and worked in law enforcement, becoming a detective on my team before landing his own lead role in Elizabeth City. He dipped his face, the corner of his mouth curling. I glanced at the body, and returned, insisting, "Well? Are you?"

"I wouldn't have taken the job if I wasn't ready." He splayed his fingers and sleeved a glove into place, adding, "Are you having second thoughts about retiring?"

I made like I was nodding, his eyes bulging at the gesture, and then sternly enforced it with a "None at all."

"That's good for the both of us." He trudged forward, an investigation kit in hand. "I think the missus and kids would have a word about another move."

"You're not going anywhere," I assured him, stopping to scan the beach. A machine echoed in the distance, the sun's glare blocking what it was. "Sand cleaner?"

"Probably," Emanuel answered. "They'd called it in—"

I stopped dead, overcome by the eerie sensation of our having been here before. Not just here on the beach. My old apartment was on the beach and our evening walks took us by here often. But there was more to it. It was the crime scene, the feel of it fleeting and unsettling. It was as if we'd stepped into a scene that already took place or maybe I'd dreamed of it. I snapped my fingers, searching for the name of the feeling, Emanuel's face filling with a curiosity. "What's that word when you swear, you'd been there before... I mean, you felt it like you'd lived through it already?"

A slow shake, his eyes searching mine. A gull cried out as it dipped, its shadow racing over his face. A moment later, his brow rose, and he asked, "Do you mean déjà vu?"

"That's it!" I shouted into the wind, clapping his arm, impressed he'd picked up on what I was asking. "You felt it too?"

"Uh-uh. I mean, the memory of the cases kinda get jumbled—"

"No, it's not that..." My voice trailed as the sand-cleaner machine chomped and churned, its rust heap rumbling away from us. "Ruby Evans! Remember?"

"The girl who had her legs amputated?" Emanuel asked. He shook his head, looking around us like we were being watched, "I wasn't here for that case."

"That's right, you were in Elizabeth City by then."

"Is there a similarity?" he asked, urging us toward the body where the medical examiner and her assistant were already busy working.

"Yeah, there is," I answered, bothered by the endless *clop-whoosh, clop-whoosh* the sand-cleaning machine clanged. I pointed to a lifeguard stand and the nearby entrance, the steps leading over the tall dunes put in place to protect the homes close by. "This crime scene, it's in the same location. And that sand cleaner, the person who'd found Ruby Evans was driving one."

"I'm sure it's a coincidence," Emanuel said, dismissing it with a wave, a blade of sunshine striking us from between the clouds. Squinting, his attention shifted to the body and Samantha Watson, our medical examiner who knelt. "But, since I'm taking the lead on the investigation, what else happened with the Ruby Evans case?"

"The lead?" I scoffed, leaning back, a flash of regret running through me like a cold shiver. I patted his arm and looked up into his face, assuring him, "It's your case, detective. I'm coming along for the transition."

"Casey, I'm hearing a lot of doubt in your voice." Emanuel stepped around until his tall figure cast a shadow over me. A rim of sunshine edged his frame like a halo, making me squint. "A moment ago, you asked if I was ready to be the lead detective. No second thoughts about retiring. That's what you said. Are you sure you're ready to let the job go?"

Since making the decision to retire, I hadn't been put on the spot quite like that. While I'm fairly young and could drive as the lead another twenty-five years if I wanted. His was a fair question. He was my replacement, and any detective will tell you, there's no room for a backseat driver.

I glanced past him to where Samantha and her assistant, Derek, worked the chain attached to the victim. I'd solved a lot of cases in my career and there was a life with my future husband and children waiting for me. There was a wedding too. Mine and my fiancé's, Jericho Flynn. He also happened to be the sheriff in this part of the Outer Banks. And as helpful as it was to be a detective and have the sheriff as your fiancé, we shared our fair helping of disagreements. That'd be behind us soon. Some of it replaced with dates with a coordinator, cake tasting, and even finding a wedding dress. This was my last case. I glanced at the victim, a familiar ache piercing my heart. I'd seen enough hurt to last a hundred lifetimes.

When I returned to Emanuel, I nodded sternly and answered, "Yeah, I'm ready."

"Good," he said, stepping aside, sunlight blasting hard enough to burn afterimages in my eyes. "Then let's get this one done."

"Let's," I agreed, shielding my eyes, loose sand kicking from the tips of our shoes until we reached the packed, wet sand. It was low tide, which had exposed the body. It wouldn't remain that way, however. "We probably only have a couple hours."

"Three, maybe," Derek said, standing to greet us. Sweat ran down the side of his round face as he swept at his stringy hair. "We started already."

"Okay, let's see what we've got," I said, raising my voice over the crashing waves. I eyed the racing foam, saw it crest and recede, a dozen sanderlings and plovers chasing air bubbles in the sand. When I reached the chain, I stopped and turned around. The victim was shy of being middle-aged, Caucasian with a slender build and an average height. Her body was face down in the sand, the clothing thin in parts, tattered and torn, which may have been from the rough surf. She wore tan-colored leggings that were short, inching below the knees like a pair of capris. Her shirt was oversized and black, large enough to have been worn at night to bed.

She had auburn-colored hair that was littered with sand. Every strand was accompanied by the yellow-white grains like she'd washed her hair in the stirring surf. In a way, that's what happened. Every part of her would be covered in beach sand, the task of removing it daunting. Her face was too far into the sand to see anything other than her ears, some gold stud earrings glinting in the rising daylight.

Her left leg was a ruin. It was shattered in more than one place below the knee, the ankle twisted in a way no joint should bend. It didn't take long to spot the cause: a length of chain coiled just above her foot, its leather buckle still cinched tight. The victim had been anchored to the seabed like dead weight, the tide beating her body again and again. Those waves didn't whisper gentle touches like a calm swell though. Instead, they struck like fists, battering relentlessly. Bone doesn't break easy, but out here, under the surf's hammer, they snapped all the same.

I knelt and took hold of the chain, the cold bleeding through my latex gloves instantly.

"We waited," Derek said, answering before I could ask the

question. He half shrugged, adding, "I wanted to pull it up though."

"How far?" I asked, the links going slack briefly when racing water reached the victim.

Derek shook his head. "One of us will have to retrieve it... whatever *it* is."

The team's focus shifted to Derek, his face in a grimace, as if suddenly blinded by the attention.

"You are the tallest," Samantha said, standing and reaching up to pat his arm. She wasn't more than five feet tall, her assistant towering over her. He nodded glumly, accepting his task. Samantha motioned to the body, "Let's turn her over."

"Sunk in there kinda deep," Derek exclaimed, driving his fingertips beneath one shoulder. The body was dug-in, wet sand accumulating around her in layers. A sand crab climbed aboard the victim's broken leg and immediately scurried to the leather strap and broken skin. Derek yelled, "Get!" swiping the crab, sending it back into the ocean with a drippy plunk.

"If the sands weren't anchoring her body here, she might have been overlooked," I said, studying the chain and the tide. "It was the timing. That's why she was found this morning."

"Who called in the body?" Emanuel asked, his knees popping loudly when taking to one side. He coordinated the roll, each of us in position, counting down, "And three, two, one."

Air was sucked into the void with a squelching burp, the suction unexpected. For a moment, there was a perfectly preserved mirror image of the victim's face and chest, her arms and hands and fingers too. But like everything on the beach, the impression was fleeting, the time temporary. A wave crawled across the sands just far enough to fill the space. We eased the victim onto her back, Samantha guiding her head gently in a caring way. That was Samantha. It was one of the reasons we loved her for the person she was and the role of medical examiner she excelled in.

It wasn't the victim's face or hair that caught my attention first. It wasn't the broken leg or torn pants and bare feet that had turned the color of a storm either. It was the shirt. All black and extra-large by three or more times her small size. It was a classic concert T-shirt with a band I recognized because we had one of these in our home. It was Def Leppard's *Hysteria* world tour. My fiancé and the father of our two children was an avid collector. When a house fire had stolen most of the concert T-shirts, I'd replaced some, finding them online, surprising him one at a time whenever he seemed to need a helpful pickup. I couldn't break my stare. It was the same exact shirt I'd given him recently.

"Casey?" I heard Emanuel say, bumping my arm. "You okay?"

"Sure, yeah." But I wasn't. What were the odds of a concert T-shirt that I'd purchased in the last year showing up on a victim?

"You look like you've seen a ghost," he said, his face cramped, eyes narrowing. "Thinking of Ruby Evans again?"

"Uh-huh," I said, lying. "Let's get pictures of her face and hair."

"Like that?" he asked, clumsily circling, stepping on Derek's foot while the shutter beat the air rapidly. He glanced at the back of the camera to view his work, the pixels all black. "Wait—"

"Lens cap," I hinted, speaking just loud enough to be heard. His face turned red, and he uncovered the lens, continuing where he left off. "Make sure to get some of the chain and the victim's leg."

"Casey?" Samantha said, a question in her voice. She puffed hair away from her eyes, her normally short crop of black hair longer these days. Against the sand, her ivory-colored skin blended, her pale blue eyes standing out. "There's injuries consistent with a puncture."

I joined to see, inviting the officer to take pictures. When he was done, I flashed my light on the area, a bruised area raised and discolored. There were multiple punctures, three that we could see. "Drugged?"

Samantha sighed and sat back onto her heels, her body seeming to shrink. I sensed how the finding troubled her. She'd been accosted once, drugged and held captive. The Samantha I knew before that happened was a different person to the Samantha we knew now. It wasn't for better or worse. She was just different. Samantha nodded and shook herself like she was freeing the chill of a ghost. "A toxicology report will confirm."

"A couple walking a dog," I overheard Derek saying to Emanuel, the back and forth covering the logistics of the morning and the discovery of the victim.

I placed a hand on Samantha's arm, turning enough to keep the contact between us. I dipped my face, looking into her eyes which had grown big and wet. "Are you okay?"

Her mouth turned down, she answered fast, "Sure sure. I'm good." Her gaze lifted to look over my shoulder. "We should hurry this up."

The tide was coming in, seawater chasing foam across the victim's legs, the sight hitting me with another memory, a stronger sense of déjà vu. Samantha must have noticed, pinching my arm, reciprocating the concern.

"This feels a lot like the Ruby Evans murder."

Her brow rose with understanding, and she looked around as if we were being watched. Her gaze landed on the sand-cleaning machine which was closer now. She cringed when its endless *clop-whoosh, clop-whoosh* reached us. "I could have gone all day without thinking of that case."

"It's eerie, right?"

"We've had other cases on the beach," she reminded me

with hopeful persuasion. When I didn't say anything, she continued, "But yeah, you're right."

"Let's get the victim back to the morgue as soon as we can —" I began to say.

"What's the case?" Tracy Fields appeared from behind Emanuel, her tall figure shaded, but her voice unmistakable. I'd recognize its sound anywhere. Sunlight glinted sharply from the badge on her hip when she turned and approached the body. She walked with a steady pace, a mist curling around her as the waves thundered behind. She slipped on a pair of gloves, circling to find a place to start. The sands were softened by the tide, each step leaving a shimmering footprint. Her eyes traced the outline of the body where the ocean foam shyly crept closer. As though still a part of my team, Tracy lifted a camera, its lens catching a reflection of the crime while the shutter announced her attendance.

"The district attorney's office is a little early?" I asked, my insides tightening. All activity around the body stopped. There was tension but that hadn't been my purpose. I cringed inside, my reaction to her arriving a clumsy one. This was her first case in her new role as an investigator, an extension of the district attorney's office. "I mean, we usually don't hear from the DA until after the autopsy."

"I know," she replied, face remaining tucked behind the lens. Tracy wasn't bothered by my initial words. She worked her way toward the chain, focusing on the broken leg. "I heard the call for the medical examiner and spoke with the dispatcher."

I forced a smile, saying, "You just can't stay away from it."

She lowered the camera, a grin appearing. "I guess the apple didn't fall far from the tree."

"Well, I don't care where or who you're working for now," Emanuel said abruptly with a stony frown. He opened his arms wide, a smile breaking, "Come over here. I need to congratulate you!"

"I hear that congratulations are in order for you too," Tracy replied happily, her voice muffled as she disappeared in the embrace.

"Seems just yesterday when we were all working together and you were only getting started."

"That's got to be more than a dozen cases ago," I said, the wonderment of years breaking in my voice. "Time flies."

"I talked to the DA about a more hands-on approach, working earlier in the case. She agreed, we'll all be working a lot together," Tracy said, carefully making her way to Samantha. They said nothing as they hugged, the two close friends outside of work. When she faced the body, she asked, "Want to catch me up?"

"Sure. The victim is early to mid-thirties," Samantha began. She returned to the neck area and pointed out the bruising. "There are a few puncture wounds consistent with a needle."

"Drugged?" Tracy asked, a flash brightening the wound. "Any other injuries?"

"It doesn't appear that she fought her attacker," I said, looking at the victim's fingernails and hands and forearms again. "There are no defensive wounds."

"Toxicology report will tell us more," Tracy commented, taking pictures of the chain. She glanced at Derek who rolled his eyes.

"Why does everyone just assume it'll be me retrieving it," he scoffed sorely. He gauged the waves up and down the coast, his hair swept in each direction as he turned. "I guess now is as good a time as any."

"Let's remove the restraint," I said, knees plunking into the wet sand. The leather around the buckle had swelled from the saltwater, the victim's flesh swollen and making it tight. When the strap wouldn't loosen, Tracy gave it a tug, the familiar smell of her hair tickling my nose. It was good to have her here. It was even better to know she'd be close and working with Emanuel and the team. *The apple didn't fall far*, I heard her say. Tracy was much more to me than just a crime-scene investigator. She was my daughter and her moving to work in the DA's office had put a small rift between us. One that I was hoping to smooth over. "Can you get your fingers in there?"

"Uh-uh." She sat back, lips pressed, and mouth curled, a dimple appearing on her left cheek, sunlight shining from her baby-blue eyes. "I think we're going to have to cut it."

"I've got it," Samantha said, a pair of medical scissors in hand that looked like garden shears. "We have to free it before Derek starts to lift whatever the chain is anchored to."

"Why would that matter?" Tracy asked, a spray from Derek's legs striking. The water ran faster and moved the victim's leg awkwardly, bending it freely. Tracy's eyelids widened, "Oh, her leg could—"

"It's already torn up really bad," Samatha answered. "We don't want any additional damage."

"Got it!" Derek yelled, having waded deeper, following the chain. His arms were submerged shoulder deep, his body hunched over. "It feels like a pair of cinderblocks."

"Hold up!" Samantha yelled back, spitting seawater from her mouth. She slipped the flat edge of the blade against the victim's leg and squeezed with a grunt. The edge of the leather began to cut free. "This is a very hard material."

"That's good. It means it's not cheap," I said. She paused, confusion appearing on her and Tracy's faces. "If it's expensive then it should be easier to find."

"Right, it'll narrow the number of stores to search," Tracy commented, taking a half dozen pictures. The officer working our team's camera mirrored Tracy's moves. She looked over her shoulder, telling him, "Get some from the other side. At your angle, the sunlight will flare across the lens."

A look of astonishment appeared, his answering, "So that's why it looks like that. Cool."

When Tracy looked at me, I muttered, "Still in training."

"Can I lift yet?" Derek yelled, his voice desperate. His clothes were soaked and clinging to show more of him than any of us ever expected to see. He shook, yelling, "The water is freezing."

"Go ahead!" Samantha hollered, the restraint coming free with a snap of the scissors. While the restraint was freed, the impression around the victim's leg remained. "Wow, look at that, you can see the letters imprinted on her skin from the inside of this thing."

"Do you think she was alive when it was put on?" A picture was forming in my head of what happened.

Samantha half nodded, uncertain.

"Assuming it was, the victim is drugged and then brought here. With no defensive wounds, she was unable to fight while her killer put the restraint on her leg. I suspect the chain was already in place, anchored. The killer timed this to the tide so the victim would drown when it was high."

"That's a terrible way to die," Samantha said.

"Whoever did this put some effort into it," Tracy said, jumping at a sudden crash. It was the cinderblocks, two of them, the other end of the chain threaded through the holes to bind them. She looked up at Derek who was shivering. "Heavy?"

He cocked his head. "Not bad. I'm going to the van. I have a change of clothes."

"I wonder if we can get an idea of where the cinderblocks and chain were purchased." I lifted the links, the gauge heavy. "This is galvanized. It could be the type for construction or a boat anchor."

"There's a Lowes and Home Depot nearby. A couple smaller shops too," Tracy offered.

"I wonder if she was targeted?" Samantha asked, her

expression soft with sadness. Samantha was the type who some-times cared more than she should in this line of work. Not that we were all callous, but there was a line and crossing it could be overwhelming. However, it was because of Samantha's partic-ular sense that she went the extra mile, her autopsy investiga-tions were beyond expert. "Who was she?"

"Her name is Violet Jones," Tracy said, surprising us. Heads turned to see her phone in hand. She held it up, but the sunlight's glare was too strong. "Her parents reported her missing late yesterday. It wasn't twenty-four hours yet, but the parents went to the station anyway."

"Alice would have seen them," I said, thinking of our station manager and the shift. A missing person report would have been on my desk and showed on my phone this morning too. But there'd been none. That meant we could narrow the hours to sometime in the last eighteen. Possibly less. "That gives us a timeline."

"Late last night would be my guess," Tracy said, announcing the time like it was a competition.

"I think you're right," I said, agreeing. "Violet Jones was abducted and drugged. She was brought here, the restraint put on her leg when the tide was low and rising."

"She drowned at high tide?" Samantha said, asking. "I may be able to confirm the time of death with a body temperature. If not, the victim's eyes should help narrow it down."

"You ready for transport?" Derek asked, returning in a change of clothes, baggy jogging pants and an oversized sweatshirt.

"We're ready."

THREE

The station where we worked was busier than expected for mid-morning. It wasn't reporters or bloggers, no cameras and microphones, the news of the victim still somewhat quiet. It was a remodel of sorts with workers in bright yellow reflective vests and heavy boots, clopping back and forth in a never-ending parade of activity. A blanket of haze clouded the air, dust lifting unhealthily when the walls and floors were gutted at the front.

Alice, our station manager, stood patiently nearby, a foot on one of the benches as if claiming it for historical purposes. It very well may have been as old as the station too, always there, used to seat the arrested who were awaiting processing. Separating the front, which was for the public, from our desks and conference room, we'd had a small gate. Old-fashioned with curvy wood slats and standing just tall enough to work well without getting in the way. It was gone, its history too, replaced with a sheet of heavy plastic that was fastened to the ceiling and hung like a curtain.

"Security policy," Alice began while digging a pencil out of her tall hair. The hairspray was thicker today, the smell itching my nose. A shorter woman with a round face, I suspected she might have been around when the gate was put in place. And from the sour expression, I was guessing she was not too happy with the decision to rip it out. Waving her arms wide, she stepped forward, explaining, "They're going to put a wall here with a heavy door. And you'll need one of those card thingies to get to your desk."

"New security," I said, glancing up and around, trying to imagine how different the station would look. "It's because of the shooting?" Less than a month ago, a man walked into a smaller police station carrying a revolver and rifle. Five people lost their lives that day. Our station was designed and built a long time before the fears of mass shootings were a part of our everyday. I motioned to Alice's receiving desk. "But you'll still be out here?"

"I'll be in that corner behind thick glass," she replied, returning to where her desk would normally be. Nodding her head, she continued, "It's kind of like that thick stuff the cashier sits behind at the twenty-four-hour Stop 'n Go."

"I guess more security is safer," I said, commenting as Emanuel joined me. "Still seems sad to lose so much history."

"Whoa," Emanuel said, waving, dust shimmering in a blade of sunlight. "They really tore into this place."

"Like it was a rotten tooth or something," Alice said with a snorting laugh. We smiled and laughed along politely as she handed out paper masks. "For when you're on this side of the plastic."

"Thank you," Emanuel said, a cough slipping while he quick snapped the elastic behind his ears. "They're not changing the office or anything?"

"Wow, look at this place," Tracy said, following behind. "What did I miss?"

"Just a small remodel for security," I replied, repeating what Alice said. I didn't wait for more and went through the plastic, the touch cool. "Come on."

Tracy emerged first, with Emanuel close behind, plastic crinkling while we moved sideways to avoid a pair of electricians.

"At least the offices look okay," Emanuel commented, working his way through the cubicles to the office next to the conference room. He looked over his shoulder, asking, "Any objection to taking this one?"

"It's your place now, pick whatever you want," I told him, plunking my bag and laptop on top of my desk. I'd never considered using the office which, on paper, had been assigned to me. I preferred the open floor and cubicles with everyone else, leaving the string of offices edging the station to the sheriff and other higher-ups.

My office sat empty for some time until we'd converted it early last year into a small crime-scene laboratory, the contents of which were now stored and stacked in boxes that nearly reached the ceiling. It was Tracy's home away from home. Her first love in this field was the forensic sciences and she excelled at it. As if hearing my thoughts, she eyed the boxes, touching them briefly before returning to her old cubicle. "Nobody is using your old desk if you want it."

Brows rising with subtle surprise, "You sure?"

"Of course, anytime," I told her, a bittersweet rush of nostalgia warming my heart. It was good to be working closely. Even if it was our last time.

A commotion and clatter rang out from Emanuel's office, him moving furniture, making the place his own. The ruckus was like a horse kicking the walls in a small barn, making a construction worker peer through the plastic curtain.

Peeking in the door, his face already sweaty, I asked him, "Are you settling in?"

"Yeah, something like that." He shoved the chair beneath the desk which was now facing a window and asked, "Violet Jones, want to meet in the conference room?"

"I'll meet you in there," I said. "I need some coffee."

"What's planned for all the lab gear?" Tracy asked. She stood next to the pile of boxes with her arms crossed and toe tapped one of them. "A lot of time went into selecting the equipment."

"Not sure," I answered with a shrug. I wasn't at all sure what was planned and admittedly had looked to do nothing, leaving it for Emanuel to take care of.

"Storage for now," Emanuel answered confidently as if the decision had already been made. Tracy put on a frown and pinched her lips the way she does sometimes. Emanuel saw it, and asked, "Unless the district attorney wants it."

Her eyes brightened at that. "I'll talk to her."

"I'd think it's a bit outside of your office's jurisdiction though?" Emanuel questioned, fishing a video cable through the top of his desk. "But I'll leave them for now."

"We're meeting to discuss Violet Jones—"

"Coffee?" Tracy interrupted, a nod of encouragement followed. "I'll bring two?"

"Thanks," I said, opening the conference room door. I entered the meeting room and took the second seat from the head of the table, reserving the first for Emanuel. It was his place to drive the review of the crime scene and who Violet Jones was. From my seat, the station looked very different with the sheet of plastic hiding the front. We call the meeting room our fishbowl on account of all the glass. It was next to Emanuel's office and behind our cubicle desks, and perfectly convenient for the team. Tracy entered, the smell of warm coffee following.

"Violet Jones," I began, laptop open with her picture. I displayed it on the main screen, the pixels turning bright with an image that was far from what we saw this morning. "I was able to get a copy of her driver's license."

"Other than that, do we have anything else?" Emanuel asked, pulling a chair out, wheels squeaking. "Online maybe?"

"I found her on some of the more popular social media sites," Tracy answered, mirroring her display on the second of three screens. "Most of the posts she makes are public, food she's cooking, some baking stuff too."

"Scroll down," I asked, eyeing the times to determine a frequency. They were distant like afterthoughts. "I'd think there would be more for her age? She posts some, not a lot though."

"Not always," Tracy said. "I mean, it might have been at one time. But maybe she grew out of it."

"Or she likes another platform?"

"There are so many of them," Emanuel commented, shaking his head. "What else do we know about her?"

"Five foot seven and lean and fit which leads me to think she might have gone to a gym regularly. We know little about her and will meet with her parents. They're with Samantha now."

"An awful time for them," Emanuel said, shaking his head. He nudged his chin, instructing, "Find out what gym and then give it a visit."

"Done," I said, listing the task. I opened the conference room door, construction noise flooding in. Slipping on a pair of gloves, I retrieved the evidence from beneath my desk, heaving the bagged chain and cinderblocks, the weight tipping me some. Tracy and Emanuel followed me as I returned, Emanuel grabbing the door. "Leave the block on the floor but put the chain on the table."

"Got it," Emanuel said, his forearms taut like sinew while he carefully worked the chain's links. "They've got a marking inside them."

"A4," I answered, having seen it at the crime scene.

"I think I got a picture of it too?" Tracy said, uncertain,

scrolling fast enough to make me turn away from the screen. When she found the picture, she zoomed in, the letters clear and large on the monitor. "What is that? The type?"

"I think it could be a manufacturer's code?" Emanuel said, questioning.

"Tracy, send me the picture you have," I asked, seeing hers was clearer. "If it's a manufacturer's code, that could help narrow down the source."

"Sent," Tracy said, keys rattling. She was searching for the letter and number stamp and looked up, surprised. "It says here that the A stands for Aqua and the four is the number of times it was coated."

"This chain was made for the saltwater, like the kind used for anchors." My heart picked up, beating harder while I peeled more of the chain from the bag and spread it across the conference room table.

"The killer could have used any type of chain," Emanuel commented. "Why get this specific type? There wasn't a risk of it rusting through before the victim's body was discovered."

Returning to my seat, turning the leather restraint end over end, I shook my head subtly. "Because they wanted us to know it was a marine-grade chain. It was intentional. The real question is, why?"

"Or it's just a coincidence," Tracy said confidently. "A selection based on circumstance and opportunity."

I turned to face her, Emanuel too. "Go on," I insisted.

"We're on an island. The barrier islands. Every other store from above Corolla down to the Cape Lookout Lighthouse carries equipment for boats, especially anchor chains."

Emanuel's brow rose slowly, the corners of his mouth turning in an agreement. "That's fair."

I sat back down, the anticipation of having found a useful clue gone. "You're right. There's got to be dozens, maybe a hundred different places carrying the same type." Turning the leather restraint around, I added, "But I doubt many carry anything like this."

"I didn't get a close look," Tracy said, slipping on gloves, powder rising with the snap against her wrist. She pinched the leather between her fingers to uncurl it, reading the inside. "The stamp says, 'Made in Mexico.' It's too thick to be a dog collar and the circumference is way too small."

"It's more like a handcuff, but it does look like a dog collar," Emanuel added.

Tracy passed it back, the sturdiness of it felt in the heavy stitching and buckle.

"Hmm," I grunted as a thought occurred to me that seemed too far-fetched. Reluctance to say what it was climbed aboard my tongue like a heavy paperweight, Tracy's dipping her chin and asking with her eyes.

"What is it?" she said finally, anxious to hear the idea.

"What... what if it's BDSM? You know, like a leather cuff?" I asked with a flutter in my chest, voice wavering. Emanuel and Tracy sat up, stirring uncomfortably around the subject, their gaze fixed on the restraint. "I mean, this looks like it might be bondage gear worn on wrists and ankles."

"If it is, it must've been bought online," Tracy said, beginning to search her computer. "There aren't any stores like that in the area."

Emanuel cleared his throat, offering, "Well, I know of a shop not far from my old place. It carries that kind of stuff." The quiet descended between us until there was nothing but the distant clamoring of construction. Emanuel cleared his voice again, focus still locked on the restraint. "That's the only place—"

"And you know about this place, how?" Tracy said, bright-eyed, a smirk appearing.

"Now now. Let's wait a minute," he exclaimed, palming the air in a whoa motion. "I passed by it all the time."

"I'm sure you did," I joked, joining in the levity, his face warming. I caught Tracy's eyes then, which only made us laugh harder, wheezing. None of us could speak, the laughter strong, my face hot and stinging with tears, Emanuel and Tracy too. An officer walked by and saw our state, concern showing briefly before we waved him along. I didn't want it to end but wiped the grin and returned to why we were in the conference room.

What we'd seen this morning was as serious as it got, but we needed the moment. We needed it with one another. And it felt good. In our line of work, we had to have moments like this to counter the bad and bring balance to what was the darkest seen in humanity. If we didn't, I'm convinced we'd rot through and through. Finding my voice, I asked, "Emanuel, did you ever go inside?"

His brow bounced, a flash of red on his face, "Well—" And that was all it took for us to get going again.

"Seriously though, did you?"

A slow nod.

I slid the restraint across the table. "I guess you'll be returning there, ask them about this."

"I can do that," he answered, tucking the restraint back into the evidence bag. "If it was bought locally, that'd be the place."

"If not, then that leaves online," Tracy said, fingers sweeping across the keyboard. She turned her laptop around, the screen filling with a dozen pictures of naked men and women wearing nothing but bondage gear. "Easy to find online."

"We get it," Emanuel said, shielding his eyes, glassy wet from the laughter.

"Don't be so bashful," Tracy joked. Her face emptied, the investigation continuing. "There's the discretion though with online, people afraid of what the mail delivery might think."

"And the shop Emanuel mentioned being local. The easier access."

"Why not use more chain?" he asked, taking hold of the links, metal on glass clanking softly as he demonstrated. "Why risk the purchase of a restraint less available over chains which are readily available?"

"I think it's because chains can slip," I answered. I poked the tip of my finger between two links. "There's not enough surface area making contact with the victim's skin."

"The bondage restraint won't slip," he said, lowering the chain. Shifting in his seat, he asked, "What's next?"

"I'll want to speak with the victim's parents." I glanced at my phone to see a text waiting from Samantha. "They should be finishing soon. I'll reach out to them."

"I'd like to join you," Tracy said, returning to the role she'd left behind. She must have sensed my questioning the request and asked, "I mean, if that's okay to do."

"Certainly, investigation has full transparency with the district attorney's office." I wanted to cringe at the response, hating how it sounded. "It'll be useful to have the help."

"What are we dealing with here?" Emanuel asked.

All smiles and levity were absent, the three of us returning to that dark place where the worst in people is evident. I flipped through pictures, the silence growing. When I landed on the concert T-shirt, a knot formed in my throat.

"Jericho has that shirt," I heard myself say.

"I know," Emanuel replied. The two had a long history as both coworkers and friends. "I was with him when he bought the original. That was before the fire when he had a collection of them."

"The new collection is growing," I commented, relishing in the nostalgia of it a moment. "I wouldn't have expected to see it here though."

"It's a coincidence, right?" Tracy said, asking. Her fingers brushed the keyboard, a screen appearing with retro-styled concert garb of every kind. "Like the BDSM stuff, it's easy to get online."

"The victim was a fan, is all," Emanuel said unconvincingly. "Right?"

"Right," I agreed without hesitation. "She's a little young for the genre though."

"A few decades too young," he added.

"I'll find out more when I visit with the victim's parents," I said, my voice catching slightly, betraying the dread that always came with this part of the job. There is nothing in the world harder than telling a parent their child has been murdered. It's a wound you deliver that they'll never recover from. Sitting with them and seeing the hope drain from their faces as they beg for answers you can barely give... it never gets easier. And it shouldn't get easier. Ever. Some of them ask for every detail, as if by knowing each moment of their child's final agony, they might somehow be closer to them. As if their pain could bridge the unbearable silence left behind. It doesn't though. The pain remains after we leave, and sadly, it'll be there tomorrow and every day after.

Tracy closed her laptop. A set of tasks established for us to follow, Emanuel's question going unanswered. As I stood, an image of the concert T-shirt in my head, I looked across the table at the leather restraint and chain. I had no idea what kind of killer we were dealing with.

FOUR

The local hardware store was a bust. I'd gone there with a hint of expectation, selecting the one closest to the crime scene. I was told near exactly what we'd drummed up in the meeting, the chain type was commonly used for anchors and could be found anywhere in the Outer Banks. I left the hardware store with a few lightbulbs I knew we needed for the new house and a slight bruise on my pride since it was my idea to determine the chain type and its source. I could only hope Emanuel was having better luck at the place where BDSM equipment was sold.

"BDSM. Emanuel." A giggle rose in my chest while I steered around our new home. It was already late when I pulled into the gravel driveway, car tires crunching softly, parking on the east side until the driveway was paved. I opened the car door, the tired shadow of the Victorian silhouette covering me like a cool blanket. My brain was fogged with the dead weight of the day, and for a fleeting moment, I'd nearly driven to our old apartment on the beach. The muscle memory of years spent there working on autopilot. But the beach apartment wasn't our home anymore—this was.

I walked around to the front and stood a second, staring up at the way the setting sun was casting a forgiving glow on the weathered house, its buttery light softening the peeling paint and sagging trim, making it look almost beautiful. Almost. I shrugged, the truth of it far less romantic.

We'd bitten off more than we could handle. This house needed work. More than that, it needed a miracle. We purchased it when the lease on the apartment was up for renewal, the monthly toll raised significantly. It was all done in a mad rush and sadly, it was becoming everything I'd never imagined as part of our first big purchase together as soon-to-be husband and wife.

Still, we had hope, and found it tucked away in the form of an old photo album left behind by the original owners. As best as we could tell, the album was passed down to every new owner since the first. Some couples even added their own, creating a beautifully maintained history of the Victorian. I'm not sure of all the details, but the bank owned it for a decade, the photo album left unkept, as was the house, the salts of the Atlantic Ocean whipping against it relentlessly, each pass stealing a little more life from the glory it had once held. But each faded picture showed what the house had been like in its prime. From the stately home on the outside, to the pristine trim and polished floors inside, the pictures were our guide.

The house stood like a relic of another era with its weather-worn Victorian facade leaning derelict against a life of salty winds whipping off the ocean. The white paint had faded to a dull gray, peeling in long strips like a bad sunburn. Its ginger-bread trim sagged in places, giving it the look of a tired smile. The wide front porch, with its groaning planks and lichen-covered railings, hinted at years of neglect. Yet, to me, there was hope that I could make it beautiful again. This house was ours—every faded shingle, every sagging beam, every scratch and scrape. It was home.

I took a breath and listened to the playful yells and hollering that came from inside, the house barely able to silence Thomas's and Tabitha's banter. This old house had a heartbeat again, a growing heartbeat that gave me pause. Thinking of where on our massive list of to-do items did we put windows and doors and staring at the weathered siding now, I wasn't so sure the photo album would help. It was suddenly feeling all too much. The project felt as big and overwhelming as the storms we'd faced at sea. And tonight, with exhaustion tugging at me, I wasn't sure I was ready to tackle it.

Jericho had stood beside me when we signed the papers, a quiet smile tugging at his mouth, his strong hand resting protectively on my back. The pen felt heavier than any weapon I'd held in my career, the moment weighted with equal parts joy and terror. I felt the same mix of emotions now and I was certain I was going to feel it when we'd meet on our wedding day.

This place needed us, and maybe, just maybe, we needed it too. I say that because of who we'd become recently. We were about to formally become a mister and missus, which was a long time coming, along with planned wedding pictures to add to the album and a few to hang on the walls. We were also the adoptive parents of a brother and sister whom we'd saved at sea, their parents brutally murdered. All at once, we were an instant family and needed a permanent place to call home.

Inside, the house exhaled its age with every creak of the floorboards beneath my shoes. The living room welcomed me first, dim and cluttered with the chaos of the move. The walls were a mismatched canvas of faded greens and yellows, where sunlight had failed to reach the more recessed parts. An ancient chandelier dangled precariously from the ceiling, its once-grand crystals dull and dusty, occasionally glinting sunlight when the sun was low enough in the sky. Cardboard boxes towered in the corners, their sharpie-labeled sides like cryptic messages: "Kitchen—Fragile," "Books," and the inevitable "Miscellaneous Chaos."

I ran my fingers over the banister as I made my way further into the house, the wood cool and uneven beneath my touch. The scent of the place hit me—aged wood, damp air, and a faint floral sweetness that must have come from the overgrown wisteria outside. The Outer Banks was waking from its winter nap and soon, more blooms would accompany the slow emergence of this old Victorian.

The house wasn't sleek like the apartment we'd left behind. I already missed that place, especially its view of the beach and the cramped coziness. But Thomas and Tabitha had been outgrowing it faster than I could blink, their boundless energy filling every corner. This house was the space we needed. It was space to breathe and to grow and to settle.

A thump riveted through the floor and was followed by a loud peal of laughter. They were playing in the den again, the one room that had resisted any attempt at order. The plaster walls were cracked and bubbled with moisture, one corner showing a dark stain that hinted at past leaks and possible rot beneath the plaster and lath. The ceiling sagged slightly, and the floor bore uneven patches of mismatched wood. It was, without a doubt, the room most in need of repair, yet it was the one everyone gravitated toward.

Inside, Thomas and Tabitha were a blur of motion. Seeing them playing gave me pause. They'd grown so much since we'd first found them adrift in the ocean. They were like two baby birds out of the nest with their light-colored hair, almost white, and pale skin with pink lips, bony and dehydrated. But their eyes. They'd looked up into mine with those vibrant, light hazel eyes and I instantly fell in love. Thomas was growing faster, his hair turning darker and needing a cut. Tabitha's hair remained light, her wiry limbs and endless energy giving her older brother a run in just about every game they strummed up.

"Whoa," I called out, stepping into the doorway. Their bare feet clapped against the floor, Thomas chasing his sister around the room, a makeshift sword—a paint stirrer—clutched in his hand. Tabitha was infinitely cleverer at times, and dodged her brother with ease, long strays of hair catching the dim light as it streamed behind her in waves.

She had freckles now, some of them standing out against her pale skin, a constellation of curiosity and mischief. She spun around, clutching her stuffed dolphin, the ever-present companion of late that had survived countless adventures. Her laugh rang out, a sound that softened the rough edges of the room.

"You guys be careful in there. That plaster's older than both of you combined. Probably older than me too."

Thomas paused, his breath coming in quick bursts. "We're just playing pirates, Mama!"

"Pirates don't destroy their own ship," I teased.

Jericho appeared behind me, leaning against the doorframe, a grin tugging at his lips. "Or maybe they do, depending on the crew."

"Hey babe." I said, turning to him, my chest warming at the sight. Jericho Flynn—the man who had been my rock through so many storms. His broad shoulders filled the doorway, the soft fabric of an old Marine Patrol jacket stretching across his chest. He had new uniforms now, his returning to the role of sheriff in our part of the Outer Banks. It was one of the reasons I was leaving the force, to take over as a full-time parent. I needed it. My family needed it. We just had this case to get through first. Inching up onto my toes to reach him, I gently brushed his lips with mine while digging my hands inside his jacket to wrap my arms around him.

"Rough one I heard," he said, asking.

I peered up, the window's light turning his hair to the color of sunlit sand. It was tousled too, as though the wind had claimed it for its own. There was compassion and a smile in his blue-green eyes—eyes that could shift from stormy to gentle in an instant.

"Are you the sheriff or my fiancé?" I asked, somewhat jokingly, wanting to know which role I was going to play. My chest warmed again, calling him my fiancé still felt new. We'd danced around the commitment a few years and even adopted Thomas and Tabitha while engaged. We both knew it was inevitable, everyone did. And everyone was there when we'd finally formalized things. A beautiful beach ceremony with us and the kids, and what was supposed to be a few close friends but ended up bringing out most everyone on a coldish spring afternoon. The gold band on his finger caught the weak sunlight filtering through the cracked windows, and for a moment, everything else—the chaos, the repairs, the endless to-do list—faded. I took him into my arms, the care of our roles falling away, the hurt of seeing that victim this morning hitting me. I felt the emotion swell in me and told him, "It was bad. Real bad."

"I'm thinking you need a break?" he asked, his voice low and steady, as he brushed a stray piece of hair from my face.

"From the case, the house or the pirates?" I asked, smiling despite myself.

"All of it." He glanced toward the kids, who had resumed their game with renewed vigor. Tabitha leaped onto the thread-bare couch, narrowly missing a stack of old picture frames we hadn't yet hung.

"We should get that couch out of here before they turn it into a trampoline," I said, though my heart wasn't in it. This one room, chaotic as it was, felt alive.

Jericho nodded, but his gaze lingered on me, studying my face the way he always did when he thought I was carrying too much. "You know, you can turn the case over to Emanuel. He's here to be the lead detective," he said quietly.

"I know," I replied, leaning into him. For a moment, I wanted to tell him about how the case bothered me. I didn't though. I couldn't put my finger on it exactly and maybe that's why. "That wouldn't be fair to him."

"You're a terrific detective," he said, hugging tighter. "And an even better friend to Emanuel."

"I'm not worried about him." The hug ended, cold air touching where his body had been. "Tracy surprised us. She joined us at the crime scene like she was still working for the team."

"A little early in the investigation, isn't it?" A nod. His grin returned. "You didn't mind, did you?"

"Not at all."

We watched as Tabitha tried to outsmart her brother, ducking behind a tower of boxes. She glanced over at us, her eyes alight with a mischievous smirk. "You two better not join his crew!"

Jericho chuckled, "She's trouble, that one," he said affectionately.

"She's ours," I replied, and the truth of it settled over me like a warm tide. "They're ours."

All of it was ours and the end of this case meant my being home full-time to raise them and restore this place. And far from perfect it was, but as I stood there with Jericho and laughter filled the room, it felt more like home to me than I'd had in a very long time.

A cramp touched my heart, the cold tip of a memory reminding me that I did have this once before. It was another home and husband and child. I could smell the memory too. I'd been cooking something in the kitchen when I heard the screen door hinges creak, or thought I'd heard it. Whatever it was, it had been enough to urge a look in on our daughter Hannah who'd planted herself in front of the television to watch SpongeBob cartoons.

"You okay?" Jericho asked, sensing something was off.

"Uh-huh," I muttered, my body rigid. Relaxing some as the initial memory passed. Tabitha let out a shrill laugh, the sound of it eerily familiar. Hannah laughed like that, and it could turn any gray day into sunshine. In the memory I saw her little feet skipping across the floor, her soft wavy hair bouncing with every step. She was everything I could have hoped for in a daughter— curious, kind, brave. But that day! God, that day!

My mouth went dry when my mind stirred up the rhythm of a motor, the mechanics gulping air and spitting fire. Its roar came with the slap of the screen door and distant giggles dancing in the air that were unmistakably Hannah's.

I ran from that kitchen like I'd never run before, my first concerns being the street and the careless drivers speeding up and down it. When I reached our porch, Hannah was already at the curb where a woman held a stuffed animal from inside the car, luring our baby. I couldn't run fast enough, Hannah's leg caught in a tug-of-war, the woman inside winning. When the car door closed with a thump, Hannah's voice silenced in an instant and split my heart open, the scars still tender.

I ran after them while they sped away. There were neighbors approaching, curious onlookers at the crazed woman screaming her daughter's name. I barely heard them consoling while cold dread wrapped around my chest as if Death himself had visited. I did die that day. Not entirely, but my soul was broken, a large part of it missing.

While death hadn't come to stay, ghosts had taken up residence in our home. We were mere shadows of who we'd been before, and life never felt right after that. Hannah's father and I split up, going our own ways. He moved on and started a new life, but I never stopped looking for my little girl. I couldn't rest.

It was fifteen years before I'd see my daughter again. By

then, she was all grown and had a new name, a family and a life with a budding career as a crime investigator. Something much bigger than us must have stepped in and decided we weren't meant to be apart forever after all. I like to think it was serendipity that brought Tracy Fields into my life. She'll always be my little girl, Hannah though. Always. Forever.

The kids' laughter echoed through the house, a chaotic symphony bouncing off the scarred walls and warped floors. Jericho's arm around me anchored me to the moment, showing me what we had today. I buried the Hannah memories back into the past and forced myself to look forward, taking Jericho's rough and calloused hand in mine with a squeeze. We said nothing and watched our children turn the den into a battlefield of imagination.

Thomas, with his wild hair and flushed cheeks, had dropped his paint-stirrer sword in favor of climbing onto an overturned ottoman that leaned precariously to one side. "This is my ship!" he declared, planting his feet wide as if to balance against imaginary waves. "No girls allowed!"

Tabitha, not one to back down, planted her fists on her hips. "It's my ship! I found it first!" she countered, her freckled nose scrunching as she stepped closer to him. Her stuffed dolphin dangled from one hand like a talisman of justice.

"Careful, Captain," Jericho rumbled, his voice rich with amusement. "Mutiny's a dangerous game."

Thomas froze mid-taunt, his bright eyes darting. "What's mutiny?"

"Something you don't want to find out, kiddo," Jericho replied, a wry smile tugging at the corners of his mouth.

I laughed softly, shaking my head. "You're going to encourage them, aren't you?"

"Maybe just a little," Jericho said, his grin widening. "But it's better than them tearing the whole place down. Barely."

"Hey, I had a question about your concert shirts," I asked,

changing the subject with a nudge. "Do you still have one from Def Leppard's *Hysteria* world tour?"

The whites of his eyes flashed, his answering, "Yep. It's my favorite." He glanced at the ceiling as if seeing through it. "It's gotta be upstairs."

"Huh," I muttered, thinking of Violet Jones and her wearing the shirt. "You don't see many like that anymore."

A shrug. "I don't know. I notice them when I'm out. It's nostalgic." Jericho entered the room, floorboards squeaking where the floor tilted slightly and the walls weren't quite square. His presence in the room was magnetic, a quiet strength that brought the kids to him in an instant. He rolled onto the floor with a grunt, laughter pealing the air when his inner tickle-monster emerged. When he came up for air, he asked, "Why?"

"The victim," I began, careful about what I was going to say around the kids. But they were buried in the throes of tickling and laughing and wouldn't hear anything. "She was wearing the same exact shirt."

"Really?" he asked, pausing with a pensive expression. "I mean, it was a huge tour for the band. I'd think there's got to be tons of them around. Online too."

"Yeah, we considered that."

"But?" he asked, hearing doubt.

"It just seemed odd to me. I mean, that shirt." Our gaze was fixed, the words not coming. "Don't you think?"

"Honestly?" he asked. I nodded. "Coincidence. Nothing more. It's a common shirt."

"Okay," I said, kneeling to join in the tickle fest. I tugged on blond hair affectionately and was met by spidery fingers tickling my ribs. "Gonna get you."

The laughs continued until there were cries for retreat, but I wouldn't let go and stayed there on the floor with my family staring up at the ceiling where it sagged deepest. Turning toward Jericho, he was looking at the same, the lines at the corners of his eyes deepening as he smiled with a mixture of amusement and something softer—something that said he knew exactly what I was thinking.

"We bought a mess, didn't we," he said with a soft laugh. "But it's ours."

"It's ours."

FIVE

The frosty air curled around my ankles and crept into my chest, hitting me like an offense as soon as I stepped into the room directly outside the morgue. It always felt like the cold was alive in here, seeping from beneath the rubber-sealed doors that separated the living from the dead. The sterile gray walls glinted under the municipal building's harsh fluorescent lights, and the faint chemical scent of industrial disinfectant lingered. No speck of dirt dared to exist here.

I risked a breath, the air sharp with the acrid tang of disinfectant, burning faintly in my throat. We joked that it was Samantha Watson's signature blend, the medical examiner's concoction to ensure nothing stained her sterile field. She insisted her morgue be cleaner than an operating room, and we'd found it best that none of us dared to argue it.

"I think my breath just froze," Tracy muttered, rubbing her gloved hands together as her paper booties slid against the polished floor. "Does she have to keep it *this* cold?"

"It's always been like this," Emanuel chuckled, pulling on a disposable cap with the practiced efficiency of someone used to suiting up in sterile environments. "You know Samantha—

anything short of a surgical field, and we'd never hear the end of it."

"Yeah, yeah," Tracy said, rolling her eyes. "Next, she'll have us scrubbing in for our own autopsy findings."

I snorted, adjusting my lab coat, a second one to double up the layers. "I imagine that is probably her dream. But until then, just make sure you're layered, buttoned, and gloved. You know how she feels about contamination."

This was the room we prepared in, and it was as orderly as Samantha herself, a row of gleaming steel lockers lining one wall, their surfaces reflecting the sterile light overhead. Hooks jutted out beneath a shelf of neatly folded lab coats, each piece arranged like an offering to her obsession with precision. We stood before the heavy double doors, their rubber seals clamped tight against the frosty air that oozed out from beneath them. Bold red stickers on the steel read:

AUTHORIZED PERSONNEL ONLY

"You ready?" I asked, glancing back at them. Emanuel nodded, his face calm and steady, while Tracy shivered visibly but set her jaw with determination. In my years as detective, nobody ever truly *wanted* to be ready for what lay behind those doors, but it was where the dead spoke to us. It was where the medical examiner was the interpreter to tell the dead's story of what happened in the minutes and even the hours leading up to death.

I pushed the door open, and we stepped into Samantha's kingdom. And as expected, the morgue was pristine, every surface gleaming as if polished within an inch of its life. White and black tiles stretched from wall to wall, their glossy finish bouncing the stark fluorescent light into every corner. Stainless steel counters lined the perimeter, each one housing neatly organized instruments, microscopes, and high-tech equipment that looked more suited to a cutting-edge lab than a basement morgue. The walls were purposefully bare, they were stark and undecorated, save for a single dry-erase board filled with Samantha's careful notes in red and black marker.

An old refrigeration unit stood from floor to ceiling with a dozen or more square doors facing us like tiles on a game board. It was the oldest piece of municipal equipment and hummed steadily, the constant low drone underscoring the oppressive quiet of this place. Each door was labeled with a small metal plate, a piece of paper and what looked like Derek's chicken-scratch handwriting, marking the identities of the dead waiting for a turn beneath Samantha's scalpel.

The heart of the room were the autopsy tables—sleek, modern, and eerily immaculate. Integrated drainage ran along their edges, leading to hidden reservoirs beneath the floor, a labyrinth of complex piping that I could only imagine funneling to protective waste disposal. Overhead, there were adjustable lights that hung from articulated arms, their bulbs casting a cold, surgical glare onto the table below. Samantha stood at one of them, her blue scrubs and mask making her blend seamlessly into her clinical surroundings. She was short like her predecessor whose stepstool remained a part of this morgue, used daily to provide Samantha the reach needed to do her job.

"You're late," Samantha called without looking up. Her voice, sharp and professional, echoed off the walls as she continued working on Violet Jones's body. "If the body could talk, it'd have told me everything by now."

"Nice to see you too. Sorry if we kept you waiting," I replied, striding toward her, regretting that third cup of coffee before leaving the house. "What have you got?"

"Plenty," she said, straightening toward us. Her gloved hands were bloodied, and she rested them at her sides as she nodded at the body on the table. Violet's pale skin seemed to glow under the harsh lights, her bruises standing out like ink stains. "And you'll want to hear every word."

It took a lot to intrigue Samantha, our small part of this sometimes-cruel world having experienced some of the grimmest murder cases. Behind me, the quiet click of a camera shutter brought me back to the moment. Tracy was already moving around the room, holding the district attorney's office camera steady to capture detailed images of Violet's bruises and the ligature mark around the ankle.

The task wasn't officially hers anymore since the move to the DA's office. I'd reassigned it to an officer from our station, an Officer Ben Stanley, the greenest of rookies. He'd only been roped in during his first week by sheer bad luck, standing near Tracy's old desk at the wrong time, his sergeant eagerly offering him like a sacrifice.

"Stanley," Tracy said, her tone firm but patient as she knelt slightly to angle her shot. "Don't just stand there. Pay attention. Watch how I'm doing this. It isn't just about pointing and snapping pictures. This isn't Instagram."

"Yes, ma'am," Stanley stammered, fumbling with our team's camera gear as he mirrored her pose. He was a wiry kid, barely out of the academy, his nervous energy filling the room like static electricity. He crouched awkwardly, his camera nearly bumping into the side of the autopsy table.

"You're doing fine," I encouraged, helping to guide him.

Samantha leered with a frown, saying, "We're documenting evidence, not playing Twister."

"Right," Stanley muttered, adjusting his grip. "Sorry."

I exchanged a look with Emanuel, who grinned faintly. "Baptism by fire," he murmured under his breath. "He had more room to move around at the crime scene."

"This isn't the crime scene," Samantha snapped. "Take care."

Tracy took another picture, the flash momentarily bright.

Turning back to Stanley, "See this angle? You want to make sure you're showing the depth of the bruises. That means you have to capture the contours. Use the light to your advantage. Like this."

Stanley mimicked her, crouching low to shoot from the same perspective. His camera clicked, and he hesitated, glancing at the screen. "Uh... is this okay?"

"Let's see." I leaned over with Tracy to check his work, her expression softening slightly. "That's not bad. But next time, adjust your focus."

Tracy nodded, agreeing, and added, "The bruise is the star of the show, not the background."

"Got it," Stanley said, nodding earnestly.

"Don't worry," Tracy added, her tone lightening. "You'll get the hang of it. Just takes practice. And trust me, you'll see more bruises and cuts than you'll ever want to in this job."

The rookie gave a nervous chuckle but seemed to relax slightly as he adjusted his camera again. Watching the two of them, I felt a flicker of something close to pride. Tracy might grumble about the cold or the workload, but she had an unshakable knack for mentoring. If Stanley stuck around long enough, he'd learn from one of the best.

"Let's keep moving," Samantha's voice cut in sharply, drawing our attention back to the body on the table. "We've got a lot to cover, and Violet isn't going to explain herself."

Tracy stepped back, letting Stanley snap a few more shots as she carefully removed her gloves and returned to her spot near the autopsy table. "All right, rookie," she said over her shoulder, "keep going, but remember to get close-ups of the needle marks on her neck. That's going to matter later when we tie this to the tox-screen results."

"Yes, ma'am," Stanley replied, his voice less shaky now, though his hands still trembled slightly as he adjusted the camera settings. He shifted angles, bending closer to Violet's still form. The camera clicked in rapid succession as he captured every detail of the faint puncture wounds on her neck.

The rookie paused and lowered the camera as if seeing a dead body for the first time. He'd seen Violet at the crime scene but may have never seen anything like this. Violet's body lay motionless on the gleaming autopsy table, her pale, lifeless skin unusually bright under the unforgiving fluorescent lights. She was completely exposed, the stark vulnerability of her form a grim testament to what had been taken from her. The Y-incision down her torso had been meticulously executed, the edges of the skin folded back to reveal the dark, hollow cavity where her heart once beat.

Samantha gestured to the organ resting in a metal tray nearby, its surface slick and glistening. When she saw me looking, she commented, "The heart was pristine," her voice clinical and steady. "Not a single anomaly—she was in perfect health. That is, until this." Her gloved hand moved back to Violet's open chest, pointing to the bruising around the ribcage. "These tell us how hard she fought before they subdued her. She didn't make it easy for them."

"Fought?" I asked, confused. "At the crime scene, there'd been no indication of defensive wounds."

Samantha adjusted her gloves as she pointed to a faint discoloration on Violet's forearms. "Post-mortem bruising usually shows up as livor mortis," she explained. "It occurs when blood settles in the lower parts of the body due to gravity, especially if the body is moved after death. But in this case, the key difference is that a true bruise from injury will present with tissue damage caused by trauma and the post-mortem bruises lack any inflammatory response seen with living tissue. In cases of injury, you'll also see ruptured blood vessels and hemorrhaging into the surrounding tissues, which are absent in simple lividity."

"These are bruises the victim sustained while she was still

alive?" I asked, the interest gaining focus with a rapid succession of camera clicks and flashes.

Samantha nodded and raised Violet's arm higher to show additional bruising that I recognized as being livor mortis, saying, "Post-mortem, the blood settling, dead tissue." She circled the peach-sized bruises closer to the victim's wrists. "Combative with abrasions and response from living tissue."

"Violet Jones fought her attacker," I said, Emanuel jotting it in his notebook. "But the extent of the defensive wounds indicates the drug worked fast."

"That is my assessment as well." Samantha, ever the perfectionist, gave the rookie a quick once-over before returning to her work. "Make sure you're capturing the symmetry of the punctures, Stanley," she said, her voice clipped. "They're evenly spaced. That's an important detail—it tells us the needle was inserted deliberately, not haphazardly."

Stanley nodded quickly, angling his camera again.

Tracy smirked, watching him out of the corner of her eye. "Relax, kid. She's tough on everyone."

"Back to the drugs," I said, pulling us back on track. "What do you think was used?"

Samantha paused while regarding the question. With a shrug, she answered, "Could be a number of things. Something potent and fast..." She glanced into the overhead lights as though the beams were feeding her answers. When her gaze returned, she answered, "Could be etorphine or ketamine. Any number of them."

"Which is why we have to wait for the tox screen," Emanuel said.

"But to clarify, Violet didn't die from the drug?" I asked, understanding the potency and its dangers. "It was a risk to use, right?"

"The tox screen will tell us for certain," Samantha said. She leaned slightly against the counter where her instruments lay in meticulous order. "The evidence before us indicates death occurred due to drowning. How much the sedation played a factor isn't known yet."

Tracy rejoined us, asking, "So they sedate Violet Jones, tie her up, and then what? Wait for her to wake up so they can start this horror show at the beach?"

Samantha nodded grimly. "That's my assessment. The bruises on her wrists and elsewhere indicate a short-lived fight. She was conscious. It's the damage to her leg that suggests she was chained to the cinderblocks, the tidal changes and waves lashing her body around for hours."

"They wanted her alive for the shock of drowning to death," I murmured, staring at Violet's pale, lifeless face. "They wanted her awake for that part."

Emanuel's expression darkened. "Psychological torture. She knew with the tide rising what was coming."

"Exactly, the psychological became physical torture," Samantha said and leaned over the table, pointing to Violet's face and chest. "There was foam and froth coating the mouth and nostrils. That's classic for drowning. It's caused by water mixing with air and mucus as the victim struggled to breathe. The throat and lungs were filled with seawater, and I found salt crystals and fine sand in the airways, consistent with drowning in the ocean, beach sediment stirring in the waves. The lungs weighed significantly more than normal, completely water-logged. When sectioned, they released frothy liquid, which is another indicator for drowning as the cause of death."

"She aspirated water while she was alive?" I asked, hating the idea of knowing the torture and horror of what Violet went through.

Samantha nodded, and I faced Emanuel. "That definitely rules out post-mortem submersion then."

"And the chains," Emanuel asked, his voice hardening. "Any leads beyond our own findings at the local suppliers?"

"Afraid not." Samantha gestured to the tray holding the galvanized links. "Like you suspected, it's a standard hardware store chain that's been cut to a precise length. There were no additional treatments applied."

"But the length of the chain indicates this wasn't a rushed job. They planned it down to the last link, knowing where to place Violet to drown in the tide's change."

"Sadly, I've seen a hundred drownings in the Outer Banks. Most are recreational accidents but this one..." she paused to take a deep breath and softly brushed the side of Violet's face. "... this one is in the top five of the worst. The extent of seawater and sand found indicates a prolonged drowning."

I let the weight of her words settle in the air, glancing over at Tracy and Emanuel. "This isn't just about murder. It's about control. Every part of this screams domination."

Tracy exhaled slowly, her arms tightening around herself. "The sedative, the restraint, the chains... They didn't just want to kill her. They wanted to watch her suffer... and control it too."

"And they succeeded," Samantha said, her voice flat but heavy.

"What's this?" Stanley asked, face hidden behind his camera. I think we'd all forgotten he was still here, turning in unison. He rose from behind the lens, standing at the victim's feet and pointing. "This thing on her heel?"

"The abrasion?" Derek asked, leaning over to inspect.

"It's more than an abrasion," Stanley said, voice cracking. He held his camera up high, showing a close-up of the foot.

Derek's brow popped and he waved Samantha over.

"What is it?" Samantha asked, shining a light and magnifier on the suspected area. We circled around as Stanley stepped out of our way, a look of achievement on his face. "The seawater did so much damage, it's hard to tell."

"Letters?" I asked, staring through the magnifier. The skin

was wrinkled and loose, a collection of small cuts on the heel. When I saw the number of perpendicular lines I straightened, saying, "That doesn't look random like something she'd stepped on."

"You think those are initials?" Samanatha asked, her eyes enormous behind the magnifier.

"Initials?" Tracy asked, stepping closer, her camera dangling from its strap. "I might be able to work from an image and reconstruct the letters."

"See what you can do," I said, Tracy's flash firing rapidly. "We've seen initials used before. Previous cases."

"Let's assess first, determine what they are before we start looking at old cases," Emanuel instructed, taking the lead. "We don't want to get spun up searching old cases when we don't know what we have yet."

The team looked at me. I gave a quick nod, assuring them of the regime change. "Assess first, you're right."

With an action taken, the possibility of initials carved into the foot of the victim, Samantha asked me, "Do you have anything yet that'd suggest why she was targeted?"

"Not yet," I said, meeting her wide, nervous eyes. "But that's what we're here to figure out."

Samantha folded her arms, sharp gaze cutting through the tension. "Then I suggest you do so quickly. Whoever did this didn't just stumble into it—they knew exactly what they were doing. And someone with this level of preparation doesn't stop at one victim."

The words hung in the icy air, stark and unforgiving. I glanced at Violet's lifeless face again, the faint bruises and puncture marks speaking volumes about her final hours. She deserved justice, and I wasn't about to let her down.

"Tracy, would you keep working with Stanley to document everything," I said, my voice firm. "Emanuel, let's go over the timeline again to see if this bastard slipped up anywhere."

As Tracy and Stanley began positioning for another round of photos, I caught a glimpse of the rookie's face. His jaw was tight, his eyes focused, the initial nerves giving way to determination.

"Good work, Stanley. And a very good find," I said, giving him a brief nod. "Keep it up."

He blinked in surprise but nodded back quickly. "Yes, ma'am."

Turning to Samantha, I gestured toward the monitor. "Send me everything you've got from the scene and the tox screen. We're going to nail this one."

Samantha gave a curt nod, her expression unreadable behind her mask. "You'd better, Casey. Because they'll do this again."

SIX

Tracy stayed with us after the grim findings from the autopsy. Her determination didn't waver, even as we decided on the next step: Violet Jones's apartment. The address led us to a modest unit perched above a worn restaurant on Corolla's bay-side. The kind of place where the smell of pizza and deep fryer oil clung to the walls, saturating the air long after closing time. The drive there was quiet, the early spring-season lull leaving Route 12 almost eerily empty. Tourists hadn't yet descended in droves to fill every rental and clog every backroad. For now, it was just us —the locals, the year-rounders—living in the fragile quiet before the chaos.

I checked the rearview mirror, catching a glimpse of Emanuel in the backseat. His face was shadowed, his chin low, and he wore the kind of expression that gave the impression he was bothered by pain. He wasn't though. He was working the case. The breaking sunlight seemed to do him no favors, his skin flickering between the laptop screen's glow and natural light. Silence pressed inside the car like a weight, and I couldn't let it linger.

"So," I said, tossing the line out as bait, "are you working more BDSM stuff?"

Emanuel's head snapped up, his wide-eyed glare practically drilling through the glass. Red flushed his cheeks instantly. "Damn, Casey. Are you serious?"

"Very," I answered, expressionless. I caught Tracy's smirk from the passenger seat which urged a smile on my face too.

"No, you're not," Emanuel muttered, shaking his head. "Can't you go five minutes without—"

"Nope," I cut him off, my smile widening. "Besides, if we can't joke about the weird stuff, what are we even doing?" My grin faded slightly as I glanced at him in the mirror. "Seriously, though. Have we learned anything else about the victim? Who was she? Who were her friends? Anything else?"

Emanuel sighed heavily. He turned his gaze out the window, watching the dunes ripple in the breeze. "Not much we didn't already know. Tracy's notes were thorough. Violet was single, no kids, kept to herself. Worked as a martial arts instructor. No enemies, at least none that show up in the usual records."

"Nothing else? You sound unconvinced." Tracy said, twisting in her seat to face him. Her hair caught the light as she moved, the strands turning auburn at the edges. "Like there should be more?"

"Because it's too neat," Emanuel replied. He waved a hand at the shoreline that peeked through the sand dunes. "Nobody's life is that simple. There's always something beneath the surface."

"Like those pelicans?" Tracy teased, pointing out the window. A group of seven flew low over the water, their wings beating in lazy unison.

"They're fishing," Emanuel said, tilting his head toward the birds. "The waters are warming up. Good time for it."

"Speaking of warming up," Tracy said, her energy sharp

and direct, "are we diving this summer or what? Emanuel certi-fied us for a reason, and you've been avoiding it, Casey."

Her words tugged at an uncomfortable memory. Our last dive hadn't been for leisure—it had been for a case. Cold, dangerous waters, two shipwrecks stacked. The search for answers to the case were at the bottom of the ocean, and Jericho nearly lost his life in the search. I hadn't put on the scuba gear since.

"We'll see," I murmured, eyes fixed on the road. "Depends on how warm it gets."

"We're not asking you to scuba for murder clues again," she said gently. "Just for fun. Like we used to."

"We'll see," I repeated. I sensed the disappointment, and quickly added, "It'd be nice to get back down there."

"A left turn is coming up," she added, pivoting back toward the windshield. She pointed at a restaurant with peeling paint and a neon pizza sign that buzzed faintly in the gray light. "Violet's place is just above that." Her stomach growled loudly, and she let out a laugh. "Please tell me they serve lunch."

"The victim's apartment first," I said firmly, though my own stomach tightened in protest. "Then we'll get some food."

We pulled into the gravel lot, the tires crunching until we came to a stop. The air was cool and damp, carrying the faint scent of the freshwater bay, Currituck Sound. At the base of the wooden staircase leading up to the apartment, a couple stood waiting. They were middle-aged, their faces etched with grief so raw it made my chest tighten. I saw the resemblance to their daughter immediately.

"They must be Violet's parents," Tracy whispered as she unbuckled her seatbelt. We were meant to meet the day before, but the weight of the morgue and the cold formality of the process in meeting with Samantha, and the unbearable sight of their daughter, had proved too much. Grief swallowed the day whole, leaving them unable to face another soul.

"They're right on time," I said, opening the door. The day wasn't getting any easier.

We stepped out of the car into the weighty silence of the gravel parking lot. The air smelled of salt and faintly of oregano, the latter wafting from the open door to the pizza shop below Violet's apartment. The couple standing at the base of the staircase looked like they'd aged decades in the short time since their daughter's murder. I'd seen what grief can do. I'd felt what grief can do. The pain of it was etched in their faces and gleamed from their weepy eyes. And sadly, there was little to nothing any of us could do or say to make it better.

Mr. Jones wore a wrinkled button-down and khakis that hung loose on his wiry frame, his posture bent as if the sorrow itself was a weight on his shoulders. His salt-and-pepper hair stuck up in uneven tufts like he'd been clutching at it in frustration. Mrs. Jones held his arm tightly, fingertips pressed white and her pale hand trembling against his sleeve. Her face was hollow, eyes rimmed red and puffy, and her thin lips quivered with every shallow breath.

"Detective White?" Mr. Jones asked, his voice rough like gravel scraping the bottom of a bucket. He blinked against the harsh daylight, though the clouds had thickened overhead.

I nodded, stepping forward. "Yes, Mr. Jones. And this is Tracy Fields and Emanuel Wilson. We're here to learn more about Violet. We're so sorry for your loss."

Mrs. Jones let out a shuddering breath, her voice trembling. "I just... I still don't understand why someone would... would..." Her words faltered, and her knees buckled. Mr. Jones held her up with one arm, nodding toward the staircase.

"Let's go inside," he said, his words barely audible. "Her apartment's this way."

We climbed the wooden stairs in silence, the boards weathered and creaking. The second-floor landing opened onto a narrow walkway. From up here, I could see the glint of the shoreline to the east, the ocean a restless strip of gray. The buzz of the neon pizza sign below punctuated the quiet with a faint hum, the smell of pizza and sub-sandwiches a constant along with the sea.

Mr. Jones fumbled with the keys, his hands shaking so violently it took him a moment to unlock the door. When the door finally widened, a string scent of vanilla and lavender washed over us, Violet's attempt to mask the restaurant food.

"This is it," he said, stepping aside to let us enter.

The apartment was small but meticulously kept and held a warmth that spoke of a new, young life just beginning to take root. The open-plan featured a couch with cheerful yellow cushions and a worn coffee table that may have been someone's throwaway. Doilies, yellow and faded, were spread across the top, a neatly stacked collection of picture books on one side.

To the left was a modest kitchenette, its counters spotless except for a jar of sugar and a single mug sitting in the sink, a ring of dried coffee around the bottom. A large picture window dominated the far wall that faced east toward the beach. Instantly, I saw why Violet might have selected this apartment. Even under the growing overcast sky, the view was breathtaking, the shoreline stretching endlessly in both directions.

"She loved this place," Mrs. Jones said softly, joining me, a weak smell of alcohol following. Her gaze was fixed on the window, trembling fingers touching a stained window ornament, blue triangle shapes glinting the outside light. "Especially this window and its view. She'd send us pictures of the sunrise every morning. Said it gave her hope."

Tracy gave her a small, encouraging smile. "It's beautiful. I can see why she loved it."

I walked slowly through the apartment, scanning for anything that might hint at Violet's life—or death. There were schoolbooks, academics on kinesiology and related materials. "Was she attending school?"

"Not for the last year," Mr. Jones answered, clearing his throat. He thumbed one of the books, lifting it to check the binder. "She was working her master's but wanted to take a break."

The binder had a label, a location in a library. "She looks to have continued some studies on her own."

"I'll have to return these," he replied, dropping the book with a hard plunk.

Violet's desk in the corner held an open laptop, a pen, and a planner with neat, color-coded entries. The bookshelves were filled with thrillers and beach reads, alongside a few framed photographs of Violet with friends, smiling brightly in the sun.

"Detective," Emanuel said from the kitchen. "You might want to see this."

My insides squeezed at the thought of finding something, and I crossed the room to join Emanuel who was staring at a small corkboard that hung beside the refrigerator. Photos, receipts, and handwritten notes were pinned there, forming a collage of Violet's routines and aspirations. It was a long Post-its tab, the kind with the perforated sheets. This one had pre-printed letters in bold that said, "Market" across the top, ready-made for jotting down things to get. On the last one, there was a date and time which matched when we suspected Violet went missing.

I touched the perforations, saying, "She went to the market that day."

"With a shopping list in hand," Emanuel agreed.

"Did your daughter have a car?" Tracy asked.

Violet's parents looked to one another, nodding and shrugging as though we'd already known the answer.

Tracy crossed the room to exit onto the landing and look around. When she returned, she asked me and Emanuel, "Was there a vehicle reported missing?"

"No vehicle. The victim"—Mrs. Jones clasped a hand over

her mouth, Emanuel rephrasing—"We don't know where Violet was abducted."

"I think we might know now," I said, commenting quietly between us. I raised my voice, asking Violet's parents, "Could you provide a make, year and model? Anything about your daughter's vehicle."

"I'll get that and put out a call to search locally," Tracy said, turning to face the victim's parents and work the details.

While Tracy and Emanuel continued with Violet's car, I moved toward the bedroom, opening the door gently. The space was as tidy as the rest of the apartment with a neatly made bed covered in a pale blue quilt and a dresser topped with a single photo of Violet and her parents. There were other pictures too that included a man, the closeness of the two indicating a boyfriend.

"He's dead," Violet's mother said, her voice strong and in my ear, startling me.

"Dead, ma'am?" I asked, stepping back to give her room. She picked up the picture and brushed her fingers over her daughter's image. The sight of it struck my heart like a cold dagger. Hadn't I done the same a million times when Hannah went missing? "Ma'am?"

Mrs. Jones was fighting the grief again, voice shuddering as she spoke, "Cancer took him before they could marry."

"I'm so sorry."

She forced a smile, the kind you put on to comfort others when the consoling turns repetitive. "Please, don't let me interrupt."

"We won't be much longer."

I opened the closet, the hangers clinking softly as I slid them aside. Her wardrobe matched what I'd expected: athletic wear in bright colors, casual sundresses, a few blouses for more formal occasions. It all spoke to her Outer Banks lifestyle—active, breezy, and unfussy. But one thing caught my attention:

there wasn't a single concert T-shirt. There was no sign of other Def Leppard tour shirts like the kind she'd been wearing when we found her body. My gut tightened.

"What is it?" Mrs. Jones asked, reading my face. It surprised me since I was usually very good at hiding reactions.

"T-shirts. Oversized, mostly black with rock bands?" I asked, offering hints of what I was looking for. I gave just enough for her to recall seeing Violet wearing them. She looked deep into the closet, repeating my search. "I'm not sure what you're referring to?"

"May I?" I asked, holding my phone. Silence fell between us while she considered it. When she nodded, I retrieved the photo we'd taken at the crime scene and carefully palmed the screen to reveal only the section showing the T-shirt. I held it out, moving slow so as not to reveal anything else. "Do you recognize this shirt?"

Mrs. Jones recoiled slightly, her brow furrowing. Shaking her head, she answered, "No. That's not Violet's. She wouldn't wear that rock and roll stuff. Nothing like that."

"Are you sure?" I pressed gently, tucking my phone into my pocket. She shook her head liberally. "Why not?"

"She only listened to country music," Mr. Jones answered, his voice firm from the bedroom doorway. He'd overheard the exchange and entered. "I grew up on Rock and roll, but Violet never liked it. She said it gave her a headache."

"Thank you," I said, more bothered than ever about the concert shirt. The pieces weren't adding up. If Violet didn't own that shirt and didn't listen to rock, why had she been found wearing it?

Mrs. Jones's hands began to tremble more as she looked at me, her voice breaking. "Why would someone do this? My little girl never hurt anyone. She… she was a kind spirit. She loved everyone and everyone loved her."

"She didn't deserve this," Mr. Jones added, his voice cracking. He looked away, his fists clenching at his sides.

"We're going to find out why," I said softly, though the weight of their grief made the promise feel fragile. We filed out of the bedroom, the mystery weighing heavier, my adding, "And who."

Turning back to face the apartment, I tried to piece together the life Violet had lived and the secrets she might have kept. But all I could hear was Mrs. Jones's whisper behind me, her voice raw and broken: "Who would do this to my little girl?"

SEVEN

Wedding dresses weren't exactly my thing. I would have been fine picking something mail order or maybe even from a department store, a dress off the rack. Tracy insisted we go to a bridal shop though, explaining I'd want the full experience. I'm still not sure what that meant, but the enthusiasm had me agreeing. Tracy knew this was my first wedding dress—my *first* wedding dress, like it was a surprise to anyone. I mean, who's got time for dress number two when the first one already comes with scandal and courthouse vows?

One night, not too long ago, we'd shared a half bottle of wine, or maybe it was a little more than half, and I ended up spilling everything to her. Not just about not having a wedding dress, but about me and her father and the whole rebellious love story that got us married against everyone's better judgment. Honestly, it was one of my favorite memories. Tracy soaked it all up like it was a lost chapter from a sappy romance novel. As my maid-of-honor, she took that story and ran with it. By the next morning, she'd organized not just the big day, but the pre-ceremonies, the post-ceremonies, and I'm pretty sure something called a "practice brunch." Luckily, Jericho and I at least got to pick the honeymoon spot. Small victories, right?

I faced the wedding dresses in front of me, indecision rising. Tracy had insisted that I pick a wedding dress that was on the formal side, and white of course. I agreed and went to take advantage of the time with her which had become sparse as of late. Her excitement was contagious, as was her promise that we'd have a great time. Almost at once, we had staff catering to us. I wasn't used to the pampering and the attention at all but that didn't stop me from soaking up every minute of it.

It was our wedding. Mine and Jericho's. We were finally tying the knot and doing it in front of friends and family, including a small bunch traveling from Philadelphia to be witness and partake in the nuptials. I could feel the nerves mounting already, the momentum gaining. Before I knew it, I'd be walking down the aisle. And it was happening soon. For a long time, it was a distant date we'd circled with thick red magic-marker on our calendar. Suddenly, that date coming at us toward the end of next week. There was no knowing that it'd overlap with Violet Jones's murder investigation either. Then again, there's never knowing when a murder is going to take place.

Not far from the bridal shop was a strip mall where Violet Jones's car was found. A report of it came in soon after we'd arrived at the bridal shop. We'd go there next, the urgency shouldered by Emanuel who told us to finish up here and meet him there. I think Tracy was in cahoots with him, maybe even Jericho, all of them making sure I picked a dress. Guys have it easy. Jericho and Emanuel had tuxedos picked weeks ago. I don't think they spent more than an hour doing it either. The tardiness was my fault, the dress selection pushed to the last minute which was ridiculously dumb of me. But like most of the Outer Banks, the owner of the bridal shop knew Jericho and offered to make any alterations needed up to and including the day of the wedding.

"It has to be something sexy," I said, and spun around to show off my figure. I lied when I said the date was suddenly here. I knew. I could feel it coming like a snowstorm and had proudly trimmed a few pounds. I wanted to look my best for Jericho. "I can't do frumpy. I want something with a bit of leg and a plunging neckline."

"Plunging?" Tracy asked, gaze dipping to my chest. Her brow rose with a smirk, asking. "Just exactly how *plunged*?"

"You know, flirty." I nodded until she acknowledged. And warned, "But not so steep that my girls pop out."

"Not so steep," she repeated, picking through nearby dresses.

"It has to be classy." One by one we searched the dresses, quickly growing tired. "Anything?"

"How about this one?" she offered, holding up a dress that I'd already looked at. I cringed and waved it off. Disappointed, she turned away and moved on to a fresh rack. "This is harder than I thought."

"I'm sorry," I said with a pinch of embarrassment. I sensed she was disappointed and hated that I'd soured what she'd thought would be more enjoyable. Truth was, it bored me to tears. I think the two of us were just wired differently. If this had been a crime scene, we'd work it until dropping. I think we both had Violet Jones's car in mind and were anxious to get there. Maybe dress shopping wasn't her thing either.

"I could browse online, pick something off-the-rack—"

"Casey, you'd never get it in time," she interrupted, the frustration carrying in her voice. She blew the hair hanging in front of her eyes, and continued, "We kinda have to find it today."

Admittedly, I was doing this more for Tracy than for any kind of need. Like I said, an off-the-rack dress would have been fine by me. "With Jericho, I always pictured wearing something simple but beautiful, you know? Nothing too flashy—just something that feels like me."

"That's what I'm looking for," Tracy said, holding up another that I quickly dismissed.

I continued talking. "I'd go for a soft, flowing gown, maybe chiffon or lace, something light enough to dance in the ocean breeze. We'll be outside so it's got to be sleeveless with delicate straps, and the plunging neckline I mentioned."

"It's called a sweetheart cut," Tracy corrected me. I'd no idea what it was called. "You want subtle. Nothing too dramatic."

"Maybe some lace details too, especially along the hem. It'd look like the ocean foam where the waves meet the shore."

"Casey!"

I looked over to what Tracy was holding, and in an instant, I knew what it was. It was my dress. I dropped what I had and joined her, gaze fixed while she turned the dress around. The back dipped just a little, with tiny buttons running down to the waist that added a hint of elegance without overdoing it. And the color wasn't a blinding stark white like the others. This one was a soft ivory, something that would complement the beach at sunset. The front of it was gorgeous too with the subtle neckline, the *sweetheart* thing Tracy had mentioned. It was sleeveless with dainty straps and had the most beautiful lace. "This is the one. Isn't it?"

"Tracy, I think you found it," I said, swooning over a dress like I'd never had before. It left me short of breath and emotional, the tips of my fingers gliding gently across the silky material. "It's... it's the one."

"Would you like to try it on?" the owner said, brow raised. She glanced at her watch, commenting, "We have plenty of time. The next appointment—"

"Yes!" I answered, interrupting. I don't even think I needed to try it on though. It looked like it'd be a perfect fit, like there was some wedding goddess looking out for me today. That sounded silly in my head, but I chuckled at it anyways. I forced myself to get serious, asking, "You can take the measurements for any alterations now?"

"What's the rush?" Tracy asked. I only had to start saying "Violet" and Tracy nodded, asking the owner, "There's some place we need to be."

"Then we best get started," the owner answered.

She opened the door to the changing room and invited me toward it while I text Emanuel, telling him we'd be there in thirty, maybe forty-five minutes. He replied that he'd stand by, grab a bite to eat and that he'd instructed a few officers to cordon the vehicle with crime-scene tape.

"You okay in there?"

"Be out in a minute," I answered.

And I was out in a minute. The owner pulled and pinned and prodded and did all the things she needed to do to make that dress fit me like a glove. Though I couldn't take my eyes off the mirrors, I'd only needed to see Tracy's face to know we'd had a good day, we'd found my wedding dress.

Ten minutes after I'd returned to my street clothes, we'd joined Emanuel at Violet Jones's abandoned car.

The afternoon sun dipped lower as we parked in the cracked, weathered lot. The light was soft and golden, the months of drab wintry grays a memory. The asphalt was crumbly, springtime weeds bursting through the fractures, nature reclaiming the site a piece at a time. The breeze carried the smell of salt and fish from the ocean and a faint, acrid tang of burnt oil from a nearby restaurant's exhaust fan. Overhead, seagulls called out in shrill cries, their wings cutting as they circled, looking for scraps.

The small strip of shops surrounding the market had seen

better days. I looked them over, hoping to find a thrift-store or one of those retro eighties shops selling classic vinyl records. That would have explained the concert T-shirt, my thinking Violet stopped in, saw one she liked, bought it on the spot and put it on. But there was nothing beneath. There was no bra, no other clothing. They could be in her car? I questioned, the unknowns mounting. The simplest explanation was that the killer put that T-shirt on her. But why?

I found no stores that would carry records or concert shirts. This was a food market. Nothing else. I'd been here before though, a fish market being one of the larger storefronts. It was me and Jericho, shopping for homemade sushi that we swore we'd never do again. I recognized the screen door immediately, and its face with paint peeling like the dried flower petals of a forgotten bloom. It creaked every time someone pushed it open. Next to it was a candy store, its sign missing two letters, leaving *ANDY STOR* to fight for dignity. The grocery store anchoring the lot stood tired but functional, its hand-painted *Local Produce* sign half-hidden behind a faded and oversized Pepsi-Cola banner with a logo that was decades old.

And then there was Violet's car.

It looked ordinary enough at first—a beige two-door Corolla that would blend into any parking lot. But here, in the afternoon light, it felt like a tombstone marking a crime scene. A breath stuck in my throat. If I was right, this was the location of her abduction.

"Let's get started," I said, my voice breaking the tension as I grabbed a crime-scene kit from my trunk. Emanuel and Tracy were right behind me, their gloves snapping into place in perfect synchronicity. Emanuel carried his usual quiet intensity, brow furrowed pensively. And Tracy beamed a sharp gaze that darted to every corner of the lot as if Violet's ghost might appear from the shadows and tell us what happened here.

The driver's door drew our focus first. Emanuel crouched, a

knee popping, his broad frame folding neatly. He motioned to the asphalt where there were scuff marks cutting across the ground. "Look at this," he said, running a gloved finger across the brittle pavement. "No doubt there was a struggle here."

"Yeah," Tracy agreed, already dusting the door handle for prints. "And there are smudges everywhere."

"This is where she fought. But it was brief," I said with a nod, feeling a familiar knot in my stomach. A sense of guilt. We should've been faster, smarter, better about finding Violet's car. It wasn't a slip or mistake. It just should have been sooner. Emanuel continued his investigation around the ground while I joined in the fingerprinting. "Sun sets early, let's get fingerprints and pictures."

We worked methodically, careful not to miss anything. The breeze picked up, rattling a tattered plastic bag that clung to the market's rusted fence, parts of it bent awkwardly, other parts missing. It was the shadows along the asphalt I glanced at, seeing they were longer, the sun inching toward the horizon.

An hour or more passed, my arms tiring. Tracy was feeling it too, but her brush continued to move with rhythmic precision, the powder revealing a chaos of overlapping fingerprints around the trunk which were likely old. "Not much clarity here," she muttered, "but maybe we'll get something from the edges."

Emanuel, testing the driver-side door handle, suddenly froze.

I smirked, trying to lighten the mood. "What? Emanuel, tell me you're getting tired already?"

He didn't laugh. His voice was low, almost a whisper. "No... not tired. Guys. There's something in here." His hand stayed fixed on the handle, and his body stayed rigid like he'd become part of the car.

A wind hit us, the weather shifting, warm air rising out of the springtime cold. I put my fingerprint kit down, asking, "What do you mean, something?"

He didn't answer but put on a face that took my breath. I stepped closer, the knot in my stomach tightening, my smile gone.

"Casey, I heard something. I felt it too. It came from the handle when I lifted it."

"That'd be the latch," Tracy said nonchalantly. She was looking up, her focus on the work. Much like me, she was a born problem solver and always fast to answer any question. "These older model cars have more metal than plastic. You'll feel the mechanicals working, especially if they're pitted from the salt in the air."

"That's not it," he answered. The tone of his voice was like ice, and it was sharp enough to pull Tracy's attention. Emanuel was a tall man, his height gaining him fame briefly in the past. This afternoon, that height revealed for him what we could not see. Carefully leaning into the door, he gazed down through its window, the whites of his eyes gleaming. "Guys, there's something between the seat and the door. I think I see wires too." His voice was steady, but the sheen on his forehead betrayed him.

"It's probably just the victim's handbag," I said with encouragement. But the look of him had me racing over to the passenger side while I continued to make excuses. "You know, hidden from sight for security."

"Uh-uh," he disagreed. "I felt a click, and it wasn't the latch."

"Hold on," Tracy said somewhat amused. "You're overreacting."

I knelt and shone my flashlight inside the car, Tracy next to me and breathing fast. The beam sliced through the dim interior, landing on what could only be described as a nightmare. It was a black trash bag that had been wrapped tightly with duct tape at the front, middle and rear. Whatever it was, it was packaged carefully and placed against the door panel.

"Jesus, Casey," Tracy whispered. She gently nudged the

flashlight toward the door panel to the space between the package and the armrest. My throat closed when the beam hit two wires. They snaked out from the bag, disappearing into the interior door handle which was near opposite of where Emanuel's hand rested.

"Emanuel, don't move," I said sharply, chest tightening on every syllable.

Tracy shifted to my side, shoes scraping the asphalt. She flicked on her flashlight, its beam joining mine. "Oh my God," she breathed.

"It's a bomb," I said, my voice hollow. With those words, time stopped. The breeze was suddenly too loud, the cries of the gulls turning into screams. Devastation was one electrical pulse away.

EIGHT

The bomb squad arrived just as the sun dipped below the treetops, the golden light fading into a bruise-colored sky. They emerged from their vehicles like soldiers from a battlefield convoy, lips and eyes etched like stones, their gear heavy with purpose. A woman doled out commands with a calm authority that made you want to trust her immediately. She strode toward us, the leader of the squad. Her name tag read, *Lt. Harper*, and her voice and gaze were as steady as bedrock.

"Detective White?" she asked, her hazel eyes locking onto mine.

"That's me," I said, trying to match her calmness.

"Here's the situation," she began, pulling off her helmet for a moment. "We're dealing with a potential tripwire system. Your officer here"—she nodded toward Emanuel, who was visibly sweating but holding the handle steady—"is likely keeping the circuit from completing."

"Completing?" I questioned. "Meaning, if he lets go, we're looking at a detonation."

"We don't want him to let go," she answered, not answering the question directly. Her brow rose until I acknowledged. Emanuel said nothing but swallowed hard enough to hear.

"We're going to approach this in stages," Harper continued. "First, we'll stabilize the handle so he can release it safely. Then we'll move to investigate the device itself. Our techs will open the passenger-side door first to avoid disturbing the driver-side mechanism. It's crucial that no one touches anything unless instructed. Understood?"

We nodded as one.

"Emanuel," Harper said, her voice softening. "You've been incredible, sir. Just hold on a little longer. We'll get you clear of this very soon."

"Soon is good," was all Emanuel could say. The fatigue was beginning with a tremor in his hand, his wrist bouncing subtly.

The process was agonizingly slow, Harper's team analyzing the handle and creating mechanical braces to secure it. Their gloved fingers were smudged black by the dust we set, the door handle looking like a charcoal mess. After the first three attempts of locking the handle in place were abandoned, Tracy joined to help. She went to the asphalt, body scraping, shimmying herself beneath Emanuel and taking pictures of the handle's underside that showed where best to place the points of contact needed.

"His fingers are blocking the lip," Tracy yelled from beneath, shifting from the squatted position. She stood and showed the back of her camera, the squad engaged and evaluating every frame. Rather than say anything else, Tracy approached, camera in hand, the bomb squad convening a few feet away. When she reached us, she looked fiercely at me and then to Harper, explaining in a voice low enough to keep between us, "He's got big hands and there isn't enough room to wedge a makeshift brace in place. Doing so will risk the switch closing."

"From the topside?" Harper asked, reviewing the pictures.

Tracy shook her head subtly, the squad leader taking a deep breath, resigning the first approach. "Then let's find another way to secure that switch."

"We could attempt it from the inside," a bomb tech said. Emanuel's head jerked, trying to follow the two conversations. The bomb technician shuffled over to us, the heavily padded gear dragging. His face was bright with enthusiasm, shiny with sweat, his eyes darting fast between the car and Harper. "There's just the two wires. They're basic switch leads. It's amateur stuff. Cut one and the circuit can never be completed."

Harper chewed on the approach a long moment before waving over one of the other technicians. "Charley, you'll be taking the lead on this. What're your thoughts on the approach?"

"Ben's right about the switch leads—" he started. Charley's lips pressed thin to form an unmistakable line of doubt, instant dread stirring my stomach. Harper motioned for him to finish. "—but they're not the same gauge."

"That doesn't mean any—" the younger technician countered.

"Shush now, Ben Jacobs," Harper barked softly. She closed the distance between herself and the young technician, saying, "We work the problem all the way through. Understand?"

"Yes, ma'am," Ben said. "Look, I'm just saying, even though the gauge might be a little different, it's probably because the guy who made this thing had scrounged for parts."

"The gauge?" I asked. "You mean one of the wires is thicker than the other one?"

"That's correct," Charley said, tone empty, save for this sole concern. There were deep lines carved into every part of the older bomb technician's narrow face, his wearing a map of the nerve-wracking pressures that came with the job. "I suspect the thicker wire could be a sheathing, a conduit with smaller gauged wires inside it."

"Smaller wires inside. They might be used to detect an interruption in the circuit," Tracy added, her eyes blooming big and round. "A booby-trapped booby trap."

"Jesus," Harper said, breaking character with a show of emotion. She wiped the back of her glove across her forehead, a smudge appearing. "We need to know what's what about that thicker wire before we attempt anything else."

"On it," the men answered in unison, leaving us.

"Someone gonna tell me what's going on!?" Emanuel yelled. His voice was heartbreaking, and the shaking had worsened.

"I got you, bud," Jericho said, the sight of him a shock. It stopped me dead, stealing my breath. I didn't want him here. God, what was he doing here? As if answering my questions, he lifted his sheriff's badge toward Harper and tucked himself next to Emanuel and the bomb.

My mouth went hot and dry like the sands after a long summer day. Jericho was fully dressed in his gear. His shift was ending soon, the shine from his sheriff's badge tin standing out even in the dimming light. He tipped his hat in my direction and continued to console Emanuel, supporting him in words only, his hands cradling the air.

"Sheriff, with all due respect, I'll ask you to stand over here," Harper said, a hint of demand in her voice. Jericho acknowledged her but continued to talk to Emanuel. Truth was, it was helping. Whatever Jericho was saying, it helped calm his old friend whose hands were steadying. They stopped speaking and lowered their heads, Harper questioning, "Now what are they doing?"

"They're praying, ma'am," I answered, their friendship a powerful one, the sight filling me with emotion. "Give them a minute, please."

When they were finished, and Jericho started toward us, Harper explained, "Sir, we're working this from the passenger side first." She instructed her team with a wave, the squad moving in choreographed precision. "Is that passenger-side door clear?"

"It's clear," they answered, door hinges creaking, the sound cutting through the heavy air. Inside, the technicians worked carefully, documenting every angle before they approached the black bag. One tech used a small camera probe to examine the wires leading to the handle, yelling out numbers that were meaningless to the rest of us.

"It's a rudimentary circuit," one of them answered the other, his voice muffled through his helmet. "But effective. Two leads as discussed that connect to the door handle to complete the loop. As for the thicker gauge, we are going to need more time to assess it."

"More time?" Emanuel said, voice breaking, the shaking in his hand returning.

"Fucking hell," someone said. "This thing would've gone off the moment the handle was released."

"Stow the commentary," Harper commanded.

"Yes, ma'am."

"What do we have in the bag?" she asked.

We watched as the technician carefully slit the tape to reveal a tangle of wires and a block of gray bricks I recognized to be C-4.

"Explosives are live," the tech confirmed. "There's no timer active, only the circuit is armed. We should be able to disarm it here."

"That was stupid," I told Jericho, reprimanding. I watched from a safe distance, my heart pounding. The wind picked up, carrying the scent of the sea and a reminder of how close we were to disaster in this beautiful and tranquil place. "Don't do it again."

"I won't," he said. "Sorry."

"Perfectly forgivable," I said, emotion catching in my voice.

As Harper's team began the long work of disarming the bomb, I saw Emanuel's legs trembling, his large frame hunched awkwardly to maintain his grip. He was holding it together, but barely. His breath came in short, shallow bursts, and sweat dripped steadily from his temple.

"Jer—I can't... I can't do this anymore," he rasped, his voice cracking. His wide eyes met mine, and I saw the terror that had taken root deep inside him. "They're numb. I can't feel my fingers anymore. I'm gonna lose my grip."

"What he say!" I heard, a commotion inside the vehicle.

"You're fine, Emanuel," I shouted, even as my own heart hammered against my ribs. "Just a little longer."

His head rocked sideways and forward, his body twitching. "I can't. Casey, I can't. Jericho, all of you! You've got to run. All of you need to get out of here."

"Out!" someone demanded. The commotion erupted like a thunderclap, reverberating through the team, padded bodies scuttling backward like sand crabs fleeing from a wave.

"I know you've been holding on a long time," I said firmly, crouching beside him. "Just a few more minutes?"

He gave a weak, bitter laugh, his shoulders slumping slightly. "It's too much. I'm done." His voice was rising, breaking with panic cresting. "I can't do it anymore. I'm sorry."

I'm not at all sure what happened then. I saw Emanuel's body lunging, his free hand slapping the top of the car, the men and women from the bomb squad hurriedly scattering. And I saw the broken asphalt passing beneath my feet in long strides as though someone else was driving me. Emanuel was next to me suddenly. Rather, I was next to him, one hand on his back and my fingertips slipping overtop his. Emanuel let go just as I took hold, his body crumpling to the ground like a marionette whose strings had been cut. My fingers slid into place, gripping the handle as firmly as I could, the weight of the moment pressed down like an anchor tied around my neck.

"Shit," I heard myself say, second-guessing my actions. But this was an explosive that would have killed everyone. I don't think there was any second-guessing anything. Still, the touch of the car handle was sickeningly warm and damp with sweat. And now I had the burden of holding it in place to save us. To save us all. I looked down at Emanuel, saying, "You're safe now."

His breathing hitched, his lips trembling as he stared at me. "Casey..."

"It's okay," I said softly. "I've got this."

"Casey, what did you do?" Jericho whispered harshly, his eyes snapping from mine to the handle and back. "Casey, what the hell did you do?"

Emanuel crawled back, his breaths coming in shallow, uneven gasps. Jericho rushed to him, pulling him further away. "You've done enough, man," Jericho said, his voice hoarse with emotion. "You're safe now—"

Jericho stopped talking when he returned, our eyes meeting and speaking volumes, reciting leaping fears, but no words spoken. "Casey?"

"I just did it. I didn't think—" I said through gritted teeth, not daring to shift my grip even an inch. The shock of it tore my insides as everything we had as a family hit me like a thunderbolt. *Oh God! What the hell did I just do?!*

"Casey?" I heard Jericho saying, the words muffled behind a soft cry.

"It'll be okay," I said, lying to the love of my life. I cleared my throat, telling him, "Just make sure they finish this. Okay?"

He was gone in a flash, his full uniform blocking all of Harper while he peppered her with a thousand questions. In a way I was relieved. They were over fifty feet away and the sting of repetition was already settling in my arms. I have no idea how Emanuel held the handle as long as he did. "Don't think about it!" I hollered, the bomb squad stopping to peer up at me through the window. The man couldn't have been more than eighteen, his face absent of age, of whiskers and wrinkles, not a single blemish. He was a baby and should have been anywhere but here.

"You okay, ma'am?" he asked.

"It's Casey," I said. I wasn't a ma'am yet. My mom was a ma'am. "We're in this together so please call me Casey."

"Yes ma—" he started, his helmet sliding over his eyes. He adjusted it, finishing, "Yes, Casey. We'll get out of this soon enough."

Time moved strangely after that. Harper and her team worked quickly but meticulously, their voices a steady murmur in the background. I wish I could say the same for what was happening inside me. It reminded me of those games in gym class or the stupid punishments a teacher would dole out to the class. *Hold out your arms*, they'd say with a grin. After five minutes, your fingers weighed a hundred pounds, and your arms would drop.

I knew the horror of Emanuel's plight. I felt it. Legs aching, stomach rolling, a bladder that was screaming to release. It wouldn't be long before I'd fail, my arm or hand drooping, the door's handle an anchor of dead weight held up by my fingers.

"Dead weight," I mumbled, the words resonating. Was that what was going to become of me? Dead weight? Sadly, I doubted it. The young man looked up, following my voice. And from the eyes behind his bomb squad gear, that package nestled between the door and the seat was big enough to incinerate us all.

"How are we?" Tracy asked, kneeling beside me, fully clothed in bomb squad gear, her eyes red and damp, but her hands steady as she handed tools to the bomb squad techs.

"You shouldn't be here," I said, evenly toned.

"Nonsense," she half whispered, trying to sound encouraging. It barely registered though, the sound of my own breathing becoming too loud in my ears. "I know this stuff."

"That's not the point."

"Shh," she said, trying to work.

Harper approached me directly, her hazel eyes calm but intense. "Detective White, we're close. We've secured the passenger-side door. Once we disarm the wiring on this side, we'll move to stabilize the explosives."

I nodded stiffly, the ache in my fingers becoming too much as though they'd been struck with a hammer. "Just tell me when I can let go."

"You're doing great," she said firmly. "We'll be ready in a couple of minutes. Hang on until then."

Tracy retreated to a safe place alongside Emanuel and Jericho. They were almost done but the minutes felt like an eternity. The sun dipped lower, and the breeze carried the cries of gulls and the distant hum of cars from Route 12. I could feel every second pass as the coolness of the ending day seeped into my bones. My mind raced, but I forced myself to focus on the handle, the solidness of it beneath my grip, the fragility of the wires brushing against my fingertips.

Finally, Harper gave the signal. "We've secured the circuit on the passenger side. You can release the handle now, but slowly. Very slowly."

A wave of nausea struck with spinning force. I knew it was the adrenaline, the buildup enormous. *Breathe into the nose and out through the mouth.* I said this over and over until it eased. When I was ready to release the handle, my fingers refused to cooperate at first, stiff from the relentless grip. I exhaled slowly, the first breath I'd truly taken in what felt like hours and began to release the handle. My movements were painstakingly slow, my muscles screaming in protest. When I felt and heard the internals of the handle click, I finally let go and staggered back, falling to the pavement as my knees gave out.

"Clear!" one of Harper's techs called out, Harper waving the all-clear, the tension breaking like a snapped cable. The wave of relief that swept over me was almost dizzying. Jericho was there in an instant, his hand on my arm to steady me back to my feet.

"You're insane," he said, his voice shaking, the glint in his eyes sharp with tears. But there was a faint smile tugging at the corner of his mouth, his face a welcoming sight. "Don't you ever—"

"You don't have to worry about that!" I replied, managing a shaky grin.

"We're still here!" Emanuel said, celebrating as we huddled together, the four of us safe.

The bomb squad turned their attention to the black bag. The passenger door was fully open now, and one of the techs moved carefully to investigate the wires. Another tech began to examine the duct tape-wrapped package, slicing through the layers with a scalpel as Harper supervised. We'd become spectators and I couldn't look away, wanting to know for certain what it was that attacked with such evilness. The earliest assessment was a C-4 explosive. My hope was that it was only a fake. Something the killer stood up as fodder to humor themselves with.

"What if they're watching?" I said, asking, spinning around, searching every corner, every shade.

"Who?" the team asked.

"The person who set that bomb," Jericho answered, realizing the same. "To watch all this go down."

"What do we have?" I heard Harper asking her team, voice clipped.

"But they couldn't have known we'd be here," Emanuel countered. "I mean, how would they know unless they were following?"

"Live C-4," one of the techs replied to Harper. "The second

wire does appear to contain multiple wires inside but shouldn't be a problem."

Harper let out a slow breath, nodding. "Proceed in disarming. If you see a complication, we'll have to remove and use the blast containment tank."

"It *was* another booby trap," Tracy said, watching intently. "Be careful..."

The tech worked deftly, snipping wires and isolating the circuit. The black bag was peeled back, revealing the payload in stark detail. It was chillingly real.

"Got it! Disarmed," the young tech finally announced. The weight of the word hit like a wave, and the entire lot seemed to exhale collectively.

Harper turned to us, her expression a mix of admiration and exhaustion. "Holding that handle, you both saved a lot of lives."

Emanuel nodded, too drained to speak, I did the same. Emanuel stood still, hands on his hips, looking at me, his eyes red but filled with gratitude. "You are one crazy lady, Casey White," he said, his voice shaking.

"Yeah," I replied. "But we're alive. That's what matters."

I didn't hear the blast. I didn't feel it at first either. But the world erupted in a flash of light and fury in that moment.

NINE

One second, I was standing with Jericho and the team, watching the bomb squad dismantle the explosive with surgical precision. The next, the car burst apart in a deafening roar, a fiery bloom that consumed the Corolla and everything around it. The shockwave hit us like a freight train, throwing the four of us backward through the air.

I barely registered the sensation of flight before I slammed into the ground, my head snapping against the pavement. Pain shot through my body, white-hot and blinding. The air was forced from my lungs, leaving me gasping as though I'd forgotten how to breathe.

For a moment, everything was still. Time seemed to stretch in a disjointed series of images that flickered behind my eyelids —the fireball spiraling into the night sky, shattered glass pelting our bodies, jagged shards of metal spinning like deadly shrapnel. My ears were useless, the explosion leaving me deaf to the world. All I could hear was a high-pitched ringing that was relentless and maddening.

Shapes moved in the haze above me, black silhouettes against the orange glow. One of them crouched down, their face resolving into Jericho's—his features streaked with soot, a thin cut trickling blood down his right temple. His mouth moved, his lips forming words I couldn't hear.

"Casey, are you okay?" I read, lips moving, the words unclear.

I blinked, trying to focus on his face, trying to will my body to respond. My head throbbed, the pain radiating through my skull like waves crashing against the rocky shores of the Outer Banks finest piers. Slowly, I nodded, though the motion sent a fresh wave of nausea through me. Jericho slipped his arm under-mine, pulling me upright. The world spun dangerously, but I forced myself to stay standing. My knees wobbled, my shoes scuffing against the debris-littered asphalt as I tried to regain my balance.

"Babe?" I questioned, my hands and fingers feeling every part of him. From the front to the back, up and down his sides and then onto his face, where there was a day of unshaven whiskers. "Just the cut?"

"I think so," he nodded, wiping at it errantly.

"Tracy! Emanuel!" I croaked, my voice raspy, the words raw in my throat. "Guys!"

They were nearby. Tracy was on her hands and knees, coughing violently as smoke curled around her, her hair matted with debris. She favored one arm, an injury where there was a sooty mark on her clothes and skin. I sucked in a breath with concern, and was relieved when she sat back assessing, her eyes sharp and focused. Emanuel leaned heavily against a bent lamppost, his face pale with one of his arms hanging at an odd angle. His eyes locked onto mine, wide with shock but alive.

"We're okay," Tracy rasped loudly, waving her good hand in the air weakly. "We're okay."

Jericho pulled me closer as the four of us turned to look at the scene unfolding in front of us.

The parking lot was a vision of hell. The car was gone,

replaced by a raging inferno, the asphalt around it heaping outward like a meteor had plummeted from outer space. The flames twisted and roared, sending plumes of thick black smoke spiraling into the darkening sky. The light was blinding, turning the dusky night into an eerie, unnatural day.

The store-front windows of the market had been shattered, their jagged remnants glittering under the blaze's unholy glow. Debris was scattered everywhere—smoldering pieces of the car, shards of asphalt blown apart by the blast, and scraps of the bomb squad's tools reduced to warped, blackened metal. And there were parts. Parts of the men and women who were disassembling the bomb. I saw them. Jericho saw them. So did Tracy and Emanuel. And it was something we'd never be able to unsee.

Emergency lights strobed in the chaos, red and blue mixing with the inferno's orange. Figures moved through the destruction, some staggering, others being carried or dragged. EMTs were shouting orders, their words muffled in the aftermath of the explosion. I squinted through the haze, trying to find the bomb squad leader, Harper, eager to see if she was okay. The sickening realization hit me like a second blow: it was more than the four bomb squad members who'd perished. Harper was nowhere to be seen. She'd been close to the car when it exploded.

"Five," Jericho murmured beside me, his voice low and hollow, barely audible over the ringing in my ears. "They didn't make it."

"Oh God," was all I could say as state agency vehicles seemed to arrive out of nowhere. This included rescue squads from neighboring counties along with news vans and even some civilians looking to help. More than a dozen were limping or crawling through the carnage, their injuries a grim tally of the chaos. Blood slicked the pavement in places, mixing with the debris, the metallic tang cutting through the acrid smoke in the air. The flames burned on, defying the dark of the night. I couldn't take my eyes away from the scene—the glowing embers where Violet's car had been, the shattered windows of the market, the flickering lights of the emergency vehicles. This wasn't just murder. It was a declaration. It was an attack on us. This was personal, and whoever had done this was far from finished.

TEN

It seemed like an hour or more since Carly Rose had left the barrier islands, crossing Wright Memorial Bridge, traveling west on the mainland away from the sea and home. The gravel road stretched ahead, a pale ribbon cutting through rolling fields of green and brown. Last season's sunflowers flanked the roadside, the field abandoned, unharvested. What the winter didn't consume was disheveled, most of the sunflowers were dried out with brown petals and drooping heads, the fully mature seeds still plump and visible on the flower head, crows and squirrels tackling the plants. Between them, she saw the young plants, the ones for the coming summer. It wouldn't be long before there was nothing but green for miles to see.

Carly adjusted the visor, squinting against the amber light of the setting sun, but still, no destination was in sight. No house. No barn. Only the endless expanse of the old sunflower fields and the anticipation of a sale. She bit her upper lip, stomach growling with a hunger pang.

She glanced at the passenger seat, where her phone sat uselessly. The spinning wheel of the frozen GPS seeming to mock her decision to drive. Tossing it aside, Carly gripped the wheel tighter, her fingers smudged with dried paint, evidence of the month's work she crammed into the last week. It was the paintings—sunflowers on canvas, vibrant and alive—thin frames rattling softly in the backseat with every bump.

"I need this sale," she muttered to herself, her words swallowed by the crackling static of the car's ancient radio. Another hunger pang, bordering on painful. It was the worrying. The career she'd sought so hard to have pivoting mercilessly, money for food and her apartment at stake.

Her stomach twisted as she thought of the rent notice tacked to her studio door, the one she couldn't afford to ignore any longer. The sunflower collection had been her labor of love, and this sale could keep her afloat for another month. But the further she drove, the more this setup felt wrong. The online marketplace had been good once before with consistent sales but that dried up like the sunflowers from seasons past. Her offerings got less visibility in front of the buyers and visibility was everything online. It remained a mystery as to why though, the marketplace tech beyond her skills.

"I can paint though. That's my gift, my daydream," she said, angrily thumping the wheel. A sweeping resignation struck, and the defiance to be who she wanted to be drained out of her. "There's teaching? It's got health benefits too."

She shook the thought away. Ahead, the gravel gave way to a dirt road. Her car jolted as the uneven surface worsened, the suspension groaning with every rut. A bitter thought rose in her mind—how the world valued frivolity over effort. A grunt. It values it over good art and bad, she thought begrudgingly.

Picking at spots of dried paint on the back of her hand, she followed the design requirements to the letter, spending weeks crafting these pieces, capturing every shade of green and yellow they requested. The commission will pay the bills, yet the art sells for a pittance while ridiculous installations earn millions.

A clank. "Oh no, no. No!" The car's motor sputtered,

coughing twice and bucking with what sounded to her like a mechanical hiccup. Carly gripped the wheel, pressing her chest against it, yelling, "Please don't. Don't do that." And as her pleas went unheard, the car bucked once more before dying completely.

Carly's breath caught as the sedan rolled to an unsteady stop. "What the actual—" She groaned with a soft cry, twisting the key in the ignition, trying to start it. The engine wheezed, clicked, and fell silent. She sat for what felt like minutes, uncertain of what to do, the motor ticking, its insides slowly turning cold.

Sliding out of the car, the dusty road as dry and arid as the air, Carly found the lever beneath the hood, popping it to a shock that made her gasp. She wasn't a mechanic but there was no mistaking what was right and what was wrong with the engine. She leaned forward, inspecting the wires that were shredded, their plastic sheaths peeled back as if by teeth.

"An animal?" she murmured, befuddled by the sight, anger stirring. "Fuck!"

Her stomach tightened as she retrieved her phone and scoured the surroundings for a signal. Any signal. When none came, she jumped onto her bumper, holding the phone high, arm trembling as she searched. The back of her neck stung with sweat, her chest heaving with what was more from anxiety than physical exertion. That's when the first of the tears pressed. There was so much at stake with this sale.

She tried again, racing across the dirt road to the other side, the old sunflower field behind her. Nothing. A dirt devil spun up as if to tease the sad predicament. It crossed back to the other side, throwing loose dirt into her car, "Fuck!"

Spent, Carly pinched the bridge of her nose, shadows from the sunflower stalks looming behind her. She glanced up and down the road, seeing how they stood against the road like sentinels, their dense brown hiding everything behind them.

A faint chill crept over her skin, goosebumps rising on her arms. The air was warm though. The sense of someone watching put her feet into motion and she moved to the middle of the road, arms crossing her chest.

"Anyone there?" she asked, a breeze rustling through the dead sunflowers. Her thoughts turned to the car that had followed her earlier, its dust trailing in the rearview mirror for what seemed like miles. She stared far, the road empty. When had it disappeared? Movement! The unmistakable crunching of dead leaves. "Who's there!"

As if on cue, a pair of rabbits appeared from the field, whiskered faces chewing innocently.

Carly playfully kicked at the road, the tip of her shoe striking pebbles, "You guys gave me a—"

A sharp sting bit into her neck, searing and sudden. *Bees!* she thought wildly, her mind tracing through the car's glove compartment, wondering if the EpiPen was expired. She let out a yelp, slapping the spot with her hand, and her fingers brushed against something small and hard embedded in her skin. It wasn't the stinger from a bee. She pulled it free, the sting in her neck turning numb, a shivering cold racing into her chest. Carly opened her palm to find a dart.

The road spun sideways, a lightheadedness making her feel drunk, an untimely laugh spilling sloppily from her lips. For the moment, Carly felt like the dirt devil had returned and picked her up, spinning her around and around like the carnival rides she'd enjoyed when she was a child. The moment was fleeting, another sting slipping into her skin.

This time, her vision blurred instantly, and the horizon tilted with a nauseating roll that made her stumble against the car. Her legs buckled, a plume of road dust exploded when her back struck the ground. *Cornflower blue,* she thought distantly, staring at the sky and picking the color she'd use to paint it. *Maybe cobalt blue too and shades of white and gray and a hint of yellow and pink for those enormous clouds.* The brief giddiness faded and was replaced with fear, every muscle seeming to cease.

"No," she gasped, her voice thin and desperate with understanding. She opened her mouth to yell, a breath escaping just as the world went dark.

Carly woke to the rustling of leaves, the sound blending with the faint chirp of distant birds. Her head throbbed with a sharp ache radiating through her temples as she forced her eyes open. Although the daylight was fading, it struck the back of her skull with punishing force. She could only squint, the muscles in her body ignoring her commands. Above, the pale blue sky was streaked with gold, the light fading into twilight.

My car? Alarm set in. It'd be dark soon. *I was attacked?*

She tried sitting up, her muscles heavy, her limbs sluggish and unresponsive. Her neck hurt fiercely where the darts had left their sting. She couldn't speak without raspy pain, her throat swollen and aching. *I've been drugged. Why? Who?*

Oh my God! the commission for the artwork? *A setup?*

The realization clawed at her chest. Her breaths came faster, shallower, as she took in her surroundings. The dead sunflowers stretched endlessly in every direction, their stalks thick and impenetrable. Staring hard, slivers of white light shining between the brown stalks, Carly spotted her car, the colors mismatched on the doors, one an original and the other from the junkyard.

I've been moved into the field.

Panic surged, but another, darker thought overrode it. Her trembling hands moved to her clothes, motion returning in time to provide truths to what happened while she was unconscious. She hesitated, her stomach knotting with dread as she pressed her fingers against her jeans and the waistband of her underwear.

She let out a shuddering breath. Everything was still there, still intact. Relief swept through her, but it was fleeting, replaced by a deeper terror when a rustling sound came from the stalks. Carly froze, her heart hammering in her chest and thumping incessantly against her eardrums. The noise grew louder, closer, the heavy crunch of boots snapping dry stems. Whatever the drug was, it was fading in time for her to scramble to her knees, her fingers gripping the sunflower stalks for balance.

A step and then another, Carly picked up her feet in a run toward the road. She stopped at a clearing when it appeared suddenly, a wide circle of flattened sunflowers yawning open like a wound. She hesitated at its edge, her instincts screaming for her to turn back.

An arrow sliced through the air with a sharp whistle, striking her shoulder with a sickening thud. Pain was instant like the guttural scream that erupted from the bottom of her lungs. Carly's scream continued, the force of the arrow's strike spinning her as she hit the ground.

When she began to claw her way back, another attack came, the arrow missing and stabbing the earth between her head and arm. The next hit her, driving through her arm and pinning it to the ground. Pain radiated through into her shoulder, hot and blinding.

The rustling grew louder, the heavy footfalls deliberate and unhurried. Carly clawed at the ground, her breaths ragged as she forced her arm free so she could roll onto her back. Another arrow struck her thigh, the tip tearing through muscle and pinning her leg to the earth.

"No," she sobbed, tears streaking her face. She twisted to see the arrow's shaft, black as coal, its neon orange and green fins vibrant in the fading light. Blood seeped down her leg in ribbons. She reached for the sky, clutching and pleading, "Why are you doing this!?"

The footsteps stopped. Carly forced herself to look up, her vision swimming. The figure stood at the edge of the clearing, a dark silhouette against the twilight sky.

"Please," she whispered, her voice broken. "Please don't."

The figure didn't answer. They raised their bow, nocking another arrow with practiced precision. Carly's mind raced, grasping for anything to hold onto. She thought of her paintings, her sunflowers. She thought of the tourists who'd never see them, never see anything from her studio. And she thought of all the unfinished work waiting on the easel and stacked against the walls.

The next arrow struck her chest, driving the air from her lungs. Carly convulsed, her body arching as a strangled gasp escaped her lips, the taste of blood filling her mouth. Her head lolled to the side. She stared aimlessly at the dead sunflowers swaying above her, their brittle, dried leaves whispering, indifferent to her suffering. The killer loomed closer, their shadow swallowing her field of vision.

Why? her mind continued. A strangled laugh bubbled up as she realized how useless that question was now. Her chest felt tight, the threat of suffocation growing. The sunflowers above seemed to turn distant, their colors bleeding together in her fading vision.

"Who are you?" she managed to croak, her voice barely audible.

There was no answer.

The killer raised the bow again, the string drawn taut. The final arrow loosed with a sharp whoosh, and everything went still. Carly's last thought was of her paintings, now forever unseen.

ELEVEN

The wind whispered through the dead sunflowers as if sharing a secret too terrible to speak aloud. The scene we were approaching squeezed my heart with fright, making me afraid to hear anything at all. On both sides of us for as far as we could see, brittle stalks swayed weakly, their brown, withered petals crumbling at the lightest touch, scattering like ash across the soil. Between the lifeless stalks, fresh green shoots pushed defiantly through the earth—a cruel juxtaposition of death and rebirth. It was early morning west of the Outer Banks, the local police contacting us about a murder. The light carried no warmth, filtered instead through an overcast sky that cast the field in shades of gray. The air smelled of decay—earthy farm soil, rotting vegetation, and the faint metallic tang of something far worse.

The drive here had been silent. Tracy, Emanuel, and I were still carrying the weight of last night's explosion. Every muscle in my body screamed with soreness, my ribs tender with each shallow breath. Emanuel's forehead bore a fresh gauze bandage, his shoulder dislocation popped back into place. Tracy's arm was wrapped tight to protect a burn, a reminder of how close we'd come to joining those who hadn't survived.

Survived. What a peculiar word it was. Just the thought of it came with a sting of guilt and sorrow for those who weren't here to say it with you.

"Doesn't get any easier, does it?" Emanuel muttered as he stepped out of the car, unfolding his hunched frame with a stretch.

"No," I said, pulling on my gloves as I eyed the field before us. "And it's not supposed to."

The realtor who'd called in about the body stood awkwardly near the edge of the dirt road, wobbling on impractical heels as she clutched her phone and talked animatedly to a nearby officer. She was tall and wiry, dressed in a beige pantsuit that looked more fitting for an office than the unyielding countryside. Her car was parked behind the police cruiser, the face of her agency—and her own heavily airbrushed portrait—plastered across the door. She gestured emphatically toward the field, her voice carrying faintly over the breeze.

"I was just putting up a sign!" she exclaimed. "I've got buyers lined up, developers, big corporations—"

"We'll handle it," I interrupted sharply, striding toward the car parked nearby. A dented hatchback sat precariously on the uneven dirt, its hood propped open. A young officer—a rookie by the look of him—was reaching for the driver's door.

"We'll check inside—"

"Stop!" I barked, the command cutting through the morning air like a whip. The officer froze mid motion, his wide eyes snapping to me.

"I wasn't—I didn't mean to—" he stammered, stepping back and raising his hands.

"Nobody touches that car until it's cleared," I said firmly. I glanced at Emanuel, who was already inspecting the vehicle from a safe distance. "The bomb squad is on its way."

"Good call," Tracy murmured, tugging at one of her bandages. She crouched near the hood, squinting at the frayed wires. "Looks like something chewed through these."

"Squirrels," Emanuel suggested, his tone almost conversational. "Had 'em tear up my wiring over the winter. Damn things love this plant-based insulation. Cost me a couple thousand I didn't have."

"Are we sure it wasn't deliberate?" I asked, joining them. When I saw the frayed insulation, the bite marks, there was no doubt what had done the damage. I glanced over my shoulder, glimpsing dark red through the dead sunflower stalks. "This looks like the case where the killer tricked their victims to come to a sunflower field."

"You mean the sunflower murders that started with Emanuel's cousin?" Tracy replied, asking.

"Charlie Robson," Emanuel said with a nod. He frowned, saying, "There is similarity."

"You think that's what happened here?" Tracy asked.

"Possibly." I nudged my chin at the wiring, adding, "Or it could just be a coincidence."

Emanuel circled to the back, calling out, "Casey, you'll want to see this."

I followed, my boots kicking up fine clouds of dust. The car's gas cap was slightly ajar, and streaks of discolored paint surrounded it. "It's got signs of being siphoned," I said grimly, noting the haphazard spill pattern. The hair on the back of my neck sprang to life, standing on end.

"The killer planned this," Emanuel said, swallowing dryly with a sickened look on his face.

Peering through the dirty rear window, we spotted something in the backseat. Unlike Violet Jones's car, this wasn't a bomb. It was a collection of framed artwork, the tag hung in a dangle, visible enough for me to make out a name and address. The name *Carly Rose* was scrawled next to an address. "Definitely a setup," I muttered. "The killer knew she'd come here. The killer may have posed as a buyer, asking her to meet them on the property."

Officer Ben Stanley approached cautiously, a camera slung over his shoulder. "We got another crime scene?" he asked, his voice loud like it was an announcement. Any indications of reluctance or hesitation since the first crime scene seemed to have disappeared. I nodded and he glanced around at us until finding Tracy.

"You've got booties on, right?" Tracy asked, pointing to his feet.

"Yeah," he said, lifting one foot for her inspection.

"Good. Gloves too," she added, a breeze lifting her hair while waiting for him to nod. "Focus on the whole scene first. Wide angles. Then work your way closer toward the body. Make sure you're circling the victim, not stepping too close."

"You'll do fine," I said, Ben nodding, his Adam's apple bobbing as he swallowed hard. He raised the camera and began snapping pictures, pausing occasionally to gape at the sight before him.

"Never seen anyone with arrows sticking out of them," he said, a flush of green rising onto his face. He spun around, facing the road. "Just need a minute."

"Take the time," Emanuel told him. "We're not going anywhere."

And he was right. We had the work cut out for us. The body of Carly Rose lay fifty yards into the field, pinned grotesquely among a bed of dead sunflowers that had been purposely trampled. The victim was in her late twenties, her frame delicate but awkwardly contorted. Her dusky blue turtleneck was soaked in blood, the fabric turned dark and glistening where it clung to her ribs. Her jeans were ripped at the knees, dirt and blood streaked across the fabric. A worn pair of sneakers, one slightly untied, peeked out from beneath her sprawled legs.

Four arrows pierced her body. One had lodged deep into her upper arm, pinning her to the ground like an insect in a display case. Another jutted from her ribs at an upward angle, likely piercing a lung. The third protruded from her thigh, where the bright red blood had long since darkened to a rusty brown. The last was likely the kill shot, the killer having put the arrow through the victim's eye.

I crouched beside her, Tracy and Emanuel standing a respectful distance away. "Check her hands," Tracy suggested softly. "Are there any defensive wounds?"

I lifted one hand carefully. Carly's fingers were slender, stained with vibrant streaks of red and blue—paint, I realized. Her nails were short and clean, no dirt beneath them. No signs of a struggle. She hadn't fought back. She hadn't had the chance.

"Nothing. No defensive wounds," I said, my voice flat. "She was either surprised or incapacitated."

"Artist?" Tracy asked, nodding at the paint stains. "Explains the paintings in the backseat of her car."

"Looks that way," I replied. "She was the artist who painted them. She might've been here for a showing—or lured into thinking she was."

Ben Stanley continued to circle the body, snapping photos from every angle, his color still a shade too green. His hands were steady, but his expression betrayed his unease. "This is... It's a lot," he muttered, his voice barely audible over the shutter clicks.

"Focus on the details," Tracy reminded him. "Get close-ups of the arrows, the wounds, her face. Every detail matters."

Carly's face was pale, her lips slightly parted. Her

remaining eye was wide and stared blankly at the sky, framed by smudges of eyeliner that had run down her cheeks. The faintest hint of a smile lingered on her lips, eerily at odds with the violence of her death.

The screech of brakes announced the arrival of the medical examiner's van. They were usually first on the scene, but we'd gotten here before them. Derek and Samantha climbed out, hurrying, their usual banter subdued as they approached the body and bickered nonsensically about wrong directions. Derek knelt beside Carly, his gloved hands hovering over the arrows.

"Nice of you two to join," I said without expression. "We're just getting started."

"Sorry," Samantha said, black bangs covering her eyes while she slipped on booties and gloves. Derek followed too, bickering about the phone app that led them in the wrong direction. Samantha stood straight and searched around the sunflowers and then the body, "Tracy, this... this is like the others you told me about?"

"Uh-huh," Tracy replied grimly. The look on her face stopped me cold. It stopped us all. I wanted it to be the kind of stillness born from nostalgia, the memories of warmth and summer light. But it wasn't. It was the quiet terror of recognition, the kind of fear you feel in your gut before your brain catches up. This wasn't new. It was familiar. Too familiar. It was happening again.

The sunflower fields were supposed to be beautiful with their rows of golden crowns nodding in the breeze. But they had become something else entirely. Lures. Traps. Like carnival lights blinking over a deep pit. The girls had come willingly, drawn in by something meant to look harmless. They never left.

We'd seen it before. The victims bore the same hallmarks. Arrows, sleek and silent, had ripped through them from multiple angles. Some were still standing. Propped up, impossibly, by the shafts embedded through their limbs and into the earth, like grotesque scarecrows in full bloom. It was always the arrows. And always a sunflower field.

What haunted me most, what I saw first in my memories, wasn't the violence. It was the color. The blood was so red. Unnaturally red against the yellow flowers. Pinpricks of it on petals, bright as neon under a crime-scene lamp. The contrast made my stomach turn every time. We stopped looking at sunflowers the same after that case. They stopped being flowers. And now, standing in a sunflower field again, I felt it come back. The dread. The weight of knowing we hadn't buried the past deep enough. The field was blooming again. And so was the nightmare.

"This field was never harvested," Tracy commented, breaking the silence. "That's different from before. There could be significance in it?"

"I don't know. Maybe?" was all I could say, still feeling the buzz of deep concern about who the killer was and why they were mirroring my old cases. "One thing that is different is the shirt. She's not wearing a concert T-shirt like Violet Jones."

"But you still believe this is related to Violet Jones?" Emanuel challenged. He was right to challenge it. When putting the facts on the table, other than similarities to previous cases, there was nothing yet to connect the two murders. "Casey?"

"As of now, I'd have to work from the facts we have," I said, watching Derek inspect the body. "We don't have any evidence to say the murders are related."

"This one, the arm shot," Derek said, focusing on the work at hand. He gestured to the arrow pinning the victim to the ground, "might be that one came first? Pinned her in place, stopped her from running."

Samantha nodded, pointing to the arrow in her ribs. "This one punctured her left lung. Possibly causing a hemothorax. She would've drowned in her own blood."

"And the thigh?" I asked.

Samantha inspected the wound closely. "It may have severed the femoral artery. If so, she bled fast. But that's not likely the fatal shot."

We turned to face the victim and the arrow jutting from her eye, "That's obvious."

"She could've been deceased already?" Derek suggested.

"Possibly," Samantha agreed. "We'll know when we perform the autopsy."

"More pictures," I heard Ben Stanley say from behind us. "Like before?"

A nod. I stood, my legs aching as I surveyed the scene. The wind rustled the dead stalks, speaking to us in hushed words we couldn't quite grasp.

Tracy stepped closer, her face pale. "Why her?" she asked, her voice barely above a whisper. "Why Carly Rose?"

"It might be as simple as her initials," I replied, speaking my thoughts. The idea of a clue stirring. "Carly Rose. Charlie Robson."

Tracy's eyes widened. "You think—" she began, frowning almost instantly. "Why CR? What about Violet Jones?"

"That's not a match," Ben Stanley commented, passing behind me to continue with the photography.

"Yeah, I know." I followed him, focusing on where the flashes landed on the victim, hoping to see something new. "Just speaking my thoughts—"

Initials, right in front of me, the weight of seeing them heavy. It would have been missed though if not for Ben Stanley's pictures. Tracy saw that I stopped, asking, "What?"

"Ben, there," I instructed.

An inch or so beneath the victim's chest, on the left side of her body, the clothes blood-soaked. But in the mass of dried blood, the fabric was torn.

"Stand by for more pictures."

"What did you find?" Tracy asked again, shining her flashlight on the spot.

Samantha carefully removed more of the fabric, exposing the skin beneath. The blood wasn't from an arrow; it was from initials carved into the victim's side.

"Shit, look at that."

"It's like the one from the other victim's foot," Ben said, camera motoring wildly with a frenzy of flashes. "What does T and F mean?"

"I don't know," I answered, searching Samantha's face for confirmation.

She shook her head slightly, answering, "I've no idea." She opened a water bottle, plastic snapping like the dried stalks beneath our feet. The first pour only erased some of the blood, diluting it enough to see what the killer had done. Brushing with her fingers, Samantha washed the dried blood until there was only the remains of the injury. There were five cuts. No more. No less. Two of them perpendicular to the other three, and forming the initials T and F. Sitting back on her heels, Samantha grunted and then continued, "Well, there's no mistaking these as a random injury. Worst part is, I believe the victim was still alive. Maybe not conscious but she had a heartbeat."

"I bet if we reconstruct what was found on the first victim's foot, it'll match," Tracy said, holding her phone next to the initials, the light bright enough to see the cruel depth of each cut. "Who is TF?"

"It might be nobody," I interrupted, my voice grim. "I think we've got a killer who is revisiting the past and dragging us back to old cases."

Tracy's sharp breath echoed in the quiet field. "Carly Rose... Charlie Robson..." She let the connection hang in the air, her voice catching at the edges.

"Are we talking about a possible link to my cousin's

murder?" Emanuel asked, his voice raised for all to hear. His boots crunched over the dried earth, his gaze darting from Carly's body to me and back again. In his face, I saw his usual calm shaken, the murder of his cousin raising the grief he'd stuffed away. "Or is this about recreating it?"

"It's a sickeningly accurate recreation," I commented from behind. My gut feel on the likeness with the victim names was that it was a coincidence. "Let's concentrate on what we have."

"Tracy? Casey? You two were involved in that case," Emanuel asked, dismissing my direction and wanting an answer. "The initials CR. Carly Rose and Charlie Robson?"

"I don't know," Tracy answered, shaking her head. "Same initials could just be a something. Or it could be nothing."

"We're going to table it for now," I said with emphasis, driving focus back to the scene. I looked squarely at Emanuel, adding, "It's noted though okay?"

"Noted," he acknowledged. "The crime scene, what's familiar from my cousin's... I mean the previous case?"

"It's all familiar. It's too similar *not* to be intentional," I answered, standing stiffly. The ache in my ribs flared with every movement, but I ignored it. The scene demanded my attention. "But look closer. It's not an exact copy."

"What's missing?" Emanuel asked, pivoting from the questions about his cousin. His brow turned rigid with concentration. "Or, what's been added?"

"It's little things. Like the season isn't right. And the arrows are different. Even the angles. These were shot with the killer at the same level as the victim. In the previous case, the arrows were shot from a perch."

"Still, the cause of death in each," Samantha began to say. "The similarity has to have been done with intent."

"While this killer isn't the same, they've got to be drawing from a playbook made from our past cases."

Samantha glanced up again from documenting Carly's

wounds, asking in a clinical tone, "Are these consistent with Charlie Robson's case?" I nodded. She regarded this a moment, and commenting, "But the entry angle is different like you said. The sequence of injuries is different too. This killer wasn't aiming for the same level of control."

"Exactly," I said, my gaze fixed on Carly's lifeless form. "Whoever this is, they're leaving a trail for us. They want us to make the connection."

Officer Ben Stanley paused, camera still in hand. "Why now?" he asked, his voice shaky. "Why copy them?"

"That's the question," I said, watching him as he lowered his camera and stepped back. "But whoever this is—they want us to feel the weight of every victim we couldn't save. They made this personal like the murder was done with us in mind."

Tracy's gloved hands brushed lightly against her bandaged arm as she stared into the field's shadowy depths. "What's the endgame, though? Are they trying to draw us out? Taunt us?"

"Maybe," I said, my voice heavy. A gust lifted my jacket, the smell of death surrounding me. I shook it off, saying, "Or maybe it's worse. Maybe they're just getting started."

Derek and Samantha finished their initial assessment, moving to document the scene further before preparing Carly's body for transport. The field buzzed with quiet urgency as officers adjusted crime-scene tape and Ben continued snapping photos, his lens lingering on the arrows still lodged in Carly's flesh.

"This wasn't a spur-of-the-moment kill," Samantha said, standing and stripping off her gloves. "The arrow placement alone shows forethought. Skill. Someone knew exactly where to shoot to maximize pain while ensuring the victim couldn't escape."

I crouched again, examining the ground near Carly's body. There were faint drag marks in the dirt, leading toward the field's edge, partially obscured by the fallen sunflower stalks. "She didn't walk here willingly," I said. "She was brought here."

"Or lured," Tracy suggested, stepping closer and pointing to the paint on Carly's fingers. "Maybe she heard something?"

"Possibly," I replied, my mind already racing through the possibilities. I glanced back at Carly Rose's body, the arrows still glinting in the pale light. The dead sunflowers surrounded her like sentinels, their decayed faces turned downward as if in mourning. The wind hissed through the field, carrying with it the faint scent of rot. Somewhere, beyond the withered stalks and budding green shoots, I could feel the killer's shadow lurking. Waiting. They weren't done. Not yet.

TWELVE

The wind chased me all the way back to the station, carrying the stale smell of the sunflower field, the ache of the explosion, and the grim weight of Carly Rose's lifeless form. Every step from the car to the door reminded me of how broken we all were. Our injuries from the explosion spoke out during the walk. There was Emanuel's stitches pulling, the bandage above his brow already smudged and fraying at the edges. Tracy cradled her arm, the wrap speckled with blood where the wound had seeped through. My ribs felt like a cage tightening around my lungs, an annoyance that wouldn't go away.

I'd hoped for a quiet moment when we entered our workplace, but it was far from quiet. Half of the station was still garbed in thick sheets of plastic, construction tape marking the remodel zones. Workers were busily darting back and forth like some high-speed film reel, the number of them many, bright yellow vests scattered throughout the open spaces. Their tools struck my ears with whirring and clanging. And the air smelled like sawdust which seemed to hang in the air as if levitating. It was all a poor mask for the underlying tension that hung heavy over the department. We had two murders in a short period of time.

Dodging and ducking and carefully taking care with each step, I stepped through the flimsy barrier, brushing it aside like the ghost of an uninvited memory. We reached our desks, the familiar fluorescent hum of the overhead lights muted by the constant noise, the plastic doing little to help in separating the front of the station from our cubicles and the conference room.

Jericho was waiting, his presence as grounding as ever. I tried to give him a welcoming smile, but his face bore a seriousness that only deepened the lines around his eyes. He had the sheriff's badge now, his jurisdiction spanning our part of the Outer Banks and beyond. But from the look on his face, a deeply bruised gash on his chin, his connection to the case and to my working it was personal. It was the fallout of the bomb, the explosion that killed members of the bomb squad and seriously injuring many others. The news had picked up the story, the entire ordeal caught on a cellphone and uploaded to every site there was. It was the worst outcome. A viral mistake with opinions and comments raining down on us from as high up as the Governor of the state.

"I heard it was a rough morning," he greeted, his tone flat. His gaze lingered on our bandages. "You all look as bad as I feel."

"We've got a job to do," I replied, leading the way to the conference room. "And it's not getting done while we're sleeping."

The team followed me inside. The room had shrunk considerably since the last meeting. Our glass-top conference table was gone. So were the chairs. Alice had them removed and placed in storage, the facelift of the station shifting to our cubicles, offices and conference rooms soon. In the place of what was missing, we had small folding tables lined up side by side, along with mismatched chairs, the kind you endured but never got comfortable sitting in for any period of time.

Our monitors were gone too, an old projector provided as a temporary measure. It flickered faintly from the corner, casting muted light on the whiteboard where we'd already scrawled disconnected leads from the last meeting. Tracy winced as she sat, adjusting her arm, while Emanuel grumbled about his forehead bandage, tearing it free to reveal five messy stitches and tossing it into a corner pail.

"I'll get you a fresh one?" Tracy said, her voice soft and motherly. Emanuel waved her off initially until she put on a frown.

"I'll get a new one," he finally replied.

Jericho sat heavily, folding his hands in front of him. "All right," he began, and held up two fingers. "Is there anything that connects Violet Jones and Carly Rose?"

"A pair of initials... at least that's what we think they are. Each victim had them carved into the skin, possibly postmortem," I answered, resting my hands on the table. "But there's nothing tying them to the letters T and F."

"T and F?" Jericho raised an eyebrow, his mind spinning to find a connection. "I've got nothing with those."

"Same. We haven't tied them to anything yet. There *is* the similarity to two of my previous cases," I explained. He already knew, but I put it on the table anyway. "With Carly Rose, it's the arrows, the sunflower field. The details are straight out of the case that began with Charlie Robson's murder."

"The likenesses are beyond coincidence," Jericho agreed, grumbling while running his fingers over the razor stubble along his jaw.

"They're doing more than just using old cases," Emanuel cut in, his tone sharp. "They tried to fucking kill us."

Tracy nodded solemnly. "The bomb squad didn't stand a chance. It was a trap."

"Mm-hmm." Jericho's jaw tightened and he looked at me briefly. I knew then why he'd joined the meeting, my heart leaping into the back of my throat. He was going to bring in outside help. It wasn't just the murders, it was the bomb, the direct assault on all the team. My pits stung with a nervous sweat while I tried to find the right words. But before I could say anything, he continued, "That's exactly why I think we need to turn this over to the FBI."

"No, that's not happening," I said immediately, landing on words that were less than professional. My voice was firmer than I intended too, Jericho's reaction saying more than words. "We need to see this through."

"Through?" Jericho's sharp gaze cut to me, concern stirring. "Casey, this isn't about jurisdiction. It's about your safety—the team's safety. People are dead. How many more are you willing to risk?"

"What about justice?" I snapped, Tracy and Emanuel staying quiet. I suddenly felt alone in the argument. "We solved those cases. I'd think this team is in the best position to solve this case!"

"Casey, this is not the same as the previous cases," Jericho answered, shaking his head. His gaze jumped to Emanuel and Tracy. "Guys? What do you think?"

I felt my chest tighten, but I refused to back down. "Those victims deserve more than being handed off like evidence to the FBI," I commented, more to myself than the room.

The room fell into a heavy silence, the tension thick enough to choke. Tracy spoke first, her voice steady despite the tremor in her hand. "I think we keep the case. We've been through worse. Like Casey said, we know these cases better than anyone."

Emanuel leaned forward, shaking his head. "No way. I'm with Jericho. We've already been burned, literally. We're too close to this and—" He stopped mid-sentence, emotions catching him with a look that made my heart hurt for him. "—Jericho, I'm feeling torn. This is my cousin's murder all over again and I'm feeling too close to it but I also want to see it through like Casey said."

"And who's going to pick up the pieces if we drop it?" Tracy countered. "The FBI doesn't care about Violet Jones or Carly Rose. They care about statistics, not people."

Jericho's voice sliced through the noise. "The victims—what if they were picked just to get to you?" His eyes locked onto mine, the weight of his words heavy. His voice shook, saying, "We might not have the hard evidence, but I think this killer is after the team and you, Casey?"

The idea had been out there, but to hear the words was like a punch to the gut. For a moment, I couldn't breathe. The room fell silent again, the unspoken truth settling over us like a shroud.

The quiet was broken by Alice, the station manager, bustling into the room. Her hair was piled into a messy bun, the ends of a pen and pencil jutting out like haphazard decoration. In her gloved hands was a package wrapped in torn brown paper, the station's address scrawled in uneven handwriting. She stopped short, sensing the tension.

"Sounds like things are getting a little heated in here," she remarked, her tone light but cautious.

"We're working through it," Jericho replied, his frown deepening as he noticed her gloves. "What's that?"

"A package," Alice said, holding it up. "It looked suspicious, so we ran it through the new security scanner. It's clear."

"For who?" Jericho asked, continuing. Our eyes made contact. It was brief and it was uncomfortable. He already knew.

"It's addressed to Casey," Alice answered and placed it onto the table.

I slipped on a fresh pair of latex gloves, my stomach knotting as I reached for the package. Everyone in the room stared intently with eyes glued to my hands as I carefully peeled back the brown wrapping. Inside was a single sheet of paper and a small, unlit candle.

I unfolded the paper, my breath catching as I read the words. It was a poem, one I knew all too well.

"'Against my mother's words, I like to walk the soggy marshes...'" I trailed off, the familiar lines tumbling from my lips. The room was still, every eye fixed on me. Tracy leaned closer, her expression one of horrified recognition.

"'I am Mudborn,'" she said, her voice barely above a whisper. "That's Jocelyn Winter's poem."

"There are maybe three or four people who even know this poem exists," I said, my voice trembling. "Jocelyn's journal was found in her bedroom. It was returned to her family after the case was closed."

"Now do you see why we need the FBI?" Jericho demanded, voice rising. I'd seen him angry, infuriated even. But this was far different. He was scared. "Casey, this is too dangerous. Whoever they are, they know too much."

I barely heard him. My eyes were drawn to the plastic sheeting that separated us from the front of the station. A figure stood there, the shadowy image on the other side was as still as the air. They were watching us. I'd first noticed it when Jericho joined us but hadn't given it any thought. They hadn't moved since. He was about my height, on the taller side and lanky, his frame slim in ill-fitting work clothes. A construction helmet sat crooked on his head, the bright yellow plastic glaringly out of place.

"Alice," I said slowly, rising from my chair. "Do we vet the construction workers who come here?"

Alice frowned. "They come in a group," she said. "I don't think—"

That was all I needed to hear. The man turned, his movements sharp and frantic. He bolted through the worksite, disappearing into the chaos of tools and debris.

"It's him!" I shouted, vaulting out of the room. "It's the killer!"

The chase was on. I pushed through the plastic sheeting, the loose material snagging on my shoulder as I burst into the station's front. I ran into a cloud of sawdust, the sound of construction tools grinding to a halt as heads turned toward the commotion. The man was already darting through the half-finished lobby, his lanky frame twisting and weaving between worktables and scaffolding like a shadow trying to escape the sun.

"Stop!" I yelled, my shoes pounding against the uneven floor. He didn't slow, didn't even flinch. He vaulted over a low stack of drywall with surprising agility, his work clothes flapping as if they didn't quite fit his wiry frame.

"Casey, wait!" I heard Emanuel shout behind me, but I didn't stop. My gut told me this was him. The killer. And he was running.

The man reached the station doors and shoved them open with both hands, the crash echoing through the construction site. I followed a second later, the chill of the Outer Banks morning hitting me like a slap to the face.

He bolted into the street, his stride long and erratic. Cars screeched to a halt, horns blaring as he darted between lanes. A delivery van slammed on its brakes, the tires squealing as it skidded sideways, gray smoke spewing burned rubber. The man didn't hesitate. He leaped onto the hood of a sedan, vaulted over the roof, and hit the pavement running.

I followed, adrenaline drowning out the burn in my ribs. A pickup truck slammed its brakes inches from me, the driver shouting something I couldn't hear over the chaos.

"Stop him!" I yelled, waving frantically at the drivers, but they were too stunned to react.

The man disappeared between two parked cars on the other side of the street. I reached the same spot seconds later, ducking into the narrow alleyway, stopping instantly, walloping heartbeats pounding. The air was damp and heavy in the narrow pass. There was the echo of water trickling, the smell of mildew clinging to the brick walls on either side. The man was fast—faster than he looked—but his movements were frantic, his footfalls uneven. He knocked over a trash can as he ran, the clatter bouncing like gunshots in the tight space.

"Stop!" I shouted again, my voice rasping with effort.

He glanced over his shoulder, just for a second. His face was pale, gaunt, with thick glasses that flashed in the dim light. The mustache looked fake, like something out of a costume shop. There was something else. A familiarity in the eyes perhaps. Barely noticeable, just a tic of recognition in the back of my mind. And then he was moving again, disappearing around the corner at the end of the alley. I pushed harder, rounding the corner just in time to see him climbing a chain-link fence. His skinny legs scrambled awkwardly, his boots slipping against the metal.

"Not this time," I muttered, grabbing the fence and pulling myself up after him. My ribs screamed in protest, but I ignored the pain, hoisting myself over the top and dropping to the ground on the other side.

The man was ahead of me again, his stride growing more erratic. He stumbled over a loose piece of concrete, nearly falling before catching himself. His movements were losing their precision, his energy flagging. The construction helmet tumbled, the hair beneath sitting askew. A wig? He grabbed the helmet and took off.

I was gaining on him, but the pain was gaining too. Every breath was like a hot blade between my ribs. He burst into a construction yard, weaving between stacks of lumber and pallets of bricks. The open space gave me a clear view of him, and for the first time, I saw the panic in his movements. He wasn't just running—he was desperate.

"Casey!" Emanuel's voice boomed behind me. I risked a glance over my shoulder to see him and Tracy entering the yard, their faces determined. The man saw them too. His head jerked from side to side, searching for an escape route. There was none.

"Corner him!" I shouted, changing my angle to cut him off. Tracy veered to the right, Emanuel to the left, the three of us closing in like a net. The man hesitated, his arms flailing as he turned in a circle. He was trapped.

"End of the line!" Emanuel yelled, his voice cutting through the noise of the yard.

The man's hand shot into his jacket pocket. My heart dropped.

"Show me your hands!" I commanded, drawing my weapon and aiming it squarely at him. "Now!"

For a moment, time seemed to freeze. The man's eyes darted between the three of us, his chest heaving with labored breaths. His hand stayed in his pocket.

"I won't say it again!" I shouted, my finger tightening on the trigger.

His hand moved—fast. I braced for the worst, my heart slamming against my ribs.

But instead of a weapon, he pulled out a small, cylindrical object and threw it to the ground. A flash bang went off, blinding us, its smoke erupting, thick and choking, swallowing him in an instant.

"Damn it!" I coughed and wheezed, waving my hand in front of my face as the smoke spread, burning my eyes and throat.

"Who has eyes on him!?" Emanuel shouted, but the smoke was too dense. By the time it cleared, the man was gone.

"I lost him," Tracy said, between coughs, her voice tight with anger.

"Who the hell carries flash bangs?" Emanuel muttered, his hands on his hips as he scanned the empty lot.

"Someone who is prepared," I answered. My eyes were fixed on the spot where the man had disappeared. He'd been in our station, watching us. Listening. The thought flipping my stomach. "He's fucking toying with us."

The chase was over, but the hunt had just begun.

THIRTEEN

Against my mother's words, I like to walk the soggy marshes and wade barefoot into the still waters. I like to feel the mud squish between my toes and feel velvety cattails brush against my wet skin. I like to float in the company of dragonflies and migrating monarchs. And I like to smell the dangling honeysuckle and the lotus blossoms.

Where others only see swamp, I see beauty. I see it in the reedy grasses topped with swaying fronds. I see it in the herons, their stilted legs reflected in the surface ripples. I hear it in the sounds that are my private orchestra. And I feel it in the soft currents crawling toward the ocean, driven by moon tides and turning over the bogs that are made up of the mud which is said to course through my veins.

'I am Mudborn'

— *JOCELYN WINTER*

It was the mudborn poem that told us where to go next. But first, we had a person of interest, a description of what they looked like, their height and approximate weight, a location with the direction they'd last been seen. My nose and eyes stung from the flash bang, and there was an incessant ring that had settled in my ears like houseflies buzzing around my head. Alice joined our efforts, researching possible locations for the purchase of the munition. But it was the package he'd left and the poem inside that was the clue.

Jocelyn Winter was the killer's next victim. However, Jocelyn was already dead. She'd been murdered a few years earlier. In Jocelyn's case, she'd died at the hands of a classmate. But it was during that investigation that we'd come across another victim, the first of many, the MO one of the most sickening we'd ever seen. Death by mummification.

The killer was seeking a person like her. And more than that, with the poem as our clue, it told us where the victim was located. Jocelyn Winter's body had been found in one of the barrier island's abandoned properties, the ones with eroding beaches and accessible only when it was at low tide.

We geared up for a trip to the beach, the new clue spurring Jericho's interest too. He put aside the thoughts of turning the case over to the FBI to visit the house where Jocelyn Winter was murdered. But his decision didn't come easy. He was coming with us *because* of the beach. Because he knew the sea and the abandoned houses along the coast of the Outer Banks. He knew the tides, the dangers hidden in shifting sands, the way a rising swell can mask footprints or swallow evidence. He'd seen what the ocean can do to abandoned properties too. The way the waves erase them in a blink.

That knowledge gave us an edge, and he knew it. And maybe, just maybe, he was coming because deep down, he felt the same cold pull I did. That this place, this house, was more than just the next stop on a murder investigation. It was where the killer might have gone. And we were walking straight into it

The tide was at its lowest point for the afternoon, giving us direct beach access to the old property. I set alarms on my phone and watch, the window of time less than six hours. After that, we'd need the Marine Patrol to fish us out of the sea.

We didn't have much daylight either, the sun hanging just over Jericho's shoulder to my right, the western sky turning bright with warming colors. There were heaping clouds above, traveling slow like grazing cattle. It wasn't the weather or the day ending that had me chewing on my lower lip though. It was the house, stilted and leaning with an imminent threat of toppling.

A breaking wave chased seabirds close to us, the foam touching my shoes. While the tide was low, the waves were high. The breaks reverberated into my legs as the birds chased air bubbles across the wet sand, tiny clams sinking beneath the surface.

The four of us stood outside the old house, its state worsened from when we'd been here last. There were other houses too, some having already fallen over, stilts uprooted, shingled roofs made bare. Some of them were gone entirely, the walls collapsed and leaving behind the original pilings. The loss of the homes was a constant in the Outer Banks. Every year, new videos appeared on the news to show homes collapsing and drifting, some seeming to walk into the ocean of their own accord.

I didn't know if it was global warming like some said. Or if it was the shallow waters around the barrier islands that had forever changed. What I did know was that they were a dangerous place, and a refuge too as had been discovered in the multiple murders we'd investigated inside them.

The wind was sharp this afternoon, cutting through my coat and chilling my bones as we continued the trek across the hard-packed wet sand. The house loomed ahead of us, a weeping skeleton, sad remains of the Victorian style it had been once. Waves broke against the stilted legs closest to the sea, sending salty spray into the air. The frame had been sturdy before, but now sagged dangerously, the timbers groaning as though in mourning for all that had transpired there.

Tracy stood beside me, her arms crossed tightly over her chest. Her face was pale, drawn with the same tension I felt. Behind us, the red and blue lights of the patrol vehicles flashed against the damp sand, their reflections pooling in shallow puddles. Two Marine Patrol boats bobbed in the waves just offshore, their engines growling low like wary dogs. Jericho's silhouette moved near the waterline, steady and unshaken. He had always seemed at home near the ocean and had even worked with the Marine Patrol for a time before returning to the role of sheriff.

"I never thought I'd be back at this house," Tracy muttered under her breath, breaking the silence.

"Neither did I." I couldn't blame the tone in her voice. This house and others were used by a serial killer who'd practiced mummification of their victims. They were a landmark of horror in all our lives. Left to crumble alone, it was years later, and it was pulling us back.

"It's not the house," Emanuel said. "It's the killer. Or whoever wants us to think they are."

"And how did they get the poem? 'I am Mudborn'?" Tracy shook her head, exasperation mixing with unease.

Jericho kicked at the approaching surf, his sheriff's badge sharp with sunlight. "If that evidence was never disclosed, it means there's internal access to the files."

"Could be the killer approached Jocelyn Winter's parents," I suggested.

"I reached out to them earlier, thinking the same thing," Emanuel replied. He held his phone with a text message. "No visitors. But they did find Jocelyn's bedroom window open last month. Nothing was missing and they couldn't recall if they might have left it open."

"Can we dust for prints?" Tracy asked, the light catching her eyes. She shaded them, squinting. "It's been a month though."

"But we can try," I answered, texting a team back at the station to work the window. "I'll let Jocelyn's parents know we're sending someone over there."

"Whoever this is, they're playing games," Emanuel said, tucking his phone away before pulling up on his boot. He stopped and looked at me, the shadow of the house covering his face. "It's like they're visiting all your old cases."

"I know," I replied, pulling my collar up against the wind. I faced the bones of what once was, the framing still resembling its former self, a beach-house. It wouldn't be long before the likeness became rubble. "Which is why we're here. If there's a body—or something else—they want us to find, it's better we find it on our terms."

Jericho ran alongside us, his boots squelching through the wet sand. "Let's keep an eye on that tide, it's on the rise," he said, pointing to the waves that had crept closer in the few minutes we'd been standing there. "We'll want to move quickly. That thing's barely standing and I'm not sure how stable it is when all the pilings are hit by the waves."

I followed his gaze to the house to find where best to enter. Its clapboard siding hung in tatters, some pieces having been stripped away by years of storms. Rusted nails jutted out like jagged teeth, and the roof had caved in on one side, the shingles peeling back to reveal the skeletal beams beneath. The stilted pilings, once driven deep into the sand, now trembled with each wave that crashed against them. My stomach filled with dread at what we might find inside.

"This place shouldn't still be standing," Emanuel said, kicking one of the stilts, his voice tinged with the same disbelief we all felt. "It looks like one good gust of wind would take it down."

"Well, it is still standing for now—" I began, my body turning cold in its shadow. Emanuel was right. The house didn't just lean—it groaned, a low, mournful sound that the wind carried down the beach. But it still stood, defiant against time and tide, like some cursed relic unwilling to disappear. "It's standing and we need to go inside."

"Let's get this over with before we're swimming," Jericho said.

I nodded, stepping to where we'd entered the house previously. We'd gone inside through the floor before, where there once had been steps leading out of a pantry. The hole was still there but it was no longer square. The sand beneath my boots was firm, packed by the tide, but around the entrance, it had softened, giving way and shifting. The rhythmic pulse of the waves became louder, the water swirling around the stilts, licking at the base of the house as though it was eager to claim it.

"We sure this is a good idea?" Tracy asked, her voice tight.

"No," I admitted. "But we don't have much of a choice."

As we reached the only entrance, I paused, looking up to the insides of the house. The memories came flooding back, vivid as if no time had passed at all. Jocelyn Winter's body had been discovered in the living room across from the fireplace. However, it was the second body in the attic that had shocked us all. That body was mummified, and I was already hoping beyond hope that we saw nothing like that today.

"The Jocelyn Winter case? That was a few years ago—" Emanuel said, grunting as he climbed "—the sea rising and the sands shifting. I bet the house was unstable even then." He hoisted himself inside and held his hand for Jericho. "Let's just hope the ocean doesn't try swallowing this thing whole today."

"I hear ya," Jericho said, ascending with ease, the two

working like a pair of circus performers. Jericho joined Emanuel, their hands extended. "Who is next?"

Tracy hesitated, guarding her sore arm as she reached for their hands, eyeing the frame of the opening, which was warped and splintered, the wood blackened with rot. Jericho waved her on, insisting, the lip creaking loudly but it held. When they had Tracy's hand, she shrieked, "Don't drop me!"

"We gotcha," he said. And in a flash, she was gone. They reappeared, arms extended, "Casey?"

The air had a chill, but their grips were warm and sturdy. Before I could say a word, I was standing inside; the floorboards were slick with moisture, their edges curled like old paper. With each step, the floor groaned and felt like a gamble. The wind howled around us, whistling in and out of the place where windows had once been.

"This place is a death trap," Emanuel muttered, his hand resting on his holster.

"Yeah, it is. In more ways than one," I said, agreeing. The kitchen floor sagged dangerously, the boards bending underfoot as we moved toward the dining room. Cabinet doors hung crooked on rusted hinges, the paint on the walls had long been stripped away by the elements. Inside the dining room, the shadows seemed deeper, the air thick with the smell of salt and decay.

Jericho was first, leading with his flashlight that cut through the gloom. "Stay together," he said, his voice firm. "And watch your step."

The house was worse than I remembered. All the floors had warped and were uneven, patches of sand and debris scattered across it. Where paint was gone, the walls were streaked with water stains, and the ceiling sagged dangerously in several places, parts of it gone. A section of the living room floor had caved in completely, leaving a gaping hole that exposed the wet sand beneath. We moved to the second floor, recalling which steps to use, the previous killer having notched parts of the structure to create booby traps. Not that it mattered, the entire house felt like a booby trap.

"This is where we found her," I said quietly, gesturing to the room. My heart lifted, the room empty, save for strips of old crime-scene tape. The others didn't need me to elaborate. Jocelyn Winter's presence still lingered here, a weight that pressed down on all of us. "Let's check the next floor."

The air was thick, the third floor was a desolate shell, its former structure ravaged by years of salt, wind, and neglect. The dormer windows, which had once let in light and kept the elements at bay, were missing, one of them left with a single glass pane which was mottled with grime and cracked like jagged spiderwebs. The air that seeped through was damp, carrying with it the sharp tang of salt and an ever-present musty decay.

The roof pitched steeply, angling sharply at thirty degrees from the center. The exposed beams creaked under the strain of the winds buffeting against the building. Jericho and Emanuel shined lights into the corner where the roof was darkened by moisture and was streaked with blotches of rot. Other than our flashlights, the space was dim, diffused daylight struggling through the windows. Shadows stretched across the room, and amidst the decay, on the warped and buckled floorboards, lay the body.

FOURTEEN

"Guys!" I exclaimed loudly, gut lurching as the team's flashlights swung across the room. The beams concentrated on the remains of another victim, a collective gasp stopping us. We stared at the unexpected, the grim thoughts rising in the back of our minds becoming a reality.

"Oh my God!" Tracy said, moving closer, the house shifting with a loud groan. She dialed her phone and yelled over the static, "Samantha?! The Jocelyn Winter house—"

"What happened?" Emanuel asked, advancing. Tracy raised her phone to the sky like it was a sacrifice. Emanuel glanced at his phone, confirming, "Signal is in and out."

"She knows where we are," I assured them, voice fading as I focused. Dust shimmered in the daylight, the four of us standing motionless a moment. The body was wrapped tightly in yellowed linen strips, the once-clean fabric now discolored with age and spotted with dark stains. The wrappings on the arm closest had frayed in places, revealing shrunken, desiccated flesh beneath. The body was mummified, frozen in a haunting tableau of its final moments. The linen was layered meticulously, the wrapping a deliberate act that spoke of ceremony or ritual. The ends were tucked with precision, as though the killer had wanted their work to remain preserved despite the ravages of time. "Whoever this is, they've been dead a very long time."

"No kidding, this wasn't recent," Jericho said, his hand on the small of my back, pressing gently. "Is it like the others?"

"Similar," I answered. With Jocelyn Winter's murder, there'd been others. They'd been mummified too. But in those cases, the murders were recent, the victims mummified as part of the killer's MO. Beneath the wraps around the victim's chest, I couldn't see breasts or flesh as expected. Instead, the victim wore a shirt. A dark shirt with a loudly colored logo. "This isn't the same though. Do you guys see that?"

"The victim is clothed." Emanuel's words were a low baritone as he slid gloves over his long fingers, snapping the lip to ensure they were fastened. "The old case—they were naked?"

A nod. "They'd also been murdered more recently and steps taken to mummify their bodies."

"I remember that," he said, working the tip of a pen to lift a wrap. He exposed enough of the victim's arm for us to shine lights. "They used salt and had drained the victims?"

I leaned over, nodding. "I don't smell the salt. Do you?"

"Not like before," he confirmed, trading glances. "Casey, I think what we've got here is genuine."

"A genuine mummy?" Tracy asked. "Not a victim?"

"Genuine, meaning, the state of the body is natural causes," I answered, clarifying. "This isn't the same as what Arnold Lidder had done to his victims."

Tracy shrank away at the mention of the name. She'd almost been a victim in that case, the killer getting the upper hand briefly.

"Sorry. I know this must be hard. You okay?"

"I'm fine," she answered, perching a finger in the air as she continued working her phone.

"I forgot," Emanuel whispered. "She'd know better than any of us about that case."

"Let's move on," I said firmly.

We returned our focus to the body, the overpowering smell of salt used in the previous case missing. Emanuel exposed more of the victim's arm, the presence of puncture wounds missing. "No signs of blood having been drained either."

He lowered himself to his knees, resting.

Jericho joined us, having finished surveilling every corner shadow with a beam of light. "Anything?"

"I think we need Samantha," Emanuel answered without looking up. There was an unsettling confusion in his expression. "This might not be a victim of mummification at all."

"Samantha! I got you. Huh? What?" Tracy said suddenly, her voice loud enough to startle. Her eyelids were peeled back, the whites shining in the dim light. "Wait! What? You're here?"

"I'd texted her before we came inside," Emanuel said, his gaze still locked on the body. "You know, just in case."

"I guess she had a sense to come out here?" Jericho commented. "Tell her I'll meet her in the kitchen."

"No need, Derek is helping her inside," Tracy answered, tucking her phone away.

"I think I hear them." As if on cue, footsteps echoed from a distance. There was a conversation too, and a startled yip and assurances that the floor was safe. When the noise reached the second level, I warned, "Careful on the next set of steps, some are missing, and a few are loose."

"I've got it," Derek called back. The pair of footsteps became one and, in my mind, I imagined he was carrying Samantha over the dangers.

"Guys," I said, their faces dimmed and shiny with a light sheen. Samantha only nodded, her gaze narrowed to the center of the room. "I'm not sure what we have here."

"Let's find out." Samantha knelt beside the body, her movements slow and deliberate as she examined the scene. Minutes seemed like hours while the examination took place. When she'd seen enough, she sat back on her haunches and said nothing.

"Another victim?" I asked.

Samantha wasn't the medical examiner in the case of the mummified victims. This was new to her.

"What do you think?"

Her brow bounced. "I think someone stole a body from a grave. This is a natural decay. They may have been embalmed too, but we'll know when we get back." Her voice cut through the stillness. She held up a gloved hand, gesturing to the intricate wrappings. "And if we get an identification, we'll have a cause of death too."

"The body was from a grave?" Jericho muttered from behind me. He started pacing, fingertips digging into his chin. "How long?"

"Hard to say without unwrapping—"

"Let's remove the wraps," I instructed, having heard enough. There was tension mounting like electricity in the air before a storm. This wasn't another victim. This was a message. I cleared my throat, instructing, "I want to remove the wraps."

"Okay... let's get some pictures first," Samantha said, hands in the air in a whoa motion. "There're some intricacies here we should record. This was done with intent. Look at how carefully it's been wrapped—every fold, every layer. Someone took their time with this."

Tracy circled the body, taking pictures. I crouched beside her, the smell of must and decay mingling with the salt air. "If I'm right, this person was placed here for us to see."

Samantha scoffed and shook her head. "What do you mean?"

"We got a message at the station," Emanuel began. "It was a

clue. We thought it was about Violet Jones or Carly Rose. It wasn't."

"It was about us. About a past case."

"Okay, I'm following." Samantha nodded, her penlight tracing the contours of the wrappings. "Then what we're seeing here is a statement. Whoever did this wanted to send you a message."

Jericho stood near the broken dormer window, his arms crossed, his expression grim as he surveyed the room. "We need to see who it is."

Emanuel's voice broke the silence. He was standing near the doorway, his flashlight playing across the warped ceiling beams. "You think we know them? Don't you?" he asked, his tone uneasy.

"Uh-huh," Jericho answered.

Samantha leaned closer, a pair of scissors in her hand, the bottom blade slipping beneath where the wrappings had partially unraveled. The mummified skin was shrunken and tight, the fingers curled. "The desiccation, the smell, the shrunken skin and discoloration suggests they were embalmed like I mentioned, approximately a few years ago," she said, struggling to cut the wraps. "But it's hard to say when that was. I'll know more with a full examination."

"Who would do this?" Derek said, helping, metal-on-metal grating with each cut.

The wind picked up outside, rattling the cracked window-panes and sending a fresh gust of salty air through the attic. The loose edges of the linen wrapping fluttered faintly, as though the body were breathing. The air's force was strong enough to lift what had been cut, revealing a black shirt beneath the wraps.

"Jericho? Look at this." I waved him closer to show the concert T-shirt on the body. It was jet-black, the logo I'd seen earlier revealed a type of scarab or beetle with wings, red and gold and purple and blue colors radiating from the center. "Do you know this one?" He didn't answer, the sudden silence replaced when he dropped to his knees. His face had gone sickly pale, pasty and damp. Instant concern filled me. "Babe?"

"No," he said, picking at a lump beneath the wrap. He cleared the gauzy material, pinching a butterfly pendant between his fingers, a silver chain dangling. I'd seen the necklace before but couldn't place it. "This shouldn't be here."

"Jericho? What is it?" Emanuel asked, voice rising.

"Keep cutting!" Jericho demanded, his jaw slack, eyes wide and unblinking. The sight of Jericho's reaction filled us with a dark notion, the kind that steals your voice. "Faster. Cut!"

"I'm sorry—" Derek stammered, his fingers clumsy big as he worked the scissors. "The bandage scissors. Too small."

"Let me," Jericho growled, taking the pair from Derek. He began cutting, straight from the necklace to the face.

"Whoa, buddy," Emanuel warned. "Let them do their job."

"Babe?" I implored.

But Jericho heard none of us, a woman's face showing a moment later. There were signs of makeup, the kind when embalmed for a funeral, the features lifeless. Her hair was a dirty blonde, but without luster, and thinning. The eyes were closed and sunken, the cheeks too, the bone structure remaining. While the remains may have been a few years old, the woman's face was surprisingly intact, enough for recognition. But I didn't know her. Didn't recognize her. Not immediately, anyway.

"Oh God!" Jericho wailed, the suddenness of his cry striking. "Who did this!?"

"Jer—" I began, but the emotions stole my words. I put my hands around him, the crazed look in his eyes frightening. "Jericho? Talk to me."

"Who is that?" Derek asked.

"I dunno," Samantha followed.

"Jesus Christ!" Emanuel blurted, peering down, his color

turning gray like ash. He grabbed his mouth, looking as though he was going to get sick. "Jericho. Man, let us—" A moment later, he was sick.

"Emanuel?" I asked, pleading, my heart pounding as Jericho seemed to disappear in front of me, his eyes locked on the dead woman's face. "Emanuel, who is it?"

"It's Jessie," Emanuel answered, cupping his mouth again.

"Who is Jessie?" Tracy asked, all eyes following Jericho who'd seemed to physically shrink, holding the woman's hand, his eyes puddling wet.

"Her name is Jessie Flynn," I answered, the weight of the sight slamming into my chest. "Someone dug up Jericho's wife."

FIFTEEN

Transcript of Paige Kotes's confession, recorded during an interrogation conducted by Detective Casey White at the North Carolina Correctional Institution for Women.

Paige Kotes:

You want to talk about Jessie Flynn? Fine. Let's talk about her. You want me to confess, to spill it all out, to lay her death bare for you? You'll get what you want. But don't think for a second I'll cry over her, because I won't. I hated Jessie Flynn. I hated her with every fiber of my being.

Do you know what it's like to love someone so deeply, so obsessively, that they consume every part of you? That's how I felt about Jericho. He was mine. Or he should have been. But Jessie—perfect, sweet Jessie—she was always in the way. Fucking bitch! I hated how she was always smiling, always standing there beside him, wearing that stupid butterfly pendant like it made her untouchable. I wanted her gone.

I didn't just want her out of Jericho's life; I wanted her erased from existence. That kind of hatred isn't something you just shrug off. It eats at you, gnaws at your insides, keeps you awake at night. It was a sickness. But like any sickness, there's a cure, and Jessie's cure came when I called her that day.

Can I pause for a second. Just a minute. I'm savoring the memory. That's what I have now. The dreamy memories I see in my head. It's nostalgic, you know? Seeing it again. Playing it over and over. Mm. I love that.

Jessie answered the phone on the second ring. I could hear the panic in her voice, the fear clawing at her as I told her Jericho was in trouble. I told her to hurry, to come to Elm Street near the pond. I made my voice shake, just enough to sell it. She bought it completely, of course. She loved him too much to ask questions.

When Jessie showed up, she was exactly how I pictured her: flustered, worried, and stupidly determined to save the day. I was in the car with Barnes, my accomplice—though I'll be honest, he was never more than a tool to me. Jessie thought she was walking into some rescue mission, but what she walked into was a trap.

Her sandals crunched against the gravel when she rushed toward us, shouting my name. "Paige! Where's Jericho?" She was already on edge, her voice cracking with desperation. I stepped out of the car, and put on a wide smile, playing the part of the concerned friend for just a moment. But I had to drop the act. You see, I was eager to get started. The sooner the better.

"And look," I said, sweeping my arm theatrically, "we're all alone."

The confusion on Jessie's face was almost endearing. Almost. Then she saw the girl we had in the backseat—Theresa was her name. The teenager was cuffed and crying, her clothes torn, pleading for help. Jessie froze like her puny mind was trying to make sense of it. She looked at me, then at Barnes, and then back at me again.

I laughed. God! I laughed so hard seeing the realization hit her like a tidal wave. I could see the registers clicking in her fucking brain like gears dialing to open a padlock. It was... delicious. Yeah, delicious, seeing her finally realize who we were. What we were.

The fight didn't last long. But Jessie was scrappy, I'll give her that. The two of us, me and Barnes that is, we were too much for her. She went down hard, her head smacking the ground with a dull thud. Her eyes fluttered as the dust settled around her. She was still conscious—barely—when we dragged her to the pond. I regretted that part. I wanted her fully alert when we killed her. She was mostly, but that hit to her head, it had to have jarred something the way her eyes were swimming around, rolling back into her skull.

HAHAHAH. Swimming. It's a bad pun, get it!

I held her under the water myself. I wanted to be the one to do it, to feel it in my fingers and hands. Skin on skin contact like we were lovers. Her skin was warm at first, her arms flailing, nails scratching at my wrists. I have to admit it. Her strength surprised me—she didn't go down easily. But that only made it better for me. The struggle is what makes the kill satisfying, you know?

Through the surface of the water, her face was distorted, her features got all twisty and contorted in ways that almost didn't seem human. I watched while her mouth opened and closed like a fish gasping for air, her eyes wide with panic. That only made me press down harder, the cool water seeping into my sleeves. I got so into it that I literally felt her pulse weaken in my grip. I save those images in my head so I can relive them over and over. It's the repetition of it that makes life bearable now, like a favorite movie on a reel. You guys can't take that away from me. You can try. But you can't. I want you to know that. Okay?

Anyway, I'm holding Jessie in the water and watching as she is fighting for air, her chest was heaving bad. That pond was unforgiving, its water filled her mouth, her throat, her lungs.

That's when her movements became jerky and then slowed. I was sad when she finally stopped moving. But that stillness and the look that was stuck on her face, it was exquisite.

When it was over, I yanked that stupid butterfly pendant from her neck. The chain snapped easily, and I held it up to Barnes like a trophy. The gold in the wings glinted in the late sunlight, beautiful.

Barnes was useless after that, muttering to himself, pacing like a scared child. I ignored him. Jessie's body sank into the muck, her arms floating lifelessly, her eyes staring at nothing. I watched her until the water swallowed her completely, until there was no trace of her left. We didn't leave her like that. I wanted to, but Barnes came up with the idea of dumping her in the ocean so it would look like a suicide. I should have never listened to him. You'd never have found her if we'd let the pond have her body.

Do I regret it? No. Not for a second. Jessie Flynn was an obstacle, and I removed her. That's what you do with obstacles —you get rid of them.

There. That's your confession. Are you happy now?

This confession, along with physical evidence, led to the conviction of Paige Kotes for the murder of Jessie Cooper Flynn.

SIXTEEN

We were greeted by an open hole in the ground, grass trampled, and the headstone toppled like a casualty of war. The row of graves was like a smile with a missing tooth—only this wasn't a smile at all. This was Jessie Cooper Flynn's grave, or what was left of it. The earth had been chewed up and spat out, its remains piled carelessly next to where her casket had been.

The headstone Jericho had picked out—a grayish-rose granite marker with delicate etching—lay cracked and broken, the top left corner lopped off, its surface uneven and raw. This wasn't vandalism. This was deliberate, legal desecration—or so they claimed. Jessie Cooper Flynn's body had been exhumed.

The cemetery stretched around us, a somber sprawl of history and grief. Towering oaks framed the scene, their gnarled limbs dressed sparsely with Spanish moss that swayed gently in the springtime air. Jericho had told me once that it was Jessie's favorite thing about the southern area of the barrier islands, the trees and moss. The muted gray sky above seemed to press down on the earth, casting the rows of headstones into shadow. Each marker told a story—a name, a date, a promise of eternal rest—but beneath these trees she loved, Jessie's story had been violently interrupted.

Jericho stood at the edge of the grave, his boots sinking slightly into the soft ground. He stared into the void as though he could summon Jessie back through sheer will. His breath came fast and shallow. His fists clenched at his sides, trembling with a barely contained fury. I'd seen him angry before, but this was different. His rage was a living thing, radiating off him in waves, but it was tempered by something even more devastating: hurt. It was in his eyes, haunted and hollow, and in the way his shoulders sagged under the weight of his grief.

The cemetery owner stood a few feet away, holding a bundle of documents like a shield. His mousy features were set in an awkward mixture of defiance and fear. His free hand fidgeted with the lapel of his tailored suit as he tried—and failed—to meet Jericho's gaze. The groundskeeper loitered nearby, leaning against the massive backhoe that had plucked Jessie's remains from their eternal rest. He chewed on a toothpick, his eyes darting around as though searching for an escape route.

"Sir, the remains exhumed—" the cemetery owner began, his voice trembling but polite, nose twitching with every word. "We have an excellent monumental mason on staff. He'll repair the headstone at no cost to you—"

"Her name was Jessie Cooper Flynn!" Jericho barked, his voice cutting through the air like a thunderclap. He tipped his hat lower to shield his eyes as he shook his head steadily, his body visibly shaking. "And you validated the request to exhume Jessie?"

"Sir," the man stammered, stepping back as though he feared Jericho might lunge at him, "it—it has your signature—"

"My signature?" Jericho's voice dropped to a dangerous growl, like the low rumble of a storm on the horizon. In one swift motion, he snatched the papers from the man's hand. "That's fucking impossible."

"See for yourself," the cemetery owner said, his voice thin. He pointed to the last page of the document, standing on tiptoes to get closer but retreating just as quickly when Jericho's glower landed on him.

"It's my signature," he said plainly. But the mystery was looming in a dead stare, confusion in his words. "I... I never saw this document."

"Thank you," I said softly, approaching and offering some words to excuse the cemetery owner. I held my hand out in a *may I* gesture. Jericho held the pages tight, fingers turning white. We'd been together a few years, and I knew him better than anyone. I also knew his signature and that he was a person who would read everything twice before signing anything.

I didn't know Jericho back when he was married, back when there was a woman named Paige Kotes who'd brutally murdered and destroyed Jericho. Emanuel knew them both, as did Samantha's aunt, our previous medical examiner. Dr. Swales knew him best, having been in most of Jericho's life and she'd confided in me once how tragic Jessie's death was. She'd also said how terrible it was to lose who Jericho was too. A part of him died when Jessie was murdered. It made me sad that I never had the chance to know that part of him. "Babe?"

Jericho stared at the document, his hand shaking as he turned it toward me. "Casey," he said quietly, but there was an unspoken plea in his voice.

I took the papers from him, scanning the lines quickly. It looked official—perfectly so. The document bore the Outer Banks courthouse header, a judge's signature, and, most damningly, Jericho's name scrawled in his familiar handwriting at the bottom. My breath caught in my throat as I held the paper up to the light, willing it to reveal any secrets but seeing none.

"It's your signature," I said softly. "But—"

"I never signed this!" Jericho roared. He took a step toward the cemetery owner, who flinched but held his ground. "And you didn't think to call me and verify?"

"Well, sir," the owner stammered, his voice barely audible now, "that's not usually part of the process when there's a court order involved. The documents seemed legitimate—"

"Seemed?" I echoed, incredulous. I gestured to the open grave behind him. "This isn't some lost parcel or a billing error. This is his wife's grave. You didn't think to double-check?"

The groundskeeper hung a thumb from his dungaree coveralls, leaning back against the backhoe. He didn't look up, but I could see the guilt in his posture, the exchange making him uncomfortable. I turned to him. "You were here," I said, keeping my tone steady but firm. "You saw what happened. Who picked up the remains?"

The man shifted, the toothpick in his mouth jumping from side to side. "A van," he muttered. "Said they were with the ME's office. Had all the right paperwork too."

"And did you open the casket?" Jericho's voice was quieter now, but the words carried the weight of all his pain. His shoulders slumped slightly, and his hat cast a shadow over his face. "Tell me. Did you open it? Did *they* open it?"

The man hesitated, his eyes darting to the cemetery owner, who offered no help. Finally, he sighed and nodded. "Yeah. They unlocked the casket with one of those keys."

Jericho took a faltering step back, his hand clutching his stomach as though he might be sick. "What did they do?"

The groundskeeper hesitated, then nodded again. "Put something inside it. A shirt, I think. Just an old T-shirt."

"The concert shirt?" Jericho said, his words like something between a gasp and a sob. I reached out, placing a hand on his arm. He didn't shake me off, but he didn't respond either.

Before anyone could speak again, the crunch of gravel announced a new arrival. A sleek black car rolled to a stop near the gravesite, and an older man in a tailored suit stepped out.

His calm measured steps seemed almost obscene in the chaos of the moment.

"Sheriff Flynn, Detective White," he greeted us, his tone overly formal. "I'm one of the owners and the proprietor of this cemetery. I assure you, I'm in contact with the medical examiner and the mason who will repair the headstone."

Jericho's head snapped up, his eyes blazing. "And Jessie?" he demanded.

"Returned at your earliest convenience," the proprietor replied, inclining his head. "We'll handle everything."

Jericho shook his head, his voice cracking. "Not without me. I'll be here when she's reburied."

The proprietor nodded again, but I barely noticed. My mind was racing. A forged court order, the desecration of a grave and a stolen body. It was the killer of Violet Jones and Carly Rose at work here. And they were going to great lengths to send a message—or worse. Only, it wasn't my past—they were recreating something from Jericho's.

A thought came to me, a spark in the dark dread of this day. Was it the funeral they wanted to recreate? Jericho had once told me that it was during his wife's funeral that he discovered who the real killer was. But Paige Kotes was dead. I was there when she'd drowned in the ocean after nearly killing me. Her body had never been recovered though. Could it be her?

I wasn't going to rest until I found out who did this.

And neither was Jericho.

SEVENTEEN

It was just past the midnight hour. And like me, the world seemed to be holding its breath. It was the anticipation of what was going to happen next that had me anxious like a dream when teetering on the edge of a cliff. There were crimes, and there were victims. We had more evidence than we'd have in most of our past cases. Yet, there wasn't a single suspect beyond the construction worker who'd escaped us in a spry run from the station.

The stairs creaked and I gripped the railing, the wood smooth and cool beneath my hand. A sting ran across the back of my neck, a nervous perspiration sprouting from the trek up and down to the evidence room. Was it the third? The fourth? I'd lost count. While the Outer Banks was in the gut of a sleepy night, I needed to work. There'd be no sleep until I had something concrete. Anything to share with the team, including Jericho and the district attorney.

The station, usually bustling with voices and movement, was unsettlingly still. The eleven to seven shift was on, eyes glancing in my direction with offers to assist. There were fewer than a half dozen and I thanked each gesture, encouraging them to continue with their nightshift duties. It was the lack of construction workers that was most evident. They'd left hours ago, their tools packed away, a skeletal framework of plastic sheeting and exposed wiring left behind. The work odors of sawdust mingled faintly with the industrial sting of cleaning chemicals. It was a mixture that felt strangely invasive in a place where the warm smells of coffee and fast food usually lingered.

The hum of the old vent system filled the silence, its rhythm uneven, as though it too struggled to stay awake through the graveyard shift. Occasionally, the vent would sputter and cough, sending a ghostly ripple through the hanging plastic. It would lift and fall gently, the motion barely noticeable unless you were staring—like I found myself doing from time to time. I was seeking answers by looking into the past, studying my previous cases and collected evidence, dusting the echoes off yesterday's memories in hopes of bringing clarity to the present.

My shadow stretched long and distorted against the walls, a smudged silhouette that seemed to follow me with an uneasy intimacy. It was the jitters. An all too familiar feeling when working mostly alone in the middle of the night. I'd been like that as a child, leaping beneath the sheets in blankets, convinced something sinister was waiting to snatch hold of my toes if I stepped too close to the bedframe's edge. I carried the last box up from the evidence basement, my arms straining from the trips that had transformed my muscles into burning cords.

By now, the makeshift conference room tables were buried under layers of old evidence boxes, each one bulging with stories too dark to forget. Some were marked with victims' names while others bore numbers only, stark and clinical, as though reducing lives to case files might make their endings less brutal. But it was the unmarked box near the edge, set aside for fear of its weight tipping the table, that I found myself staring at the most.

The quiet outside was broken by a muffled shout. A couple

of drunks lingered at the front desk where Alice's nighttime coun‐
terpart did his best to corral and quiet the pair. It didn't work,
their laughter growing louder with hollow ease, echoing down the
hallway like a bad joke no one wanted to tell. The night officer
was a rookie too green to handle such late hours alone. He waved
over two more, the three ushering the couple into the drunk tank.
I heard the heavy clang of the cell door closing and their
complaints dwindling into grumbles. Then the silence resumed,
thicker than before, my focus narrowing to the task at hand.

I set the last box down, brushing my hands off on my jeans.
The coffee I'd brewed earlier sat on the desk, still warm, still
bitter. I took a long sip, the taste sharp against my tongue, and
let my eyes wander over the disarray. The station's conference
room had become a mausoleum of my past, each box a tomb.
My gaze shifted to a single folder lying atop the heap. The
name on it wasn't written in the usual crisp handwriting.
Instead, it was scrawled in bold, heavy strokes that seemed to
press through the paper: *Paige Kotes.*

My stomach lurched, a knot twisting tightly beneath my
ribs. Paige Kotes had nearly destroyed the man I loved, and her
name was like a curse, rarely said aloud for fear of conjuring the
evilness from the depths of whatever hell she resided in now.
Even seeing it in handwritten print was a warning, a scar on my
soul that would never heal. I reached for the folder, my fingers
trembling as they brushed the edge of the tab. Somewhere in my
mind, her voice echoed, sickly sweet and sharp as broken glass,
whispering to me from beyond her watery grave.

"She's dead," I whispered aloud, needing to hear the words
spoken, needing them to be true.

The station vents sputtered again, the plastic sheeting
lifting in response. The movement drew my eye, the faint sound
like fabric rustling in a phantom breeze. For a moment, I
thought I saw a shape, a shadow behind the plastic. My pulse

quickened, but when I turned, there was nothing. Only my own paranoia reflected in the darkened glass of the door. I gripped the folder tighter, repeating, "She's dead."

But it was a lie. I hadn't seen Paige Kotes die. I had assumed, hoped, and then built my life on the fragile foundation of presumption. The reality I was facing in digging up all these cases like Jericho's dead wife had been exhumed, I was trying to convince myself there was someone else who could be responsible for the murders of Violet Jones, Carly Rose, and the men and women in the bomb squad. A dark notion cut through my guts like a knife opening a wound. I slammed my eyelids shut and admitted to myself that Paige was the one criminal from our past who could do all this.

The chair groaned as I sat down heavily, my exhaustion amplifying its pitiful protest. My hand drifted to my stomach, to the place where life had once grown before Paige took it from me. It was a new life. An innocent life that came from mine and Jericho's union. And it was stolen from us. Tears pricked my eyes, but I blinked them back. The past was a tide I couldn't stop, pulling me under, dragging me back to the night that changed everything.

That last meeting with Paige Kotes nearly killed me. It did kill our unborn child though, the memory of that moment as fresh as the wound of our loss. I'd been taken captive by a criminal pair, bludgeoned unconscious and held against my will. I'd woken up on a boat, an older luxury boat, my head feeling like it was packed with rocks. A heavy, unrelenting throb pulsed at my temples too, each beat sharp enough to drag me into wakefulness. The smell of salt and gasoline clung to the air, and the cold bite of sea spray misted my skin. I couldn't focus, blinking, my vision sluggish, the edges of the world shifting with the boat's sway.

I was lying on the lower deck, half-curled against the hard edge of a wraparound vinyl couch. The chill of the fiberglass beneath me seeped into my bones, intensifying the aches in my body. Every breath came shallow and sharp, my lungs rebelling against the effort. My face was a swollen mess, the skin taut and hot. I tried to lift my hand, but my wrists were tied behind me, the rough fibers of the rope biting into my skin.

Above me, the two who'd taken me stood at the helm, silhouetted against the faint glow of moonlight. Paige was there, her golden hair catching the sea breeze, framing a face that looked almost serene. Next to her, the guard from the prison where she was an inmate handled the wheel. He was more than a guard. He was her partner in a series of heinous crimes—a hulking man with broad shoulders and brutish movements. The engine roared beneath their conversation, cutting through the rhythm of the waves slapping against the hull.

My stomach churned, not just from the nausea but from the memory of his boot driving into my abdomen. The force of it had stolen my breath, leaving an unrelenting pain deep in my core. I swallowed against the rise of bile, panic clawing at my throat. My hand instinctively pressed against my middle, searching for a reassurance I couldn't find.

My baby.

The thought hit me like another blow. Had his kick done more than crack a rib? My fingers trembled as I tried to feel for any sign—any hope. Paige turned suddenly, her green eyes gleaming as she caught my movement. She brought a single finger to her lips, signaling for silence. Her smile was faint, a mockery of reassurance, but her eyes were alight with something darker. Sinister.

I wanted to scream. Instead, I glanced around, taking in the pristine condition of the boat. It was a bowrider, high-end and meticulously maintained, and not as old as I'd thought. Every surface gleamed, the polished chrome and spotless canvas seats an eerie contrast to the dread clawing at my chest. Whoever the guard was, he kept his tools of death immaculate.

Was this it for me? Was I just another victim to be dragged out to sea, tossed overboard like garbage? My gaze landed on the GPS unit glowing at the helm, its display showing a plotted course. The lines were clean, precise, each route marked with timestamps. They weren't improvising. They'd done this before, plotting their victims' final moments with methodical care.

"What are you staring at?" Paige's voice cut through the roar of the motor, sharp and amused. Her blonde hair danced around her scarred face as she moved closer, her expression twisting into mock curiosity. I couldn't take my eyes off the scar, a ragged crease that ran the length of her face. It was put there in a battle with Jericho when he'd brought her to justice, discovering who she really was, the person who'd murdered his wife. Her eyes flashed wide with a threat, and I lowered my head, my body curling tighter as the boat hit a wave, the impact jarring my bruised ribs.

"What is it? Cat got your tongue?" she teased, crouching in front of me. Her grin never wavered as her gaze roamed over my battered face. "Or are you finally realizing how badly you've lost?"

"Please," I croaked, the word barely audible. It wasn't strength she saw in me—it was desperation.

Paige leaned in, her lips brushing close to my ear. "I told you, Casey. You should've listened to Jericho." Her voice was a venomous whisper, dripping with satisfaction. "But now, here we are."

The guard interrupted, his voice a low rumble. "You better check her ties. Can't have her getting any bright ideas."

"Aye aye, Captain," Paige called, giving a mock salute. She

reached into her sleeve, pulling out a crude blade—thin, sharp, and unmistakably homemade. A prison shiv.

"Stay still," she said, her tone almost sweet as she reached for my wrists. I could smell her. I could smell the prison she called home as her weight pressed against me. She worked fast, her hands quick but careless. The boat jarred to the left, the blade slipping into my forearm like a hot knife through butter. The pain was instant with a sting that made me bite back a cry.

"How bad is it?" I asked, my voice trembling. Blood warmed my skin, soaking into the rope.

"It's okay," Paige answered, her voice quiet, almost apologetic. She stood abruptly, leaving the prison shiv behind. I found part of the blade still in the knot and though my fingers had begun to go numb, I cut. I cut as fast as I could. And all the while, I wondered, why was she helping me?

The boat slowed, its engine dropping to a steady hum. The guard barked instructions, his voice tinged with impatience. Paige leaned back, her expression hardening as she stood.

"It's time," the guard said, stepping closer.

"Not yet," Paige replied, her tone turning coy. "Let me do her the way I want to."

His face twisted in suspicion. "You mean like Jericho's wife?"

"Exactly like that," she said, running a hand over his shoulder. "You'll help me, won't you?"

"Yes," he answered, his voice softening under her touch. "Anything for you."

Paige's gaze flicked to mine, her lips curving into a knowing smile. She motioned for him to lift me, her movements deliberate as she positioned herself at my knees. My heart raced, the weight of the shiv still in my hand hidden by the slackening ropes. I tightened my grip, waiting for the opening I knew would come.

"Get her near the edge," Paige ordered, her tone cold now. "When I say the word, you drop her headfirst into the water."

"Won't last a minute," the guard said with a cruel chuckle.

"That's the idea," Paige replied, her laughter dark and jagged.

The world tilted as they hoisted me, the boat rocking. My mind raced, each second a countdown to the moment I would have to fight. Paige adjusted her grip, her eyes locking with mine for an instant.

"Detective," she whispered, her voice barely audible over the crash of the waves. "Now would be a good time."

The shiv in my hand moved before I could think. I drove it into the guard's shoulder with every ounce of strength I had left. He bellowed in pain, his grip faltering as I twisted the blade. Paige stepped back, her laugh cutting through the chaos as the guard staggered.

"What the hell?!" he shouted, his blood dripping onto the deck.

Paige didn't answer. Her gaze was fixed on me, her smile widening as if she'd been waiting for this. The guard lunged again, his fury doubling his strength, but Paige moved faster. She grabbed the cleat with one hand, her other driving her elbow into his face with brutal precision.

"Kill him!" she screamed, her voice breaking through my haze of panic. "Casey, kill him now!"

My arm was heavy, the blade slick with blood, the guard stunned and reeling. He stumbled, his massive frame teetering before he fell overboard, disappearing into the churning water. The boat lunged forward, the heel of his foot had struck the throttle, putting us in motion. Paige had gone overboard too, but I was quick to take hold before the sea had all of her. With her body plastered against the side, she let out a scream, her partner holding onto her legs, threatening to drag her under. Paige ended her partnership with the guard, ending his life too, burying a boat cleat into his skull with a sickening thud.

I helped her on board, the boat rocking violently, the engine sputtering, a nearby vessel sounding an alarm. Paige grabbed my arm, her grip steel tight as she steadied me. For a moment, I thought she might pull me into a hug, the relief in her eyes almost tender. But then her expression shifted, and I saw the fire in her gaze reignite.

"Did you ever hear the story of the scorpion and the frog?" she asked, her voice low.

"What are you talking about?" I panted, barely able to stay upright.

"I tried to do good. Truly, I did. But evil, it's in my nature, Casey," she said, her lips curling into a wicked grin. "I can't change who I am. The miracle of it is, I don't want to change."

Before I could react, she lunged, her hands wrapping around my neck. The force of her attack sent us both sprawling, the edge of the boat looming dangerously close. The world blurred as her grip tightened, the stars overhead fading into darkness. My fingers fumbled for the shiv, my strength dwindling with every second.

With a final surge of desperation, I struck. The blade found its mark, sinking into her flesh. Paige let out a guttural scream, her grip loosening as blood poured from the wound. I struck again and again, tears streaming down my face as I fought to stay alive.

One of the last things I remembered was the sound of the ship's horn, loud and blaring, as a massive spotlight swept over us. Then the world tilted, and we were thrown into the water, the icy embrace of the ocean swallowing us whole. Paige never resurfaced, our assumption she was dead. A rescue helicopter found me at daybreak, the search involving the Marine Patrol and headed by Jericho. But by then, our baby had passed, leaving me to feel like an unworthy failure for not protecting them from Paige Kotes. I was alive but often questioned if I'd truly survived that day.

———————

I snapped out of the memory, gasping as though I'd surfaced from drowning. My coffee had gone cold, its bitterness forgotten in the wake of my racing heart. The folder lay open in my lap, the papers inside untouched but radiating menace. The station's vents coughed again, the plastic sheeting billowing once more. This time, I didn't look. My gaze stayed fixed on the name in bold letters, the name that refused to let me go.

Paige Kotes wasn't dead. I could feel it now, like a cancer growing in my chest. She was alive, somewhere out there, wait-ing, watching, planning. It had to be her. It was Jessie's body and the butterfly pendant. Who else would do this? The station around me seemed to close in, the quiet more oppressive than before. The distant laughter of the drunks in the cells was gone, replaced by the whispering hum of fluorescent lights. I felt the weight of Paige's shadow, not just in the room but in my mind, in my very soul. A shiver ran through me, and I let out a sob I hadn't realized I'd been holding back. Paige Kotes was alive. And I was still her prey.

EIGHTEEN

I crept into our makeshift bedroom, the third of four on the second floor of the new place. It was almost three in the morning and the house was asleep, the dim light revealing our bedcovers rising and falling slowly, Jericho's soft snore from beneath. Thomas and Tabitha were out too but would be up in a couple of hours and looking for breakfast. I'd promised pancakes. Pandycakes, Tabitha called them for the longest time. Jericho usually made them from scratch with his mother's recipe but with the events of the day, I thought to step in on his behalf. My recipe was from the side of a box, and I was sure that with enough butter and syrup, the kids wouldn't notice the difference.

My clothes slid off me with each step, leaving small piles, before diving beneath the sheets. Jericho was on his left side, facing away and I wanted to feel him. My heart hurt for him. Seeing his wife like that, seeing her face years after she'd been murdered? It was the stuff nightmares were made of. It had to affect him. How could it not.

"Babe," he said, voice scratchy, rolling onto his back. I didn't hesitate and draped an arm and leg across him. "Station?"

"Uh-huh," I said, lips brushing across the stubble on his cheek.

"How many?" he asked, knowing exactly what I'd been working tonight. "How many cases?"

"All of them." His chest rose with a sigh, and he covered his face with his hands, shaking it back and forth. "It was the only thing I could think to do."

"This can't be the last case you work before retiring." He placed a hand on mine, patting it as if to comfort bad news. A rattling stirred above us, a pattern of steps running across the ceiling. In the gray light, his gaze locked on the ceiling. I followed it to where there was a crack in the plaster. If I didn't know any better, it had widened some since moving in. "I'll get the ladder from the shed tomorrow. See what's going on up there."

"The attic?" I asked, curious about it. I'd never been. Neither had he. The home inspector would have, I hoped but couldn't be sure. A nod. "What do you think it is?"

"Squirrels got in. Or a family of raccoons."

"In the attic?" I asked, skin prickly with a sudden itch.

"Could be mice," he joked, knowing my position on the rodent thing. Just the thought had me shake, a shiver racing through me. "Don't worry, I'll put some traps up there."

"The humane ones. Okay?"

In the dark, I saw the whites of his eyes. "Seriously?"

"Yeah, seriously. They don't mean any harm."

Eyes rolling, "You might not think that when you see the damage they can do."

"Jericho?" He heard the tone and instantly looked as though I was about to deliver the most awful news. "I'm sorry. But I must ask."

"The pendant," he said solemnly. He sat up, the sheets rolling from his chest. In the gray light, the moon full and peering through our window, I could see the scars. Deep reminders of his altercation with the woman who'd killed his wife. That battle had nearly killed him. And it nearly killed his career. I wasn't thinking and ran my finger along the crescent shape that ran the length of his shoulder and arm. He flinched at the touch, the skin beneath my fingertips was oddly smooth and shiny. He closed his hands around mine, rubbing them softly. "Your hands are cold."

"It's still more like early spring than early summer." I moved closer, laying my head in the on his chest. A part of him I swore was made for me, the fit perfect. "Tell me about it."

He sighed, his breath light. And though I wasn't facing him, I sensed the warm smile the memory of his wife had brought. "She'd worn that pendant since high school when she was a cheerleader. I still remember how she'd tuck it in safely before they went onto the field."

"Was it a family heirloom?"

"I think so. I can't remember asking. She just always had it on." There was nothing for a moment, save for the scurrying in the attic, the thought of rodents giving me a chill. The room went quiet, the house speaking its pre-dawn chatter that often woke us after we'd first moved in. We knew what sounds to expect now and what to question. "But the pendant was missing the day her body washed up on the shore."

"You believed it might have been lost in the waves?"

"That's what we thought," he replied, his chest rising and falling faster. "Emanuel was with me when her body was recovered. And what the waves did to her—"

"I'm sorry," I said, not believing there was anything else that could be said that'd help ease the pain, even if it was a little. I swiped at a tear, the sound of emotion in his voice tugging on my heart. "I can't imagine."

"It was at her funeral that the truth of it all came to light." Jericho shifted. I followed, laying my head back onto his chest, his heart inches from my ear. "Paige had a flower, a rose I think it was. We were placing them on Jessie's casket and when Paige bent over, the butterfly pendant slipped from her blouse. I saw it. But didn't see it. You know what I mean?"

"Like it was a dream," I replied cozily, eyelids getting heavy.

"It was dangling on a thin chain. Probably the same chain I'd bought Jessie, replacing the old one when it broke."

"The pendant was taken as a keepsake," I said, shifting the discussion to a trait of serial killers. "That's what they do. They take keepsakes."

"What? Huh?"

"Paige took the pendant as a kind of prize," I continued. "Sometimes they look at them as a way to relive the murder."

"Relive it? Jesus," he grunted. "There isn't a day that passes I don't think about Jessie."

"Really?" I asked, his words surprising, even painful. It wasn't a jealousy thing. It was sadness, hearing the relentless longing and the grieving ache he carried for Jessie. In a way I knew what he was talking about, having felt similar for my daughter after her kidnapping. It was every day. Sometimes every minute of the day.

That's why there are ghosts. It's what ghosts really are. They're not some ethereal being that haunts us. Instead, they are the love we still carry for them after they're gone. Loving someone to the point of inseparability is both a gift and a tragedy. Jericho felt that for his wife and the weight of it in her absence was so immense that it nearly took his life. He'd become lost after her murder, a shadow of his former self. If not for his solving the case and arresting Paige Kotes, he might have been lost forever.

I sat up, our eyes meeting, "I'm so sorry you're still in pain."

Jericho picked up my hand, placing it on the worst of the scars from the battle he'd waged against Paige. "That's all it is now. A scar. I live with it, sometimes forget about it a little. But it never goes away. Not fully."

I returned to snuggle closely, curling into his body, skin on skin as he dressed the sheet over us both. "Your son had the pendant? He had it at school?"

A nod. "I called and he checked his dorm. It was gone. But he never noticed it went missing until I said something. What are you thinking?"

I hesitated to answer, uncertain of how he'd react. Jericho could read me like a mystic reading tea leaves and when I didn't answer, he squeezed my shoulder gently. "I went back through every case."

"I figured you would," he replied. He cleared the frog in his throat, adding, "This killer has gone back through them too. They must've gone back through mine as well. How else would they have known about Jessie and her butterfly pendant?"

"Because they killed your wife. They killed Jessie," I said, looking up at him. The moon's full shape shined in his wet eyes. Gray pouches puffed beneath, his blink slow, his expression in disagreement. He'd aged ten years since the meeting at the cemetery, the stress of Jessie's exhumed body too much.

"Come again?" he said, asking with disbelief. I didn't answer immediately, and he dipped his chin, "Casey, Paige Kotes is dead."

My eyes stung and a phantom cramp swept across my middle where our unborn baby had once been alive. The emotions welled inside me, closing my throat as I tried to find the words to speak. "I... Jericho, I think Paige Kotes is alive."

His eyes narrowed and his lips thinned and drew poker straight like his brow. He shook his head, disagreeing strongly. "It's impossible. She died that day."

"Babe, I..." I had to stop, voice hitched in a swell of emotion. He saw my fingers splayed on my belly and pecked the top of my head with a kiss.

"I'm so sorry. Paige Kotes would have never been in your life if not for me." His voice broke then with the struggle. "Paige would have never brought you so much pain if it weren't for me—"

"It's not your fault. The irony is, I might never have met you if Paige wasn't in your life, if she wasn't your partner and murdered your wife."

"She has to be dead," he exclaimed. "She just has to."

"There was so much debris, and I never saw her body." I scratched through the memories of that day, peeling them back like the rind on a fruit, hopeful in finding any semblance of usefulness. A swath of hair adrift, or her bloodied clothes, a glimpse of an arm or the ragged scars across her face. Anything. "The baby was dying. I was dying too. I could have missed something and that's how Paige escaped."

"Well..." His voice was shaky and his mouth dry. "I-I'm not at all sure what we do now."

"Paige Kotes is a suspect. That's what we do. We assume she survived and that she's come back to finish what she started."

"Finish what she started," he repeated, his lower lip trembling. "Casey, none of us are safe."

"I know," I said, hating that there was vulnerability in his voice. He was a rock. Our rock. But this shook him.

NINETEEN

The station felt like it belonged to someone else. Morning sunlight had begun creeping through the gaps in the plywood covering the windows, its rays cutting through a dusty haze that lingered semi-permanent in the station's air, the ongoing renovations never-ending. The air smelled of sawdust and the acrid tang of old coffee left to scorch in the break room. Somewhere, a hammer clanged rhythmically, each strike a reminder of how much work this place needed.

The temporary conference tables were mismatched, scratched, and gouged from years of being shoved into storage closets. Papers and photographs spilled across their surfaces, covering even the gaps between. They bore the distinct smell of printer ink, old paper, and a faint dampness from the basement where we kept the files. Alice's voice filtered in from the front, sharp and no-nonsense as she handled a pair of drunk-and-disorderly arrests from the night before.

Tracy leaned back in her chair, one foot propped on her knee, leg bouncing and her arms crossed tightly over her chest. Her light brown hair, usually immaculately styled, was tied into a messy ponytail, a testament to her sleepless night. Her voice carried an edge—firm, clipped, and dangerously skeptical. When she spoke, it felt like she was daring you to challenge her.

"This is insane, Casey," she said flatly, pointing a manicured finger at the photographs scattered before us. "Paige Kotes drowned. The currents in that area would've pulled her under and dragged her out to sea. You know that as well as I do."

"I have to agree," Emanuel said firmly. He leaned forward, his elbows on the table. His voice was deeper, steadier, but tinged with exhaustion. He rubbed his temples, his dark eyes narrowing as if he were piecing together a puzzle he didn't want to solve. "Tracy's right. We're chasing ghosts here. If Paige somehow survived that wreck, why hasn't she surfaced before now? Why wait this long before coming back? And why come back at all?"

"Because she's Paige Kotes," I snapped, slamming my palm on the table. The noise startled both, though neither spoke. I didn't expect this much pushback and gestured at the files spread between us, the crime scenes, the graves of victims, and even the fresh murders. "She's not some amateur criminal looking for a quick payday. She's methodical. Calculating. She's waited because she knows the timing has to be perfect."

Tracy rolled her eyes, her foot dropping to the floor with a thud. "Or maybe this is just some unhinged copycat. Someone who got access to police records. Someone who studied these cases."

"She knows things no one else could know," I countered, my voice rising. "The exhumation of Jessie Cooper Flynn's body? The placement of that butterfly pendant? That wasn't public knowledge so who else knew to do that? That's not a coincidence. That's Paige."

Emanuel leaned back in his chair, arms crossing slowly over his broad chest. "Casey, even if you're right—and I'm not saying you are—how would she have survived? You were there, Casey. You fought her. You saw the wreckage."

I eased into the seat, taking a deep breath and forced myself to stay calm. The memories clawed at the edges of my mind with their usual threats. "I didn't see her die," I said softly. "And neither did you. After the collision, there was debris everywhere. Pieces of the bowrider, chunks of wood and fiberglass. It was enough to keep someone afloat. If Paige was smart—and we both know she is—she could've hidden behind that debris until she floated far out of sight."

Tracy let out a sharp breath, her phone clattering onto the table. "You're asking us to believe in a ghost, Casey. Do you know how ridiculous this sounds? You were there. You fought her. Hell, you almost died. And now, you're telling us she's back from the dead?"

I met her gaze, unflinching. "I am." Unknowingly, I'd pressed my hand on my belly, the ghost of my baby squeezing my heart. "I survived it, she could have too."

The room fell silent. Outside, the construction workers had begun their day in earnest, the low rumble of a power drill dimming the overhead lights while competing with the muffled conversations from the front desk. The sunlight had grown stronger, casting long shadows across the conference room tables, accenting the tired lines on all our faces.

"I was bleeding out," I continued, my voice quieter now, almost a whisper. "I was cramping so badly I thought I was going to die right there in the water. The baby was... I lost so much blood I couldn't move. But I still floated. The sea went still, just for a moment, and it was like the world was holding its breath. Thinking back on that moment, I realized she could've made it too."

"Casey—" Tracy began, but I cut her off.

"She's alive," I said, more forcefully now. "And she's the only one who could pull this off. Look at the precision in these killings. The intimate details. By now, I think she knows these cases better than anyone because she's been planning them for years."

Emanuel's frown deepened, his hand rubbing the stubble on his chin. "Let's say you're right. Let's say Paige survived. How does that help us now? Where do we even start looking?"

I exhaled slowly, forcing myself to focus. His question was a bite. Not a lot. A nibble perhaps. But it was what I needed to hear. "Her last known location was the ocean, near the coordinates of the collision, close to where I was found. We start there. Hospitals within a fifty-mile radius of the shoreline. Someone with injuries like hers—broken bones, lacerations, burns from the gasoline fire—would've needed medical attention."

"There's that scar on her face, from when Jericho arrested her," Emanuel commented. My insides lurched. He was on board. "That's a hard one to hide. People will remember seeing her."

Tracy snorted again, leaning back in her chair. "You think she just waltzed into an ER with wounds from a fight and a fake name? Hospitals report that kind of thing, Casey."

"You're right. She's smarter than that," I said. "But even Paige couldn't heal herself. Most of the injuries were from the boat collision. To an emergency room, she'll appear to have been in an accident."

"It's a lead," Emanuel said, tiring of the discussion. "And it's the only lead we've got at the moment."

Tracy wasn't convinced though. I pushed, saying, "Listen, Paige would've had to seek help somewhere, even if it wasn't a traditional hospital. We pull admittance records from urgent care centers, private clinics, even unlicensed facilities if we have to."

Tracy nodded slowly with reluctance. "It's a long shot."

"Long shots are all we've got," I fired back. "Unless you have a better theory?"

She sighed, leaning forward again, her hands spread wide

on the table. "No. I don't. The district attorney is asking questions. She's my boss now and I've got to report the direction
we're headed."

"Report it," I challenged, annoyed.

Slowly shaking her head, "You're sure about this, Casey? If
we start chasing Paige Kotes and she's not our killer…"

"She is," I said firmly, cutting her off. "And if we don't act
fast, more people are going to die."

For a moment, neither of them spoke. The air in the room
felt heavy, thick with the weight of doubt and unspoken fears.
Finally, Tracy sighed, picking up her phone again.

"Fine," she said, her voice clipped. "I'll start pulling hospital
records. But if this doesn't pan out—"

"It will," I said, standing up. My legs felt shaky, but I
ignored it. "It has to."

The first rays of sunlight had begun spilling fully into the
room now, bathing the papers across the table in a warm,
buttery light. It was a stark contrast to the icy dread curling in
my chest, having convinced myself and others that Paige Kotes
was out there. And if I was right, she was just getting started.

Tracy still didn't look convinced as she scrolled through her
phone, her fingers moving with practiced efficiency. Emanuel
remained quiet, his brow furrowed as he tapped a pen against
the table. The rhythmic clicking was grating, but I didn't have
the energy to snap at him. I needed them on my side, and right
now, it felt like I was trying to drag two boulders uphill.

I got out of my chair and paced the room, my boots scuffing
against the worn linoleum. The thick air was beginning to give
me a headache with its ever-present mix of construction dust
and stale coffee. The renovations made everything feel temporary—patched walls, exposed wires, and the faint rumble of
power tools adding to the sense of unease.

Emanuel raised a hand, his tone measured but firm. "Casey,

you didn't answer the question earlier about why now? Why not come after you the moment she was back on her feet?"

"Because, I don't think this is about me," I said, stepping closer to the table. My hands found the edge of the nearest chair, gripping it until my knuckles turned white. "Not entirely. Paige doesn't just kill for revenge. She kills for control. Every murder is a message, a statement. This"—I gestured to the photos spread across the table, the patterns too deliberate to be random—"This is her masterpiece. She's been building to this moment, waiting for the right time to strike."

Tracy leaned forward, her voice low and edged with skepticism. "And what? You think she's some kind of criminal mastermind? A ghost pulling the strings from the shadows?"

"Yes," I said, meeting her gaze head-on. "That's exactly what I think."

The silence stretched thin, broken only by the distant whine of a power saw. Tracy's fingers drummed against the tabletop, her expression unreadable. Emanuel rubbed a hand across his jaw, his eyes narrowing as he studied me.

"Beyond the theory, we're going to need more," he said finally, his voice heavy with reluctance, "We're going to need proof. Something tangible."

"That's what the DA is going to need," Tracy said, joining Emanuel's argument. My hope of having convinced them was suddenly in jeopardy. "I know you have the butterfly pendant. But if a copycat reviewed these files, they would have reviewed any from Jericho's time as a sheriff too."

I nodded, raising my hands and motioning to her phone. "Can we at least continue with the hospital checks, the urgent care clinics, even morgues if we have to. The evidence you guys are asking for could be there."

"And if we don't?" Tracy asked, her voice sharp. "If we don't find anything?"

"Then we keep digging," I said, my voice unwavering. "Because I'm not letting her get away again."

Emanuel exhaled deeply, the sound more a growl than a sigh. "This could be a needle in a haystack."

"It's what we have to work," I said, straightening. "And it's better than sitting here waiting for her to strike again."

Tracy exchanged a look with Emanuel, something unspoken passing between them. Finally, she picked up her phone again, her lips pressed into a tight line.

"I'll complete the calls with the nearest hospitals," she said.

Emanuel stood, gathering the nearest stack of files and tucking them under his arm. His movements were slow, deliberate, as if he were still processing everything I'd said. "I'll start pulling records from the night of the collision," he said. "See if there's anything unusual."

"Thank you," I said simply.

As they moved to begin their work, I sank into one of the rickety chairs, the weight of the moment pressing down on me. Outside, the sunlight had fully pierced the horizon, bathing the station in a soft, golden glow. But inside, the air felt darker, heavier, the specter of Paige Kotes casting a kind of gloom over us all.

For the first time since I'd uttered her name, I allowed myself a moment of doubt. Could I be wrong? Could this all be a product of exhaustion, grief, and guilt twisting my memories into something they weren't?

No. I shook the thought away. I wasn't wrong. Paige Kotes was alive.

And she was waiting.

I sat in the worn chair, watching Tracy and Emanuel as they dispersed. Tracy was already on her phone with one of the hospitals, her voice sharp and authoritative as she navigated the bureaucracy of hospital records. Emanuel lumbered slowly to his desk, the injuries of the bomb still felt with each step. He swiped his computer screen and pulled up the first list of contacts for urgent care centers.

The faint hum of the fluorescent lights buzzed over the sound of construction workers hammering into drywall. Dust motes floated lazily through the sunbeams streaming from the high, partially boarded windows. I opened the conference room window, the sea air blowing in to rid the room of the renovation smell.

I rubbed my head, feeling the weight of the cases, old and new, pressing in from all sides. It was the station too; it was a graveyard of memories. I could still see Jericho pacing these floors, his voice a steady rumble as he reviewed cases. The echo of his boots against the floor lingered, a phantom reminder of everything we'd lost. His absence today was almost unbearable, the weight of his grief over Jessie Cooper Flynn's desecrated grave leaving him at home, sifting through his own demons. He didn't talk very much about it, but her spirit was with him. I could feel it.

It was Paige Kotes too. I was going out on a limb with this one and her name alone was a lead weight in my gut. If I closed my eyes, I could see her face—sharp, calculating, and glinting with that unnerving mixture of malice and intelligence. She'd always been a step ahead, a master manipulator who thrived on chaos and control. Her absence had felt like a reprieve, but now, the pieces were falling into place, and her specter loomed large over everything.

Emanuel returned first, carrying a fresh pot of coffee that smelled better than the earlier batch. And it was exactly what I needed. He poured me a cup without asking and handed it over, his expression neutral but his eyes sharp.

"I got a list of urgent care centers within fifty miles," he said, setting a notepad on the table. "It's a start. A few of them don't keep electronic records for anything older than a few years, but they'll pull paper files if we ask nicely—or subpoena them."

"Good," I said, taking a long sip of the bitter coffee. It scraped against my throat, but it brought a spark of clarity. "What about private practices? Clinics?"

"They're on the list too." Emanuel sat down heavily, his chair groaning under his weight. "But Casey, let's be real here. Even if we find something—some mention of a Jane Doe that fits Paige's description and injuries—it's not going to be a smoking gun. We'll still be chasing shadows."

"Then we chase them," I said firmly. "Every shadow. Every lead. Until we catch her."

He sighed, running a hand across his head. "You've always been stubborn."

Tracy returned, her phone still pressed to her ear. She waved us off as she finished her call, her voice tight with restrained frustration. "I don't care if the records are archived. We need them. Get me the hospital administrator." She hung up with an exaggerated tap, muttering under her breath.

"Red tape everywhere," she said, slumping into a chair and tossing her phone onto the table. "One hospital said they might have a report on a possible drowning victim matching Paige's description, but the person I need to talk to isn't in until noon."

"That's something," I said, leaning forward. "What else?"

Tracy gave me a sharp look, her skepticism still etched into her features. "Don't start celebrating yet. It could be anyone. I still don't think she survived, Casey. And if she did, how do we know she didn't disappear for good after getting patched up?"

"It's Paige," I said, growing frustrated with repeating myself. "Disappearing wouldn't be her style."

Tracy's eyes narrowed, and for a moment, it felt like she might argue. But she shook her head instead, exhaling a sharp breath. "I'll work it until there's nothing left to work."

Emanuel flipped through the pages on his notepad, circling a few entries with a red pen. "Let's continue to divide the workload, continue making the calls. I'll stick to the urgent care centers. Tracy, you keep to the hospitals."

"And you?" Tracy asked me, her tone bordering on accusatory.

"I'll follow the thread of her last known associates," I said. "Anyone Paige might have reached out to after the collision. We'll cover every angle."

Tracy and Emanuel exchanged a look, their doubts still hanging heavy in the air. But neither of them argued further. The room felt quieter now, the tension palpable. Outside, the sounds of the station waking up filtered in—radios crackling, boots scuffing, and the occasional burst of laughter from Alice handling yet another minor crisis.

I stood, gathering the files closest to me. "We'll find her," I said, more to myself than to them. "And when we do, we'll stop her. For good this time."

TWENTY

A tall woman approached our table like she owned the sunlight. She carried two more plates with the practiced ease of someone who'd done this a thousand times and had judged each cake personally. Her frame was graceful but strong, like a former volleyball player turned bakery goddess. She leaned over slightly, placing the next round of cake slices in front of us with a precise sort of care, like each one deserved its own ceremony. Blonde streaks laced through her chestnut ponytail, catching the late afternoon light and turning it to gold. Her smirk said she'd seen couples like us many times. I hated to admit it, but we'd come to the cake tasting overconfident, sugared-out, and wildly underestimating the power of buttercream.

"Here you go," she said, sliding the plates between Jericho and me with a wink. "Round six. Or maybe seven. Honestly, I lost count after the praline blackout. You two are troopers."

You'd think after everything I'd seen in my career—the blood, the bodies, the constant presence of death—I'd know how to pace myself around cake. But as it turned out, buttercream was the real killer. I nudged Jericho's shoulder and picked a cake crumb from his chin. "What do you think of that one?"

"I dunno," he answered, sounding swelled and overstuffed. He leaned back in his chair with a pained expression, rubbing his stomach. "I swear, if I have to taste another frosting that ends in 'whipped vanilla cloud,' I'm going to pass out."

"You've said that after every new type," I said, failing to keep a laugh from slipping out. "You're going soft. How can I marry someone so soft?"

He groaned with a chuckle. "You try sitting through twelve varieties of the same sugar delivery system and not hallucinate colors."

"You literally just asked the baker if one of them was bourbon-infused."

"I was hoping for rescue," he answered with a laugh.

The woman joined him, letting out a warm chuckle and tapped his plate with her fingernail, the sound just this side of flirtatious. "The bourbon one's coming up, deary. If you're still conscious, you'll love it."

The venue itself was adorable. Airy and rustic, tucked along a treelined road not far from the beach. It was one of those weathered-chic barns turned wedding venues that also offered goat yoga and fourteen-dollar smoothies. I'd passed the location a thousand times and had no idea what it was. Not until learning from Tracy that cake tasting was a real thing and a must when planning a wedding. For today, the three of us had taken over a picnic table just outside the tasting hall, three large trays of cakes between us, each slice impaled with a miniature numbered flag, like sugary corpses awaiting autopsy.

Tracy sat nearby, cross-legged and looking far too serene for the chaos happening across the table. She'd taken exactly one bite of an almond raspberry swirl an hour ago and was now sipping water like it was a martini, watching us both with a smug grin that said we'd brought this on ourselves.

"It's not even the sugar," I said, stabbing my fork into a suspiciously cheerful-looking lemon chiffon with poppyseed cream. "It's the names. 'Sea Breeze Citrus Drizzle'? To me, that sounds a Crayola color, not a dessert."

"You're both weak," Tracy said, mocking us while taking another tiny, dainty sip from her water bottle like it was a performance.

The cake coordinator—Mel, according to her rhinestoned name tag—rested a hand on her hip and chimed in with a grin. "When I got married the first time, I ate two dozen slices in one sitting. Didn't blink."

Jericho perked up just enough to raise an eyebrow. "What happened to that marriage?"

Mel deadpanned, "The cake was the best part."

I burst out laughing, nearly choking on a mouthful of vanilla bean sponge. Across the table, Jericho caught my eye with that warm glint I knew too well. Affection, amusement, and something gentler, deeper. This was us. Us outside the chaos, the murder scenes, the late-night callouts. And as I got closer to retiring from the police force, I was seeing more of it. Better than that, I wanted more of it too. We didn't get enough of these moments, the ones where it felt like we belonged to a quieter life. One where picking a wedding cake was the only urgency.

Mel leaned in a bit closer, nudging Jericho's elbow. "If he keels over before he decides on a cake, I'll revive him. Mouth-to-mouth's free. But only for grooms."

Tracy's eyes bugged out of her skull, her surprise joining my shock, the flirting a little over the top.

"The only mouth-to-mouth would involve my lips," I quickly answered.

Jericho smiled with the easy charm that still made my chest ache, even after everything. He looked up at Mel, answering politely, "Tempting. But I'd hate to have to fight off Casey."

"Smart man," I said, tapping my fork against my plate. "And still alive—for now."

"Well, Sheriff, there will be one less good man available in the Outer Banks." Mel turned to me, saying with a wink, "You picked a true winner."

"I know."

"She does," Jericho said, chuckling.

Just as I reached for another bite of something dangerously called brown sugar blackout, my phone buzzed. I glanced at the screen and felt a chill slip down the back of my neck. It was from Carly Rose's mother, the text indicating that she was at her daughter's apartment. "Guys," I said, lifting my eyes from the screen, "we've got access to Carly Rose's place."

Tracy was already on her feet, the serenity gone, replaced by focus. "Got it."

Jericho wiped his hands on a napkin, pushed himself up from the bench, and shot a parting glance at the tower of cake slices. "Let's go."

Mel gave us a sympathetic nod as we stood. "You didn't even get to try the bourbon one."

Jericho smirked. "Keep it warm for us."

Carly Rose's apartment was on the second floor of an old building near the boardwalk, the kind with warped stairs and floral carpeting that hadn't seen a shampoo in twenty years. The entire hallway smelled like old paint and damp paper. The door was already cracked when we arrived. I eased it open slightly, dust drifting in a blade of sunlight, the air still.

"Mrs. Rose?" I knocked gently and pushed it open further.

Inside was like stepping into an art exhibit abandoned mid curation. Canvases leaned like forgotten promises against every wall. Unfinished paintings covered the small room in broad brushstrokes of vibrance. There were beach scenes, lighthouses, even a city skyline done in swirls that reminded me of Van Gogh. But most were incomplete. There were even a few with sunflowers. My eyes were drawn to them instantly.

A woman sat cross-legged on the floor in front of a low table, her back to us. Her hands moved slowly, folding a sweater with the deliberateness of someone using the task to anchor herself. A duffel bag lay open beside her. Most of it was still empty.

"Mrs. Rose?" I said again, quieter this time.

She turned. Her eyes were red, lips chapped. There was a picture frame in her lap. She clutched it like a lifeline, and the moment her eyes met mine, the fragile composure she'd built cracked.

"She was going to repaint this one," she said, holding the frame up. Inside was a photo of Carly, maybe sixteen or seventeen, standing barefoot in front of a canvas, hair pulled up in a messy bun and paint streaking her cheek. She was smiling and had that wild and free look we lose when life takes over in adulthood.

"She said it was too perfect," her mother added, the laugh that followed edged in sorrow.

"Ma'am, we're sorry for your loss," Jericho said, kneeling by the door, his broad shoulders filling the frame like a silent guardian.

"Sorry for your loss," Tracy added, moving slowly through the space, careful not to disturb anything.

I stepped inside and lowered myself across from her, close but not too close. "We can't imagine what this is like."

"You can't," Carly's mother snapped, her voice trembling. "She was... light. You know? She came into the world kicking, full of noise and mess, but she always found a way to turn it into something beautiful." She looked at me then, raw and hollow. "Who would do this to her? What kind of monster could leave her in a field like that? Like she was nothing?"

I swallowed the lump in my throat. "We're going to find them. I promise."

Her shoulders trembled. She reached for a tissue and dabbed at her face. She leaned back and looked around as if seeing her daughter's apartment for the first time. "This place is her. It really is. Everything she owned is covered in paint," she whispered. "She didn't even buy furniture. Said it was too permanent. But she did care about her work. She cared so deeply."

Tracy stepped forward, gently lifting a sketchbook from a corner table and flipping it open. Inside were quick pencil scrawls, studies of light and shadow, notes about color theory. One page stood out though and drew my focus. I muttered the words aloud, "'Commission, March seventeen. Sunflowers, golden tones, use that ochre blend.'" Beneath the words, there was a time written along with a location I knew to be where Carly's body was discovered.

"We know what time she arrived there," I said, nodding toward it. "It was for a sale. She was delivering the painting in her car."

Her mother nodded slowly. "Yes, Carly mentioned that one. She was so happy. I wanted to give her money to pay the bills, but she was so proud. She was so happy someone finally got her vision. They wanted to meet in the field so she could capture the exact light for another painting. She told me that she thought it was... romantic."

Jericho frowned. "It was a setup."

I stepped toward a canvas near the window. It was unfinished and had a woman at the center posed against a swirl of tall sunflowers, but the face was blank which gave it an almost macabre and eerie look. Only the outline remained, as if Carly hadn't yet decided who it would become. Or hadn't had time.

Beneath the canvas, tucked into the baseboard, I spotted the corner of a photograph. I pulled it free. It was a reference photo, printed on glossy paper with sunflowers in full bloom, but the shadows were wrong, too long. I flipped it over, reading, "'Deliver by sunset. Don't be late. TF.'"

"The initials," Tracy said. "TF."

"She got a note for the commissioned work?" I asked, looking up. I showed it to Carly's mother, asking, "Did she mention who this was, who she was meeting?"

Her mother shook her head. "They messaged anonymously. That note was slipped under her door with some cash as an advance."

"It's from the killer," Tracy said. Carly's mother fell backward slightly with a look of offense as though Tracy had given her a shove. Jericho was there to catch the woman, her frail body landing against him. Tracy quickly replied with a regretful tone, "Sorry."

"Ma'am, I'm going to take this."

She nodded encouragingly as I pinched the corner and turned the photo over again. The handwriting was angular, deliberate. Male, most likely. My heart pounded as I pinched the corner and slipped it into an evidence bag Tracy held out.

Jericho's voice was a quiet steel behind me. "We're going to hunt him down."

Mrs. Rose nodded, eyes shining. "Please. Find him before he does it to someone else."

"We will," I said, hoping it wasn't an empty promise. As a detective, I meant it. I always meant it.

There's always a moment in an investigation, usually early on, when you think maybe the answer is right there, just beneath the surface. And then it vanishes like a breath on glass. We were back at the station, fluorescent lights buzzing faintly overhead, adding clues to the murder board which was still mostly empty. I tacked a copy of the newly found picture from Carly Rose's apartment and circled the words SUNFLOWER FIELD in bold red marker.

Tracy was seated nearby, laptop open, glasses perched on her nose in that sharp, analytical way that told me she'd been tunneling through a mountain of data. Jericho leaned against the file cabinet, arms crossed, watching her work like a sentry ready to jump at the first lead. I dropped into the chair beside her and handed over a lukewarm coffee. "Anything?"

Tracy didn't look up. "Yes and no."

"Define yes and no," Jericho said, his voice low.

She pushed her laptop toward us. On screen was a digital art marketplace called ArtFuse, a slick site that looked part Etsy, part Dark Web and bordered on questionably legitimate. It was the kind of website that didn't just sell art, it sold mystique.

"I found Carly's portfolio here. She had a profile with her own name. Most of her commissions were for small stuff like pet paintings and beach abstracts. But this one stood out."

She clicked a tab. A blank user profile appeared. Username: Sunflower-TF. "It's the TF again, but no real name. Was there anything with Paige Kotes and the initials TF?" Her question went unanswered. She continued, "There's no payment source that matches a registered user either. Other than the case her mother mentioned, there isn't anything digital like a crypto-wallet that'd help us."

Jericho's jaw tightened. "Anonymous. They covered their tracks. If Paige is involved, she'd want us to know it was her."

I backpedaled on our earlier discussions and suggested, "Assume this has nothing to do Paige Kotes, a new suspect with the initials TF. They're working anonymously, remaining hidden?"

Tracy nodded. "Completely. There's no messages after the confirmation either. All the communications were done through an encrypted chat. The buyer even routed their connection through three proxy servers."

"Proxy servers?" I asked, vaguely understanding what it meant. "The messages between them bounced around different servers?"

"Uh-huh," she nodded without looking up. "Making them untraceable."

I exhaled through my teeth. "So, we've got a ghost with the initials TF."

"A ghost who knew exactly how to cover their tracks," Tracy added. "I sent a trace request to ArtFuse's backend support, but unless we get a court order, it's doubtful they'll even reply."

"Couldn't we go there?" Jericho asked, tipping his sheriff's hat, the badge on it glinting.

"The company is in New Jersey, and I did a trace route and IP lookup. Best I can tell, it'd take a two-hour flight for us to physically get there."

I stood and paced to the whiteboard. "TF knew how to find her. Knew her patterns, her work habits. Knew she wouldn't think twice about meeting someone in a scenic location if the art was involved."

"He exploited her kindness," Tracy said bitterly.

Jericho moved closer, his eyes dark with quiet fury. "He hunted her."

We were silent a beat too long, the air becoming stuffy and uncomfortable. I turned back to Tracy. "You can decrypt the chat?"

"I was able to login as Carly Rose; she used a weak password," she began to answer. "But every message was already scrubbed. There's only the history it existed, the content deleted within minutes of being sent. Whoever this was? They knew what they were doing."

I looked back at Carly's face on the board and a picture of the paintings. The bright yellow sunflowers she'd turned into brushstrokes. "I don't care if this guy built his network in the damn shadows," I said, "he had to have slipped up somewhere. No one's invisible."

Jericho's voice was steady steel. "And if he's done this before, it won't be the last time."

Tracy finally looked up, her eyes tired. "We'll find him. But this won't be fast."

"It never is," I said, hating the sound of my words. And in the back of my mind, a reminder chirped like a dying bird, the name Paige Kotes coming into my thoughts like a whisper. The initials TF. If she was involved, what did those letters mean?

TWENTY-ONE

I was getting used to the station's construction zone feel and noise, the hum of it buzzing in my ears and the muted roar of power tools that vibrated into my feet. The occasional clamor had me on edge though. It interrupted the little quiet time I had to work at my desk. It seemed every moment a search query presented results, another noisy interruption rang out. It was trying my patience fiercely. The sharp ping of a hammer echoed harshly, jarring, and had me turning my head. It was a short reminder of how far the station was from feeling normal again, feeling whole.

At Alice's insistence, fresh sheets of plastic hung limp between our cubicles to cut the dusty air down. While it added privacy, it also turned Tracy and Emanuel into fuzzy moving pictures, mosaics of them working at their desks. A nearby fan kept the sheets waving gently every time it swung its mechanical gaze in our direction too.

Sunlight filtered in through the windows, catching dust motes suspended in the air, tiny flecks that danced and twirled as if mocking the chaos surrounding them. Even with all the noise, my insides were uneasy with the weight of unfinished work—the need to move this case along was pressing down on me.

The faint murmur of the station televisions along the walls and in the corner barely registered as I scrolled through the hospital records on my monitor. It was still early in the day, but my eyes were already tired, each line of text blurring slightly before snapping into focus as I blinked hard. It was the dead ends. Each finding was another dead end in a string of many.

Over and over, the hospital records produced zero listings of a Jane Doe matching Paige Kotes's description. The voices on the television grew a little louder, a male news anchor laughing in a good-natured way as he bantered with his co-host about last night's game.

"And what about that fourth quarter?" he said, his voice broadcaster bright and conversational. *"I mean, did you see that throw? The guy's a machine!"*

His co-anchor, a woman with a warm, honeyed voice, chuckled in response. *"He's not a machine, Mark. He's human. Barely human, but human all the same. Honestly, I think it was the defense that really made the difference."*

I barely paid attention, the cadence of their voices blending into the station's noise. Sports weren't my thing. They were more Jericho's and Emanuel's the two often shouting at the television on any given Sunday or cheering joyfully over a win. Still, the broadcasters' lighthearted exchange created a strange contrast to the tension I felt, scrolling through file after file, each new window offering nothing but frustration.

"... and now let's take a quick look at the weather," the female broadcaster continued, her tone shifting seamlessly. *"We've got clear skies for most of the day, but don't put away those umbrellas just yet. A low-pressure system is moving in this evening, bringing with it a chance of thunderstorms."*

I tuned them out again, focusing instead on the search parameters on my screen. Fifty-mile radius, urgent care centers, hospitals, private clinics. The radius covered a lot of ground—too much ground. I felt the familiar creep of doubt curling in my chest. I'd put myself out there with Jericho. I'd done so with Emanuel and Tracy too. But what if I was wrong? What if Paige really had drowned that night?

I shook the thought away. No. I couldn't be wrong. The evidence was too specific, too intimate. The murders weren't the work of some random copycat. This had to be Paige. There was a sense she was out there too. The kind of sense that sat in my gut like a hot stone, a burning reminder that something bad was amongst us. She was alive and planning something worse.

My fingers hovered over the keyboard, poised to tweak the search parameters yet again to adjust the dates and times, when the tone of the broadcasters' voices shifted. The sweet and warmly light voice was gone now, replaced by a sharper, more serious one.

"This just in," the female broadcaster said, her tone steady and deliberate, a red banner flashing along the bottom of the screen. *"Authorities are investigating the possibility that former police officer and convicted serial killer Paige Kotes may still be alive."*

My head snapped up, the words yanking me out of my focus like a physical jolt. The screen on the wall filled with an image, and my stomach dropped. It was Paige.

Not the Paige I remembered—the one with scars carved across her face and rage burning in her eyes. This was an older photo, one I hadn't seen in years. She was in uniform, her hair neatly pinned back, her features sharp and composed. Her expression carried an unsettling calm, the kind that spoke of control and certainty. The broadcaster's voice continued, unwavering, as if she didn't realize the picture on the screen was enough to freeze me in my chair.

"Paige Kotes, once a decorated officer, later became one of the most infamous serial killers in recent history," she said, her voice

calm but urgent. *"Convicted of multiple murders, including that of Jessie Cooper Flynn, the wife of then-Sheriff Jericho Flynn, Kotes was presumed dead after a failed attempt to apprehend her several years ago."*

The photo changed, replaced by another—this one a mugshot. Paige's features were harder, her eyes sharper. As I sat frozen, the glow of the television flickered across the station, my attention was no longer on the anchor's polished words. It was on the latest photograph of Paige Kotes.

Her face was unforgettable, and not for reasons anyone would want. A jagged scar ran a cruel, relentless path from the top of her head, carving down across her left eye, which now hung in a permanent droop, before trailing along her cheek, past her ear, and ending at her chin. It wasn't just a scar; it was a statement, a brutal reminder of violence so profound that her face looked like it had been ripped apart and then carelessly pieced back together with whatever was at hand—tissue glue and band-aids, perhaps.

The scar had come in the battle she had with Jericho. He'd won, barely, the evidence of that fight riddled across his arm and chest. Those injuries weren't just physical; it spoke of a life forever marked by pain and survival.

The television droned on, recounting the details behind the image, but I barely heard it. My focus stayed on Paige's expression, that mix of defiance and weariness etched into her features. She wasn't hiding it. She couldn't. It was written across her face, raw and unfiltered. There was something colder about this version of her too. This was the Paige who had begun her descent, the Paige who had already started killing.

The broadcaster didn't pause, her words slicing through the haze of my thoughts. *"New evidence from two recent murders in the Outer Banks has led investigators to believe Kotes may have survived the wreckage of that fateful night. Officials have yet to release specific details, but sources indicate a connection between these murders and Kotes."*

The station suddenly felt colder, the air heavier, even harder to breathe. I stared at the screen, my hands clenched tightly in my lap.

"If you see this woman," the broadcaster warned, her tone dropping slightly, *"do not approach her. Contact authorities immediately. She is considered armed and extremely dangerous."*

The image of Paige lingered on the screen for a moment longer, her cold eyes seeming to pierce through the glass and into me. Then it was gone, replaced by a smiling weather anchor talking about incoming rain. The words still echoed in my ears, louder than the sounds of construction or the hum of the monitors. Paige Kotes. Alive.

My pulse pounded, and for a moment, I couldn't move. To the rest of the Outer Banks, Paige wasn't a ghost from the past anymore. She was real, she was alive, and she was back.

I forced myself to stand, the chair scraping loudly. My hands shook as I reached for my coffee, the bitter liquid sloshing over the edge of the mug as I took a gulp. It was hot, too hot, but I barely felt the sting. My cubicle felt too small, its walls and the plastic sheets pressing in as the weight of the broadcast settled on my shoulders.

The news anchor's measured voice still echoed in my ears as I pushed the construction plastic aside. My heartbeat was loud and erratic, each thud reverberating in my chest. It fluttered away from my fingertips in the draft from the fan, its edges curling like an invitation—or a taunt. Annoyed, I tore the plastic aside, the rip and snap of it only fueling my fury. My shoes hit the ground hard as I strode toward Tracy's desk. She sat there, oblivious to the storm heading her way, her head bent over her phone as she tapped furiously at the screen.

"Tracy!" I barked, my voice slicing through the noise of the station. Heads turned, but I didn't care. She'd told the DA what we were working, and the DA took it to the press. Why? "Tracy!?"

Tracy flinched but quickly recovered, glancing up at me with a raised brow. She yanked a pair of white earbuds from her ears, the plugs leaving her oblivious to the news just broadcasted. Her light brown hair, tied hastily into a ponytail, shifted as she tilted her head. "What?" she said flatly, her tone laced with irritation.

"You want to tell me how the hell a broadcast about Paige Kotes being alive just happened? Maybe I wasn't clear, but I thought we were going to continue working the initials and the picture from Carly Rose's apartment?" I jabbed a finger toward the television mounted on the wall, Paige's mugshot still burned into my mind.

Tracy blinked, clearly caught off guard. "What broadcast?"

"Seriously? You could have told me your boss's plans," I snapped, stepping closer. "The news just announced that Paige Kotes was alive."

An understanding dawned in her eyes, and her posture stiffened. "Casey, I had nothing to do with that!" She raised her laptop, adding, "I'm working the new evidence."

"Well, your boss leaked it, and somehow she knew we'd been discussing Paige Kotes," I spat, the accusation hanging heavy between us. My pits were stinging hot, the back of my throat tight too. I was mad. I was confrontational. I was yelling at a most cherished loved one. And this wasn't me. "You've been feeding her updates about this case?"

Tracy stood abruptly, her chair rolling back with a clatter. "Really? You'd think I'd compromise a case? Do you really think I'd go behind your back like that?"

"Well," I shot back but quickly bit my tongue. I couldn't let anger fuel the words. "You didn't know?"

Her brow rose, eyes widening as the heat between us lowered. "I only reported it. I mean, Casey, the DA is my boss."

"Why would the DA release it?" I demanded, my voice rising again. "Until this morning, the only people who knew about the possibility of Paige being alive were sitting in that conference room."

Tracy crossed her arms, her jaw tightening. "I can't explain what the DA does or will do." She frowned, picking up her phone and scrolling through texts. "She wouldn't have gone public without consulting me—or you. If that broadcast aired, it wasn't because of anything I said."

"Then who else could it have been?" I challenged, my hands balling into fists at my sides. I glanced into the office where Emanuel was working. His height had him towering above a pair of monitors, the desk still short from when Tracy worked from it. I turned back and put on an apologetic face. Tracy saw it but I wasn't sure if it helped. I asked, "That leaves Emanuel. But why would he do that?"

"He is the lead. I mean, I know it was your idea, but this case is his," she said, her tone remaining sharp. She was right too. I might have been soft balling ideas, but this case was his to lead, my transitioning everything to him. "It could be that Paige left more breadcrumbs than we thought, and someone else followed them."

"I don't think that's it," I said, taking a step back. "I know an investigative report when I hear one. This wasn't a reporter digging up dirt. This was calculated. Controlled. Someone fed them this story."

Tracy's eyes flashed briefly. "I can't believe you'd think I'd leak it?" Her mouth opened to continue, but before she could speak, a familiar voice cut through the tension.

"What's going on?"

I turned to see Jericho standing near my desk, his presence commanding like it always was. He was clean-shaven, his uniform immaculate, the badge on his chest catching the station light. His eyes were bright, clear, and focused—a stark contrast to earlier.

"Hey," I replied, my anger momentarily faltering. "What are you doing here?"

He approached, his shoes silent against the floor. "I have a meeting with the DA and the mayor."

"You do?" Tracy asked, folding her arms tightly across her chest. "Maybe you can ask if they leaked anything to the press."

Jericho's gaze shifted to me, his expression calm but unreadable. "It wasn't the DA."

"Then who did?" I demanded, the fire in my chest reigniting.

He met my eyes, his voice steady. "I did."

The words hit me like a physical blow, my breath catching in my throat. "You what?"

Jericho nodded, his tone unapologetic. "I leaked your idea that Paige was still alive."

"Babe?" I asked, my voice barely above a whisper over the betrayal welling inside me. "Why? We don't have enough yet to make that claim."

"I know what we found in Carly Rose's apartment, but this could open the case fast. Because if you're right, and you usually are, then it might bring Paige out," he said simply, his eyes steady on mine. "Paige isn't the kind of person who can stay hidden when the spotlight's on her. She'll want to control the narrative, to stay ahead of us. And if she's alive, this will force her hand."

"Oh Jericho," I said, my voice trembling. "I'm not sure this was the right direction."

"It was," he countered, his tone firm. "This isn't just about you, Casey. This is about everyone she's hurt—and everyone she's going to hurt if we don't stop her."

"You should've told me and given us time to work the

evidence from the apartment," I said, the betrayal cutting deep. "If I'd had some idea, then I would have—"

"I didn't have time for a debate," he interrupted, his voice softening. "We need to act, Casey. And if Paige is involved then this is the best way to draw her out."

There wasn't time to argue what he'd done, the news was already out there. I looked into his eyes and saw the determination, the unwavering resolve that had always defined him. And I wondered if he might be right. Maybe this is what we needed to pull Paige from whatever shadows she was hiding and face her once and for all.

TWENTY-TWO

I was alone, Tracy and Jericho continuing the conversation while Emanuel plugged away at his computer. A red banner with bold white text ran across the station televisions, Paige's name flashing. If she *was* alive, she'd see it. I had no doubt. I tapped another search in, keys pressing softly, the letters appearing one after the other. I couldn't shake the surprise of what Jericho had done. Why didn't he say anything? Why not tell us what he'd planned before calling the press?

Glancing over my shoulder, Jericho stood over Tracy working together. A muted voice was a third in the conversation, the woman's slight twang telling me it was the DA, Tracy's boss. A fourth voice chimed in that I recognized as the mayor, the tone on the negative side. It was the meeting Jericho said he was going to, opting to take it from here, and to include Tracy as well. His words were fast and sharp, commanding even as he explained his actions to them, justifying the move. It was clear nobody knew.

This was about Jessie and the pain of losing her. That wound was deep. It was almost fatal. My notion of who was behind the crimes and exhuming Jessie's remains had struck a chord in Jericho. It was raw and wringing loud with abrupt decisions whose ramifications hadn't been considered. In their conversation, I overheard the word "reckless" used more than once, the mayor's voice filled with disappointment. It might have been a little reckless, but it might also work favorably too.

For now, the news broadcast was already having an impact. I heard it first in the sound of ringing phones, the station's phones were lighting up with calls. Commotions were subtle at first, officers picking up receivers, others racing to their desks as new calls came in. I picked up one of them, a timid voice on the other end telling me how they'd spotted the woman on the news. I stood up, stretched onto my toes to see Alice holding two receivers while another officer offered a free hand. At once, it seemed that every phone line the station had was occupied and I could only imagine what was happening at the 9-1-1 center.

Jericho stepped out of Tracy's cubicle, staring broadly, his jaw slack with awe. This wasn't what he'd expected to see happen. It wasn't what he'd wanted for our small municipality. As I answered a second call and then a third, it was becoming clear that getting to Paige was going to be like finding a needle in a haystack. Only, now that haystack had grown tenfold.

Jericho looked over in my direction, a subtle apology in his eyes. Now wasn't the time and I nudged my chin to the empty cubicle next to me. On the desk was a phone, lights blinking rapidly like it was some kind of Christmas decoration, callers on the other end waiting. He took to it with immediate understanding, answering with the station's name and a, "How can we help?"

"Thank you," I mouthed, fielding another call. I listened to the call, questioning it and finally answered, "No, ma'am, Paige Kotes would not have been involved with the damage to your fence. I'll transfer you."

Jericho's brow rose with another apology. The news broadcast and the announcement of Paige Kotes to all the Outer Banks was bringing in every trouble call. It was burying that needle fast and deep and robbing us of time we desperately needed. Emanuel was having better luck though, the sound of his hand slamming the desk pulling my attention as he shouted, "I got something!"

"Thank God!" I said, placing the phone's receiver back into its seat. I didn't give the lights on it another look and got up to ask, "What do you have?"

"A fishermen picked up a woman late on that same day while they were heading back to docks," he answered. He approached his door, frowning when he saw the phone activity. "What happened?"

"Jericho happened," Tracy said, trying to soften the moment.

Emanuel nudged his chin, asking, "Jericho, what did you do?"

Jericho sighed, mouth turned down. He glanced up at one of the monitors, the bold white text highlighted in a bright red banner scrolling across the bottom. Emanuel said nothing immediately, his brow furrowing deep, "That'll stir some noise."

"Alice is on top of it," I assured him. "Tell us about this fisherman?"

"Scott Moore. He's got his own fishing charter out of Wanchese Harbor. He does some commercial fishing too, probably supporting local restaurants."

"He was out that day?" I heard myself ask, the feel of floating in the ocean hitting me. Debris was scattered, the soft lull of a calm sea rocking me gently while death circled like a great white shark. Would the fisherman have been nearby? "Did he see anything else?"

"I didn't speak to him yet, just the hospital administrator." Emanuel flipped his phone around to show an address on it.

"Road trip? I checked the guy's website. No charters and there's nothing in season."

"It's downtime," Jericho said, him and Emanuel nodding.

"What's that mean?" Tracy asked.

"It means he's probably fixing his boat," Jericho answered. "Downtime is when you prep the boat for the season."

"Road trip," Tracy repeated, glancing over her shoulder at the phones. When she turned back, she asked, "Mind if I join?"

"You can ride with me," I said, the sting of my earlier accusation still sore. "I've been to the harbor a few times. There's a coffee shop on the way if you're interested."

"Interested?" she quipped. "Always."

"It's a pass for me," Jericho said, his gaze fixed on the monitors, his meeting with the mayor and DA a continuation of earlier discussions. "And apologies, guys, for the noise that news broadcast stirred up. I still think it'll work."

"It very well may," I told him. "This'll die down... just might take time."

The smell of salt and diesel hit me with a suddenness that made my stomach turn. The air was heavy with gray smoke from a nearby fishing boat, two men working the motor, one of them yelling to the wheelhouse to shut it down. We stepped onto the weathered planks of Wanchese Harbor, passing boat after boat, searching for the one that Paige Kotes may have been rescued by. The cry of gulls overhead mingled with the groan of ropes pulling taut against rusted cleats. Boats bobbed in the brackish water of Pamlico Sound, a body between the barrier islands and the mainland. Among them, *The Betsy* stood out, its name scrawled in faded blue script across a peeling white stern.

Emanuel's broad shoulders cut an imposing figure in the low-hanging fog, the weather damp today and riddled with a springtime chill. He adjusted his glasses and scanned the dock,

Tracy joining him with her gaze. Sharp-eyed, she saw the owner of the charter boat first, snapping a picture of him with her phone, her mouth set in a line of quiet determination. I glanced at *The Betsy*, anchored snugly against the dock. The boat was a rough-looking, no-nonsense workhorse, about fifty feet in length with a wide beam for stability. It had seen better days. Its deck was scattered with signs of its dual-purpose nature—tackle boxes and fishing rods secured to one side, heavy-duty winches and crab pots stacked neatly on the other. The wheelhouse, with its weatherbeaten windshield and antennas, stood like a sentinel in the center of the boat.

"I think I see him over there," Emanuel said, gesturing toward a man on deck.

"Is that Scott Moore?" I asked, adjusting the holster on my hip. The name carried weight, it might finally bring clarity to what happened that day at sea after the collision.

"Must be," Emanuel answered, holding up an advertisement for chartering *The Betsy*.

We approached, the creak of our footsteps drawing attention. A bark interrupted our steps, sharp and lively. From the deck of *The Betsy*, an old golden retriever bounded down the gangplank with surprising energy. Its golden coat was streaked with silver around the face and muzzle, giving it the look of an aged sailor who'd seen countless sunrises over the water. The dog's tail wagged furiously, slapping against its sides as it approached, letting out another bark before stopping in front of Tracy.

"Well, look at you!" Tracy said, her voice soft with delight as she crouched to greet the dog. The retriever gave a pleased grunt, nuzzling its head against her shoulder before settling at her feet, as though she were its long-lost companion.

"That's Hiccup," the man's gruff voice called out. Scott Moore leaned against a stack of wooden crates. A cigarette dangled from his lips, the smoke curling lazily around his head.

Moore looked every bit the seasoned fisherman, his face as weathered as *The Betsy*'s hull. His skin was sun-beaten, leathery, and mottled with age spots. Thick salt-and-pepper stubble framed a mouth that didn't look like it had broken a smile in years. He wore a tattered cap pulled low over his eyes, the words *Outer Banks Fish Company* barely visible above its brim. Hiccup glanced back at his master but made no move to leave Tracy's side. "He's my first mate."

"Mr. Scott Moore?" I asked, needing verification. My voice was firm but even, a hint of friendliness too. There was no point in antagonizing him before we'd even begun.

"Yup. That's me," he replied, his voice a gravelly rumble. He straightened, flicking ash from his cigarette and tucking his thumbs into the straps of his overalls. "Who's asking?"

"Sir, I'm Detective Casey White," I said, holding up my badge and petting Hiccup. "This is Detective Emanuel Wilson, and investigator Tracy Fields from the DA's office. We're here to ask you about an incident that occurred a few years back. You picked up a woman floating off the coast."

Moore's eyes narrowed, and he took a long drag of his cigarette before letting the smoke escape through his nose. "The Jane Doe I found?"

"That's the one," Tracy said, stepping forward. Her tone was clipped, professional. "We believe she might've been an escaped convict, Paige Kotes."

Moore's expression darkened. He stubbed out his cigarette against the heel of his palm and let the butt fall into the water. "Thought that name sounded familiar. Wasn't sure it was her when I saw her face on the news earlier. That woman I found was beat to shit. Worst thing I ever seen come out of the sea."

"Let's talk about that day," Emanuel said, his voice low and commanding. "What exactly happened?"

He motioned us onto the boat, Hiccup following. When we reached the captain, Hiccup sat on Tracy's shoes and gave her a big, doe-eyed look, tail sweeping. "Aren't you the friendliest thing."

"He sure is fond of you," Moore said, smirking. "Guess he's decided you're his new favorite."

"I'm honored," Tracy said, laughing as the dog shifted its weight to sit squarely on her feet.

"Paige Kotes," Emanuel said.

Moore leaned against the crate again, his hands resting. "It was late afternoon. *Betsy* and I were heading back to harbor after a slow day trolling offshore. I think we was about ten miles out when I spotted something bobbing in the water. There'd been alarms radioed about a commercial vessel nearby. It was a collision. We'd come upon the scattered wreckage but didn't see anything. A mile or so, I seen it drifting. At first, I thought it was a piece of driftwood, but as I got closer, I realized it was a person holding onto remains of a hull."

He paused, his eyes fixed on a distant point beyond the harbor. The gulls squawked overhead, dipping and rising in a steady flow.

"Thought she was dead at first. The woman was barely alive," he continued, his voice softer now. "Looked like she'd been out there for hours, maybe longer. Skin was sunburned, lips cracked. Her clothes were shredded. There were injuries too. I didn't think she'd make it."

"What did you do?" I asked, listening intently, reliving that day. I'd been in the water with Paige. Drifting. Dying. I'd believed she'd succumbed to the battle and sank to the depths of the ocean. She'd escaped though. She'd escaped in the debris. "Did you realize she might have been involved in that collision?"

He shrugged, "Figured she might, and the authorities would straighten that all out." Moore shrugged again. "Only concern was what I could do. We hauled her aboard, wrapped her in some blankets, and hightailed it to the nearest dock. Called ahead to the hospital so they'd be ready. Don't know much else. They took her from there."

"Did she say anything?" Tracy pressed, Hiccup staying close to her, occasionally tilting his head as if he were listening. "Anything at all?"

Moore shook his head. "Not a damn word. She was unconscious the whole time. But I'll tell you this—she was lucky. Another hour out there, and she'd have been fish food."

Emanuel nodded, his jaw tight. "You didn't think to report this to the authorities?"

Moore bristled. "Of course I reported it! Told the Coast Guard everything I knew. They said they'd take it from there, so I didn't see the point in sticking my nose in further."

"You didn't hear anything back?" I asked, weight pressing onto the balls of my feet. I forced myself to back down. Moore was a fisherman. He wasn't a detective. I softened my voice, asking, "Or maybe, you followed up about her?"

"I never heard a peep from any authorities till now," he said, crossing his arms over his chest. "Figured she was some tourist from that boat collision who got herself in trouble. Happens more often than you'd think."

"Did you contact the hospital they took her to?" Tracy asked, circling back to my question.

"Sure, I followed up. I wanted to know how she was doing," Moore said. "The Outer Banks Medical Center in Nags Head. Can't forget it—sons of bitches sent me a fucking bill for the ambulance used to get her there."

The corner of Emanuel's mouth twitched, but he said nothing.

Moore dipped his head, shaking it. "I got out of that one, Good Samaritan kind of thing. They told me the woman checked herself out and that was that."

"Did you see anything else unusual?" I asked, wondering if he'd passed me. Try as I might to avoid the thought, I couldn't help but believe that maybe if Moore had come across me, my baby might be alive today. My voice broke, asking, "Anything else in the debris? Anyone else?"

Moore rubbed his jaw, his beard rasping against his calloused hand. "Now that you mention it... there was a slick in the water. Oil, maybe. Didn't think much of it at the time."

"Likely the fuel from the collision," Emanuel said. "It'd travel along the surface."

"Yeah. Could've been," Moore admitted. "Or it could've been from any of the other wrecks out there. Ocean's full of ghosts."

His words hung in the air like a warning, heavy and unresolved. I exchanged a glance with Emanuel and Tracy, both clearly thinking the same thing: this was no ordinary ghost story. This was the beginning of Paige's return.

"Scott," I said, stepping closer, "what you've told us could be the break we've been waiting for. If this woman was Paige Kotes, and if she was still alive when you found her, then someone out there knows where she might have gone after the hospital."

Moore's gaze met mine, and for the first time, I saw something flicker in his eyes—regret, maybe, or something deeper. "If she's alive," he said quietly, "I hope she ain't done nothing bad, you know, since she was a convict and all." He lit another cigarette, his features disappearing behind a veil of gray smoke. "But to me, she looked like she'd been through hell. Even recovered, those were injuries that stay with you. I don't imagine she'd be in any shape to do much of anything."

"We're going to find out," I said, my voice firm with conviction. "One way or another."

Moore nodded, his jaw tightening. "Good luck, Detective."

Hiccup followed us to the end of the dock, his tail wagging lazily as though saying goodbye. "Take care of your first mate," Tracy called to Moore, a smile playing on her lips.

"Don't worry," Moore replied, lighting another cigarette. "He takes care of me."

As we turned to leave the docks, the harbor seemed to shift around us. *The Betsy* bobbed gently in the water, a silent witness to Paige's story. I was right to believe she was still alive.

TWENTY-THREE

We were back at the station working with the information from Scott Moore about what happened after he'd plucked a woman from the ocean and delivered her to a hospital. Confirmation of the identity remained lacking as did the doubts about who she might be. But I think the team was leaning heavily on the possibility of it being Paige Kotes. It was the timing. The coast guard and marine patrol reported when the collision occurred and included thorough reports of the debris. They also reported the number of souls on the other vessel that struck us. That's what they called them, souls. And all were accounted for. The only soul unaccounted for was Paige Kotes..

Armed with the date, we had a rough estimate of the timeline now too, Emanuel busily verifying against the defunct bills for the ambulance service. Tracy pulled records from the hospital, discovering an AMA, an Against Medical Advice form, signed by the woman. We even had copies of the form, but these were useless. They were scans of a scan, black and white and pixelated so bad the legibility was near impossible. The name and signature at the bottom could have been from anyone. However, it was the record on file from the hospital, indicating the woman had refused further care after she was well enough to leave. And leave she did. But where did she go?

The area around my cubicle was laden heavy with the smells of cheeseburgers, French fries and onion rings. Which was far more appealing than the ever-present construction we'd been subjected to. We had milkshakes too, both strawberry and chocolate, the tops off so we could share when dipping our salted fries. Tracy joined me in a meeting of fast-food debauchery the likes of which we hadn't entertained in quite some time.

The impromptu luncheon was much needed too. It was a means of mending any hard feelings that might have been lingering between us from the earlier accusation I'd made. My heart cramped thinking about it, the feelings of a lost baby, of the woman who was responsible returning from the dead. And there were the cases Paige Kotes was copying, new victims in the morgue whose lives had been ended abruptly, senselessly, or possibly, as a message to me and to Jericho, perhaps all of us.

Tracy dunked a fry, burying half of it in the strawberry shake, the slurry clinging as she moved to the chocolate and dunked again. "You gotta try both." Her eyes were huge. "It's so good!"

"I told them extra salt," I commented, the small talk helping. We'd barely spoken while browsing through old security footage, commenting on the food and the footage. It wasn't much, but it was something. "Hiccup."

A smile. "What a cute dog." Tracy moved to her burger, devouring a bite, sautéed onions dripping from between the buns. Mouth full, she laughed, "I had no idea what that guy was saying when he called out 'hiccup'!"

"None of us did," I said, chuckling with her. I tapped the keyboard, advancing the video footage. The view of the hospital included the front and the rear exits, the main entrance as well. In the video, days passed with the sky changing, the sun rising in the east, the moon chasing stars in the evenings, an endless number of people entering and existing. "There!"

"What?" Tracy asked.

"The timeline. I advanced the footage to when we think she would have signed the AMA."

"Got it," Tracy said, mouth full again. "Slow it down. Normal speed so we can watch each person."

"Agreed," I replied, slowing the footage enough to really watch each person. We couldn't always see the faces but used whatever there was, including evidence of injuries, the person's height (like me, Paige was tall), the hair color, anything. "How's that?"

"Good, I'm tracking them."

"You're gonna miss this," I said plainly, the words out before I could filter them.

"Me!" She gaffed. "What about you?"

"I've got Jericho. I'm sure he'll bring a case around the house now and again that I can chew on."

"I've got the DA spot as an investigator," Tracy challenged. This wasn't a new conversation. I'd brought it up before. But her luck in the new position wasn't going to last. There were going to be the other cases. The ones Tracy wouldn't ever want to work. "I think when you hit the case preparation, the interviewing, court prep, all those pesky chores a DA needs, you'll be bored out of your mind."

"I don't know." She tilted her face and wrinkled her nose the way she does when holding back on something.

"What?" I asked, curiosity brewing. "Does the DA have another role for you?"

She shook her head, answering, "None at all. I've got all the investigator duties I signed on for—"

There was a *but* and she was holding on to it like it was a cliffhanger in a movie. "Come on, give."

"I wasn't going to say anything, but you're kind of forcing

my hand here." With paper napkins, she wiped her fingers, crumpling them into a ball before tossing onto the table. From her bag she retrieved a large manila envelope and quickly pressed it against her chest. I'd only seen one word which confused me. It was *LAW*. She flipped the envelope around to face me, announcing, "I've gone back to school. Law school. That's where I've been most nights and every other weekend."

"School?" I asked, even more confused. I had to sit back and give what Tracy just said a think. Never had I met anyone more educated. And now she was going to pursue a law degree. I gazed hard for a moment, looking into her beautiful face, seeing my wavy brown hair and her father's baby-blue eyes. And those dimples of hers, appearing every time she smiled. They were from her father's side too, and I'd often caught her trying to hide them. She was doing that now, forcing away a smile.

"What?" she said asking when I didn't respond with more. "I've got the time, and I think that's where I might want to go in my career."

"Wow. A lawyer? You've already got degrees in biology and criminology. Your master's is in Forensic Science, along with a certification as a crime-scene technician. Incredible."

"Yep, I'm an overachiever," she joked. The smile faded and she shrugged, her expression serious. "Casey, I think I can do more as a lawyer. You know what I mean? Like, I can get into cases that really make a difference, helping people who can't help themselves."

"A public defender?" I asked, feeling proud, her sense of civic duty strong and rooted in the same principles I shared as a law enforcement officer. I leaned in, joking, "I think I love it... as long as you're defending the good guys."

A fresh smile. "I haven't decided on that yet." She shoved a fry in her mouth. It dangled from between her lips, her countering, "I might try working for the bad guys a while. You know, more money and all. That way, you and Jericho can arrest them, and I'll get them off."

"Aren't you the funny girl! You'd never work for a criminal," I said, sweeping a fry across my milkshake like it was ketchup.

Her face blanked and she raised her brow. "Casey, I was serious." When I didn't laugh, she spat a loud chuckle. "You should see your face."

"Ha-ha, funny. But just to warn you, there's no money in being a public defender."

"What? Really?" She was laughing again, only now it was mocking. Her face pinched with sarcasm, "Casey, there's not much money in what we're doing now."

"That's true," I said, glancing at my shoes, the tops scuffed and the soles uneven. They'd seen better days. I dared a touch. A soft one. My hand on top hers. She didn't back away and I let myself relax and pinched her fingers. "I'm proud of you. You know that, right? I have no doubt that you'll be a fine public defender."

"Thanks, Casey."

We turned back to the monitors and our food, attentions refocused. The grainy black and white video frames scrolled across the screen at a fast rate, the vehicles and people moving back and forth like something out of an old film reel that had been restored. "Casey? Even if we see Paige in this video, what do we do? Where do we go from here?"

I shook my head, the early levity snuffed. "I'm not sure." Turning back to the work, I jogged the mouse wheel to the next date. I couldn't think that far ahead. What I needed was to see something. See anything that told me we were on the right track. As we continued to work, the smell of fast food hung thick in the air while we finished all but the milkshakes and fries.

Tracy continued dunking fries into her milkshake with a ritualistic precision. She alternated between strawberry and chocolate, her eyebrows raised with glee every time she took a bite. The urgency of the case had left little time for proper meals, and this greasy indulgence felt like a small, well-deserved rebellion. But if I'd been home with Jericho and Thomas and Tabitha, it would have been carrots and broccoli and lean protein. A far cry from the gluttony I just poured down my throat.

When she caught me staring, she commented, "It's an art," and licked a dollop of chocolate from her thumb. "Salty, sweet, and probably clogging my arteries as we speak. Totally worth it."

"Yeah, I get it," I said without argument.

We'd been watching hospital security footage for hours, the screen flashing scenes of people coming and going. The lull in our work had started to feel like defeat. My doubts about Paige being alive, about this clue leading anywhere, had begun to weigh heavy on me. I'd begun to think that maybe I was trying to keep the atmosphere light, the theory believable by using junk food and humor as armor against a relentless grind that wasn't going to get us anywhere.

Then, something caught my eye on the screen. A flicker of movement. A shadowy figure, limping, disheveled. It could have been any woman matching Paige's description, but having been so close to her in facing death, there was an intimacy that could only be shared between victim and killer. My heart vaulted into a run, the neurons firing in my brain in a sprint of identifying markers. I saw the hair. Check. The relative height. Check. The lean build. Check. And then I saw the scar. It was a bunch of jumbled pixels but the face on the monitor had it. I took a deep breath, afraid to jinx the finding. Leaning forward, brushing the food aside, I turned the brightness on the monitor to one hundred.

"Tracy," I said, my voice sharp enough to cut through our banter. "Look at this."

Tracy stopped chewing, a fry halfway stuck out of her mouth. She leaned closer to the monitor. The figure on the grainy footage shuffled forward, each step unsteady. Her face was battered, her hair tangled in a way that spoke of violence and desperation.

"Is that—" Tracy started, her voice dropping to a whisper. "The resolution is shit, but that woman's height and build are a hit."

"Is that Paige?" My words were a forced whisper, heart pounding in my chest hard enough to hurt. I needed it to be her. I focused on the scar, having seen it up close, face to face. I jumped with confidence, saying, "It's Paige. Look at her. That limp, the scar too."

"And the timing of what Scott Moore reported." We both sat in stunned silence for a moment, the gravity of the discovery sinking in. Tracy broke it with a sharp breath, patting my shoulder. "Holy shit, Casey. I can't believe you were right. She's alive."

Tracy's words hit me like a tidal wave, and I gripped the edge of the desk to steady myself. "What do you mean by can't believe?" I said, half joking but suddenly overwhelmed with emotion.

"It's okay," Tracy said, seeing the emotion. Her eyes were wet too. She put her hand to her chest, saying, "I wasn't out there in the ocean with you, but I can feel it. I'm sorry for what happened, for what she did."

"Thanks," I was able to say. I stared at the frozen image. Stared at this woman who'd done so much damage to so many, and who was thought to be dead. After weeks of pushing against doubts, of feeling like I was chasing shadows, here she was.

"What do you want to do next?" Tracy asked, cool air rushing over where her hand had been. She started creating a video snippet like an old-school film editor, slicing and splicing only the parts needed. "I'll circulate the video."

"She's alive," I repeated, my voice quieter now, almost reverent. "We have to figure out where she's been holing up."

"What else do we have?" Tracy fast-forwarded the footage slightly. The figure limped toward the edge of the frame, where a rusted white pickup truck rolled into view. The truck had more rust than paint, which told me it might be parked regularly near the water. There was a high level of salt spray everywhere near the ocean which was a problem for older cars. "Looks like a work truck."

"Keep going." We watched as the truck stopped, the door swung open, and Paige climbed inside with visible effort. The car lingered just long enough for us to catch a partial glimpse of the license plate before driving off.

"Rewinding..." Tracy said, rolling the video backward and forward, trying to find that one frame that'd deliver the best plate read. "There."

"Yeah, hold that spot," I said quickly.

Tracy froze the video, and we both squinted at the screen. The plate was maddeningly blurry, the resolution too low to make out the final digits. The first four characters, though, were legible: XK3T. "It's a partial read."

"Damn it," Tracy muttered, leaning back in her chair. "It's like the universe is freaking toying with us right now."

"It should be enough," I said, more to reassure myself than her. "Outer Banks. A rusty work truck. I'm guessing a long-time resident. That plate has to be enough to get a list from the DMV."

"Possibly, as long as it's still registered," she said, her tone skeptical but hopeful. "I mean, the old trucks around here? Half of them are clunkers like that."

I turned to face her, the spark of determination rekindling. "How about the municipal cameras all over the Outer Banks now?" I pegged the screen with the date and time stamped in glowing numbers. "We've got a timestamp. This truck left the hospital and had to pass through a few intersections that have cameras. All that footage is archived by date and time."

"We can find that footage and get the full plate." Tracy tilted her head, a sly grin creeping across her face. "And here I thought all this fancy new tech was just for catching speeders."

"Not just speeders today. We're using it to catch a ghost," I replied, already jotting down notes. "Let's pull up the camera locations near the hospital and start narrowing it down."

The lull from earlier was gone now, replaced by an electric buzz of urgency. We worked in silence for a while, the only sounds occupying the time were filled with construction, our keyboards and mouse clicks. Finally, Tracy let out a triumphant laugh and spun her monitor toward me.

"Got something!" she said, her voice alight with excitement, baby-blues gleaming and dimples piercing. On her screen was footage from a nearby intersection, captured just minutes after Paige entered the car. The truck came into view, the plate visible from a better angle. Though still slightly blurred, the final two characters were just legible enough to make out.

"XK3T27," I said, writing it down, my hand shaky with nerves. "That's the plate. And we've got the make and model of the truck. That's all we need to run it through the DMV."

Tracy let out a whoop, clapping her hands together. "We did it! Casey, you freaking did it."

Emanuel's office door swung open as he appeared in the frame, his arms crossed and an amused smirk on his face. "I could hear the two of you celebrating from my office," he said. "What's going on?"

"I think we found her," Tracy said, grinning like a kid on Christmas morning. "Paige Kotes. Or at least, we're damn close to finding her."

Emanuel stepped closer, his expression softening as he

looked at the footage. "You have confirmation? That she's alive?" he asked, turning to me.

"We have confirmation." I swallowed hard, my throat tight with emotion. "We've still got some ground to cover."

"No kidding," Tracy said, her grin never faltering. "But we know where to go from here."

"Close to knowing," Emanuel said, correcting her. He knelt between us, asking, "Keep going through DMV links to see who owns that truck."

"Drumroll, please," Tracy said amidst keyboard and mouse clicks. A driver's license appeared, the face and name familiar. It was Scott Moore. Tracy sat back, frowning, "Someone wasn't telling us everything they knew."

"Someone certainly wasn't." It was a step closer to finding Paige, but why did Scott Moore hold back on telling us everything? "He went back to the hospital."

"You don't think she's still with him?" Tracy asked, voice wavering, half disbelief, half shock, each syllable weighted. Eyes widening, she shook her head and spoke faster. "If she is still with him, that means Paige Kotes was at the boat when we were there!"

"Hold up," Emanuel said steadily, taking the lead. "We go back, and we question him again."

"Agreed," I said, following. But my insides were already running out the door. What if she was there? What if Paige heard us asking questions? Was she scared? Did she laugh? "He... Scott Moore may have been acting as a good citizen, civic duty and all that."

"Casey, you don't believe that!" Tracy jabbed, white-knuckling the mouse.

"Well, this video isn't new," I began, not sure what to think, my fingers trembling. I tried not to show it, but the thought of Paige being close scared me. If they'd faced her like I had, they'd be frightened too. "Still, Scott Moore should have told us he went back."

"We'll need another road trip to the marina to cover our bases," Emanuel said. "I'll get a search warrant prepared."

"Search the boat?" I asked, voice fading mid-sentence when a jumble of unexpected nerves twisted in my gut. They looked at me with surprise, our next step an obvious one. I fought what was rearing inside me, adding, "Yeah, cover our bases. All of it."

TWENTY-FOUR

The marina where Scott Moore's *Betsy* was docked looked dramatically different when we returned at dusk. Pelicans were perched on pilings, their feathered bodies framed in silhouette. Behind them, a purple and red and orange ribbon crossed the horizon, growing wide and tall as the clock approached evening. Stars blinked into existence, their shine muted while the sun crawled down the earth's western slope. The last of the sunlight ignited everything it touched, warming them with a buttery color. At any other time, the setting would have been ideal for a walk on the beach, barefoot in the sand, sea foam crawling across our toes. But I was nervous. I was more nervous than I think I'd ever been. It had my legs weighing heavy and my breath coming quick.

Could I face Paige again? I thought I could. I mean, I had to. It was my job. It was my duty, and I owed it to the lives unduly taken during the course of this case. I guess I'd never thought of actually facing her again though. The idea of it terrified me. Tracy must have sensed there was something wrong. She stopped and touched my hand, fingers pinching, her chin dipping enough to catch my eyes.

"Hey," she said, baby-blues big and round and beaming the sun's reflection. Emanuel walked ahead, boards beneath him creaking alone with each hollow footstep. A pelican nearby bobbed its head, gauging us as a threat. When it was satisfied, it gave us a cursory look before tucking its head and returning to the sleep we'd interrupted. "Casey?"

"I dunno," I said, beginning to shake some. Had I ever felt this afraid? I tried walking it off, but my legs were suddenly stuck in place. The voice in my head said to keep moving but my muscles were like stiff wood. Tracy tugged again, Emanuel stopping. He turned around, curiosity and concern planted on his face. My insides were shaking uncontrollably and my heart beat heavily and vaulted into my throat. I waved off the team, saying, "I... I can't go."

This had happened once before, the memory a powerful one. So powerful in fact that it didn't matter how deep it had been buried. I was seven years old and had gotten stuck on the playground's jungle gym, my arms and legs stiff like they were now, fingers clutching the cold metal until they ached. It was high too, feeling like a hundred feet off the ground. A few feet was all it really was. But in my mind, I was one slip away from certain death. That's what this felt like now. Like I was going to die if I got any closer to that boat.

"Casey, there's nobody there except Scott Moore," Emanuel said, frustration replacing the concern.

"What if she's there?" I asked, hands trembling violently. I held them up as steady as I could, but it didn't help. "I... I don't know if I can do this."

"Think about it. That video of her at the hospital was a few years ago," Tracy said, trying to ease the fears. Her brow rose with the explanation, her hand cradling the butt of her gun. "We're safe. Casey, you are. Nobody is going to hurt any of us."

"Tell you what, how about you hang back a little and we'll clear it first?" Emanuel said, asking. "Does that work?"

"I just need a minute," I answered abruptly, kicking one foot into motion. I had to go. Not just for the team. But for me. There was the guilt of staying back too. We don't do that. We go as one or as none.

"We'll wait," Tracy said with an assuring smile.

She was right too, we were only here to talk to Scott Moore. That video of Paige was older, but it was unlikely he'd forgotten about having picked her up. So, what was he hiding? As though listening, the pelican woke again, turning to eye us. He fixed a stare as though wondering why we hadn't moved yet. I moved. It was just a step, but enough to tell him, "Fine, I'm moving."

"Shall we—" Emanuel said, his words cut with the sharp interruption of a bark.

On the deck of *The Betsy*, a familiar graying and gold face appeared, bouncing above the deck rail, ears flopping. "There's no way that dog knew you were out here," I said to Tracy.

"Dogs know," she replied, grinning. But the grin disappeared when we reached the boat. "What the fuck?"

"Emanuel, call for backup!" I demanded, metal sliding against leather as I drew my gun with a single swift motion. It was Hiccup, the golden retriever, panicked, bloody paw prints trailing behind him. There were no visible signs of injury, but the blood looked like it could be fresh, horribly bright under the cast of a sodium light flicking on overhead. "It's not the dog!"

"Scott Moore!" Emanuel shouted. He held his gun high, perched in his hands. "We're coming aboard."

"Let's go," I said, voice timid with the bitter taste filling my mouth. It was the adrenaline, and it moved me like some kind of magic elixir. Fear of Paige remained like a hot stone burning in the pit of my stomach. I held out a hand, taking hold of Emanuel's who'd already boarded. I reached behind me, "Tracy?"

"Coming," she answered, gaze fixed on Hiccup who wore a

smile on his face the way dogs do. The fur on his legs was stiff with blood, some of it still wet.

Tracy shook her head, kneeling, running her fingers over Hiccup's body. "It's not from him."

"Yeah, I didn't think it was," Emanuel said, face damp with a nervous sweat. He swiped at his eyes and squeezed his gun. He was scared. He was feeling what I'd felt moments earlier. He clutched his middle where a bullet had found him not so long ago and cringed. Voice wavering, he asked, "Forward."

"Forward," I said, replying with a step ahead of him. A distant wail rung in my ears. It was the call for backup, but it was far. Motioning to the paw prints, I commented, "It's a clear path."

The water's surface was calm, ripples growing around a fish's jump. Every fiber of muscle was strung taut while I stepped around a bundle of ropes, following the paw prints. We could see where Hiccup had stood to watch the dock and then raced back and forth in anticipation of someone arriving. There were old footprints and new footprints, wet and glistening; it was enough to tell us the dog had to be stepping in a pool of blood. Around the corner from the bow, a larger area of the deck was cut in half with streaks as wide as a body. I raised a fist, stopping Tracy and Emanuel behind me.

"Looks like they were dragged," I said, pointing out the deck and the rail. "Possibly murdered in the wheelhouse, dragged outside and hoisted over the rail."

"Where's the body?" Emanuel asked, gun held high while peering over the edge of the boat. He pointed at the water, "Guys, look at the side of the boat."

I followed his lead, Tracy too. Only there wasn't anything there. "What am I looking at?"

"It's low tide, it was outgoing when we were here earlier," Emanuel answered.

"If a murder took place, there'd be a body," I said, thinking it through. Emanuel nodded. "If this is what we think it is, the murderer could have gone out to sea, dumped the body and returned."

Tracy's brow furrowed. She cradled her gun and slipped a pair of gloves over her fingers. Rubbing the edge of the stains, most of it already dried, she inspected her fingers and said, "With an outgoing tide and returning to the docks, even with the wind as still as it is, the sea spray would have wiped this away."

"That's a good point. Barrier islands and shallow water, they'd have to go quite a way to throw a body overboard," I said, agreeing. We'd been on boats a hundred or more times, leaving the safety of the Outer Banks. Windy or no breeze at all, there was always sea spray. Especially when riding against an outgoing tide. "Why the mess then?"

"Body goes over. The water here is shallow—" Emanuel began, leaning over the rail, shining a flashlight. "—it's unlikely but could be beneath one of these other boats."

"Drifted and clothes caught on something," Tracy said, the beam from her flashlight swinging broadly across the surface.

"Scott Moore?" Jericho asked, arriving with the backup. He didn't look at me, his focus locked on the bloody path, assessing as we'd just done. He leaned over the railing, flashlight in hand, the end of daylight kissing the crease in the horizon with a final wink. "I'm thinking we need a dive team."

"Exactly. I'll put the call in," Emanuel was quick to agree. He turned to me, adding, "Want the medical examiner?"

"If a body turns up?" I answered, uncertain at first. "Samantha and Derek can start working the bloodstains, make sure it is human blood we're looking at and not something else."

"Copy," Emanuel said, dialing.

"I've got a kit," Tracy said, passing by me.

"What's your thinking?" Jericho asked, joining me, his arm brushing against mine. It was the closest to affection we allowed in a professional setting, and I needed it. This case had jarred me sideways like I'd never felt on a case before. If not for the other officers, Tracy with her forensics kit and Emanuel talking to Samantha, I would have wrapped my arms around Jericho and held him until he pleaded to be let go. Before I could tell him what I thought happened here, he narrowed his eyes, locking them with mine, and asked, "You okay?"

My lower lip began to tremble. I turned away from the scene, facing the empty space behind us where I could whisper into his ear. "I froze. I froze bad. Really bad."

I looked up, his eyes going soft and his mouth pinching. "Paige."

"Uh-huh," I answered.

He lowered his face, rolling up a sleeve where the scars from a handful of operations drove deep into his skin like a wrinkled roadmap. It was the remains of his battle with the woman who killed his wife. He swiped at them errantly, saying, "Sometimes I think the P in PTSD stands for Paige. She'll do that to you. She did that to me."

I touched my middle where Paige had done the most damage, and confessed, "I'm... Jericho, I'm afraid of her."

"That's good," he answered, the response a confusing one. "We need to remain afraid of her. It's when we get complacent, she'll come and finish what she started."

"This is likely human blood," Tracy said, holding a test strip, the bottom of it indicating positive. "We have an antigen-antibody reaction, which is a good indicator."

"You asked what I was thinking?" Jericho turned and waited. "That release you did for the press? It did bring Paige back."

"Why kill Scott Moore?" he asked, raking his fingers through his salt-and-pepper hair before returning his sheriff's hat. "What's the thinking in it?"

"What's the thinking in any murderer's mind?" I said, questioning. "I don't think Paige Kotes has ever needed a reason to commit murder."

Jericho didn't like my answer, Emanuel shaking his head too. "It's got to be more than that."

"It is," I said, gaze returning to Jericho. "Scott Moore was the only person who knew where Paige was staying. He was a witness. She wanted to stop him talking."

"Shit," Jericho said, understanding. His eyes dipped to where our child had been and then returned to mine. "After he picked her up at sea, and then from the hospital, they stayed in touch."

"The scorpion and the frog. That's the story she told me once." I had to stop a moment, breath sticking in my chest.

"Story?" Emanuel asked.

"Scott Moore carried Paige to safety," I said, understanding flashing on their faces.

"He's the frog and Paige is the scorpion," Tracy said with a nod.

"And it's in her nature to kill."

TWENTY-FIVE

When the sun had gone down for the night, we made our way to Scott Moore's house. A rain followed us, peppering the wind-shield at first, and turning heavy as the car wove through traffic on Route 12. Samantha and Derek remained on *The Betsy*, treating it like it was a crime scene. I'd no doubt it was, but if it was a murder, Scott Moore's body was missing. Jericho stayed behind as well, suiting up with the dive team, taking turns to search beneath the docks and the boats.

"What are you expecting?" Emanuel asked, flipping the turn signal in response to Tracy's directions. "Do you think he would have brought Paige back to his house?"

"I have no idea," I answered, eyeing the small home, thick raindrops blurring the view of it. Windshield wipers brought the house back while Emanuel pulled up behind a rusted white pickup truck. "That's the one we saw in the video."

"Same plate number too," Tracy said from behind. "Does the warrant cover it?"

"The warrant covers Moore's house, truck and the boat," Emanuel answered, leaning forward and staring up at the black sky. He cringed, adding, "Neither snow nor rain nor heat nor gloom of night stays these *detectives* from the swift completion of their appointed rounds."

"Uh okay," Tracy said, sliding an arm through a bright yellow rain parka.

"You never heard the postman's motto?" Emanuel asked, sliding his gun into his holster. "I think we need a motto too."

"I think you just gave us one," I told him, opening the door and shielding my face. I stepped into a puddle, deep enough for water to seep inside my shoe, wetting my toes while I searched the home's front windows. It was a single level ranch-style, a garage off to the side of the property with barn-style doors that were locked. While the house was dark, a faint light seeped through the edges of the doors. "Does the warrant cover other structures on the property?"

"Shit," Emanuel said, shaking his head. He turned away and ducked his head back inside the car, his face aglow from the phone's light. His voice was echoed like in a cave, calling out, "The wording is for the premises, and has language that says residence and any outbuildings."

"That's an outbuilding," Tracy said, hugging herself, appearing smaller. With the rains there came a springtime cold front, our breath foggy. "The warrant probably won't cover any other residences if on the same property. But a garage for this house is an outbuilding."

"Might be good to have a lawyer joining our team once in a while," I said, but remembered this was my last case. "I mean, joining future cases."

"Let's get inside and see what we see," Emanuel said, clapping his arms. We followed, running toward the front door to huddle beneath a portico, the concrete pavement dry. Emanuel jiggled the handle, metal clacking, the door locked. "Yeah, figured as much."

"Someone is here," I said, glancing over at the truck, taking a chance and racing back into the rain. The hood was wet and cold but provided nothing to tell me how long the car had been there. I went around the side to where the tailpipe was, kneeling next to it and lowering my head. There was smoke. A tiny amount, wispy trails rising out of the pipe and disappearing into the air. When I got up, I mouthed to them, "Someone is home."

Emanuel frowned, explaining on my return, "Warrant covers entry."

"Knock and announce," Tracy said. She shivered and added, "If we don't hear a response, or if we have reasonable cause, then we can open the door forcibly."

"Forcible won't be a problem," Emanuel commented, running his fingers above the door handle. "I'm not even sure there's a deadbolt installed. Just the lock on the handle."

"Police department!" I yelled loud enough to wake the dead. "We have a search warrant for the premises and requesting the door to be opened!"

"I'd open it," Tracy joked, the three of us turning when a neighbor's front lights flicked on with an amber glow. A minute passed, Moore's house remaining silent. "That's long enough."

"Long enough," Emanuel agreed, stepping back and raising his leg. The motion was swift, the bottom of his foot striking solidly against the door, landing just above the door handle like we'd been trained. The door flew open with a crash, wood splintering where the lock had been nestled inside the frame. He went to the damage, picking at the remains. "See, no dead bolt."

"That was easy," I commented, swallowing the lump in my throat, the inside pitch black. Flashlights on, our three lights beamed inside, landing on dead space. "I don't think anyone is home."

"I guess Scott Moore wouldn't be if he's dead," Tracy said.

She walked ahead of us, gun drawn, flashlight perched above. When she reached the first light switch, she flicked it, the foyer suddenly bright, one side in shade due to a burnt-out bulb. The kitchen was ahead of us, our piling inside, stepping around a water and food bowl that had Hiccup's name on them. "There's food and water in the bowls. Scott Moore and Hiccup have been home recently."

"Probably not since we met with them on the boat—"

"Casey!" Emanuel's voice was sharp, his call sounding panicked. "You gotta see this."

"What did you find?" I asked, turning to see what he was looking at.

The kitchen table was filled with evidence bags, the handwriting on some of them recognizable. It was mine, the evidence collected in past cases, torn open, their contents spilled across the table. These were the missing evidence bags. All of them were here. Tracy joined him at the table while I stared, a wave of shock racing up my spine like a strongman peg racing to strike the bell. Carefully, I opened a notebook that had been famous once. It was a journal filled with the crimes of multiple serial killers. A diary of sorts which had been passed around and thought lost. Paige had it and was using it again.

With the end of my pen, I picked through the bags, recognizing what we'd labored to collect. It was the wires and the casings that interested me more, a second table against the wall was outfitted like a workbench. A spotlight with magnifying glass stood on an articulating arm. I flicked its switch, swinging it over the bundle of unspent solder which sat coiled like a silver snake. There was copper braid too along with small integrated circuits that would require an electrical engineer's help deciphering. "We've got bomb making equipment along with old case evidence."

"The construction worker," Tracy announced, hoisting a cardboard box from beneath the workbench. Inside it, a yellow construction vest and wig, along with a fake mustache and tissue adhesive. "The clothes and the disguise used."

"It's got to be Paige. Right?" Emanuel asked, continuing to pick through the evidence. "She's been here all along?"

"If that's the case, it makes Scott Moore an accomplice." My words fell into silence while we each questioned the statement, thinking about the danger we'd been in when first speaking with the captain of *The Betsy*. "The news story exposed her but why kill him?"

"Scorpion and the frog," Emanuel said, reminding us. "Like you said, it's in her nature."

I wanted to buy it but couldn't. Paige was smart and if she'd been here all this time, then why kill Scott Moore now? "He saw the news report and decided to turn her in."

Tracy poked through the wiring on the workbench, adding, "Do you think he knew what she was doing?"

"He must have. He knew and decided to turn her in," I answered. "That's got to be it. Why else would she kill him?"

"I've got a team coming," Emanuel said, phone in hand. "The bomb squad too. They warned not to touch anything."

"I don't see any explosives," Tracy commented, poking and shoving the materials. "This is the wiring we saw in the bomb though. Fairly certain it was built here."

"Step away, Tracy. Okay?" I asked, voice rising. My words broke with fright and my legs grew weak. "What if this house is a trap?"

"Fuck! Like the car," Emanuel barked, the whites of his eyes turning as big as saucers. "I'm ordering us to leave, slow and steady, taking the same path we entered."

"No argument from me," I told him, backing away a step at a time. Images of the kids and Jericho flashed in my head, a floorboard creaking beneath my foot. Why was it loose? Was there a bomb wired beneath it with a spring joining a switch to an explosive, waiting to close the circuit and cause certain death? "Easy."

"Careful," Emanuel said, repeating the words until we were beneath the foyer again.

"Better safe than sorry," Tracy said. "But I don't think the house was wired. It's got that lived-in feel, you know what I mean?"

"I think you're right. The water and food in Hiccup's bowls is fresh," I said, nodding to agree. "Still, we can't be too careful—"

Silent blue light skipped through the front windows and painted Tracy's face, her focus lifting to a car door shutting. "I think Jericho is here."

"Good," I said, moving to a living room and flicking on the switch. The door opened, the smell of rain following Jericho indoors. "Everything okay with the sitter?"

"She can stay a couple hours," he replied, leather creaking from his belt and shoes. He tipped his hat toward Tracy and Emanuel, a habit formed since returning to the role of sheriff. "I heard the call to the bomb squad. You found something interesting?"

"That'd be an understatement," Tracy answered. She held up the wig and construction vests and then gracefully presented the table of bomb making equipment, waving her arms like a model at a car show. "We found everything."

"I'd say yes, that'd be everything," he said with a slow nod while slipping gloves onto his hands. Jericho's eyes narrowed when he approached the far wall, a collection of family portraits hanging. He turned, pointing to the workbench next to the kitchen. "In this picture, Moore has a wife and daughter."

"The only sign of family we've come across so far is Moore's dog," I said, commenting, curious where Moore's family might be. A stack of mail sat untouched on a small table next to a reading chair. I sifted through the top ten or so, reading the names of the addressees. Again and again, there was only Scott Moore. There were no mentions of a wife or child. "Appears he lived here alone."

"Maybe they're divorced," Tracy said, searching a nearby bookshelf. She pulled a large book from the top, a dozen stickers and drawings on the front, saying, "I found a girl's scrapbook."

"Maybe the daughter left it here," I said, thinking the couple had split, the wife moving out. We'd have to notify her soon after confirming Scott Moore's status.

"I think the daughter died," Tracy said, her words stopping our search and turning heads. She held up a prayer card, a name at the top and a pair of dates. "Looks like she died a couple years ago."

"That's sad," Emanuel commented, shining a light on the scrapbook and card. "Lots of couples fall apart after a tragedy like that."

"Different last name," Tracy went on to say. "Maybe she was a stepdaughter or kept her mother's name?"

"What's the daughter's name?" I asked while we continued searching for any evidence that Paige Kotes was here.

"Theresa Franks," Tracy said, reading the card.

"What!?" Jericho asked, his voice like a bark.

"Can't be!" Emanuel questioned, snatching the card from between Tracy's fingers. His head shook with disbelief, Jericho approaching them with a heavy foot. "It's her."

"It's who?" I asked, trading confused glances with Tracy. "Who is Theresa Franks?"

"What the fuck is going on here?" Jericho asked, dropping to his knees as though bumped by a ghost. He yanked the scrapbook and turned the pages rapid enough to move air. When he found what he was looking for, he sat back on his heels. "Her birth certificate reads, Theresa Franks Moore. She kept her mother's and father's names but had only used Franks."

"So?" Tracy asked as we gathered around the scrapbook.

"Jericho?" I asked, concerned, his shoulders trembling. I helped him back to his feet, asking, "Who was she to you?"

"Theresa Franks Moore is the girl Paige murdered the same day she murdered my wife." His voice trailed and a look of defeat filled his face. "Theresa was used to help lure Jessie to her death."

TWENTY-SIX

"Paige Kotes murdered Scott Moore's daughter—" I stopped mid-sentence when I opened the front door. "Tracy, anything?"

"This is sad," she said, her face blue from the phone's screen. "Soon after the death of her daughter Theresa, Shelly Franks Moore succumbed to a sudden cardiac death."

"I know that one," Emanuel commented, tapping a finger to his lips. "It's broken heart syndrome."

"Losing a child and then his wife," I said, thinking more than the mother's heart was broken. Something else broke after Scott Moore lost his family. "Theresa was an only child?"

"Looks to be," Tracy said, stuffing her phone in her pocket. "What are the odds of Scott Moore finding Paige in the ocean that day?"

"Probably the same as winning the lottery," Emanuel answered, blowing out a sarcastic laugh. "I know I'm not the only one asking that question."

"It's not possible," Jericho exclaimed, his expression fixed in a grimace. He hadn't said a word since the scrapbook, but I could see in his eyes that thoughts were spinning in his head like a top. "Not at all possible."

"Odds aside, I'd say it was closer to impossible," I added, making room on the narrow porch, raindrops finding my eyes. I blinked them away when the team looked at me. "I think Scott Moore was always wherever Paige Kotes was."

"As crazy as that sounds, I think you're right," Jericho agreed, nodding slowly. He scratched at the stubble on his chin, another tell he was thinking. "Moore must have been following that day Paige took you. For all we know, it might've been his boat you hit, causing you and Paige to go overboard."

"You think?" I asked, disbelief rising. But didn't that make sense? The possibility of it anyway? "What's even crazier is that as much as Paige was obsessed with us, Moore was obsessed with her."

"But why help her?" Tracy asked, wiping her face, the rain gaining. "What's the reasoning?"

"I don't know," I answered, the explanations not adding up. "Moore saved Paige. Later, he picked her up at the hospital. Then she stayed here with him—"

"Maybe she did to him what she did to the others who'd been involved with her," Jericho said, interrupting. "I knew Deputy Barnes a long time before Paige. Yet, she convinced him to help her murder my wife and Moore's daughter."

"And then she murdered him," Emanuel said, phone in hand. "Divers haven't found a body yet. They confirmed it was human blood on the boat though."

"Finally," I said, looking into the gray sky, the rains letting up enough for us to return to our cars. Faint music reached us as it mixed with the steady patter against the roof and pavement. We didn't hear it earlier, the passing storm pummeling the area. I followed a guitar solo, drums kicking in with bass beat. It was a song from the eighties, classic rock that I recognized once the synth sounds accompanied the chorus.

"Where we going?" Emanuel asked, following.

"Do you hear that?" I couldn't recall the name of the band

but knew the music from one of Jericho's concert T-shirts, a standout from his usual classic rock music. I stretched my fingers across the white garage doors, light bleeding around its edges, the music thumping into my palm. Keeping my voice low, "I think there is someone inside."

"Cutting Crew," Jericho mumbled. He added, "'(I Just) Died in Your Arms Tonight.'"

"What?" Tracy asked, confused.

"The music," I answered and made room as Jericho pressed gently against the doors. He stepped back and unclipped his gun, metal rubbing on leather when he raised his weapon.

"Careful," Tracy warned, guns drawn together while we worked our fingers around the doors searching for trip wires. I took to one door with Jericho. Tracy took the other while Emanuel searched the top lip of both. They were barn doors that opened from the middle and swung out. The door Tracy worked opened slightly when she dug her fingers into the gap. "Guys, it's open."

"Police department, we have a warrant to search the premises!" I announced, knocking hard enough to rip the latex covering my knuckles. "We're coming in."

Emanuel opened the doors, swinging them wide in a quick and swift motion. The garage was brightly lit inside, the overheads blinding. There was a workbench to the left, a hundred assorted tools, most old and a few new that had been collected over the decades. Oily patches of grease stained the concrete where a car had been parked once, decades or more producing a collage.

The right side of the garage had a white curtain hung from a shower rod, the shadow of a bed or gurney behind it. There were also poles with medical bags like intravenous fluids and there was a body, the shape of a figure that wasn't moving. I waved for the team to move closer, carefully entering with weapons at the ready. I saw everything and nothing at the same time, uncertain if a booby trap or camera was hidden. Though the walls were open to the studs, there were plenty of pictures and calendars, some older than my team. No wires or cameras to be found. My focus shifted to the gurney and body as we migrated closer.

"Police department," I repeated, taking hold of the curtain and sweeping it open.

"Jesus Christ!" Emanuel blurted, peering down.

I froze. We all did. Small gasps escaped our lips. We were staring at death, or as close to death as could be imagined. It was a woman, and she was about the most tortured a person I think I'd ever seen.

Her eyes swam lazily, barely focusing as her gaze reached Tracy and Emanuel. She peered up at Jericho then, her brow rising so slight it was almost missed. She watched him a long time before her stare landed on me, the haunted appearance sending fright through me like a bolt of electricity. Another victim, barely clinging to what was left of her humanity.

Her mouth was covered with tape, the adhesive torn and chewed at the edges as though she'd tried to scream and gnaw her way to freedom. She was naked, her frame skeletal, the sharp ridges of her ribs stretching the skin like a drum. Thick leather straps crisscrossed her chest, abdomen, and thighs, their edges biting into her flesh, some so deep they merged into a network of oozing gashes. New wounds overlapped old ones, creating jagged scars that traced her body like a morbid map of suffering.

Her hair was a filthy curtain that hung in greasy strands, so sparse her scalp glared through unbearably bright. Her green eyes were too large for her skull, dark and sunken into bruised sockets. The skin around them had turned leathery like a corpse left in the sun too long. The victim's arms and legs were mere twigs too, mottled with sores, her gray skin as thin as tissue, each joint knotted and grotesque.

A filthy blanket, too small to offer any dignity, lay half covering her lower body. But nothing could hide the brutality carved into her. Every rib stood out, the breastbone a sharp peak jutting forward, threatening to pierce her skin from within.

And then I saw it. I saw the ragged scar that had visited my dreams and haunted me for years. It had faded and shrunk in the transformation, but was unmistakable, running across her eye and down her cheek. The skin had turned waxy, the mark a twisted trophy from a battle she'd fought with Jericho. The sight struck me like a fist to the throat. Staring at it, my breath caught, my stomach flipped. This wasn't just another victim. Scott Moore was behind this. Behind all of it. He had kept Paige Kotes and had tortured her. For how long? Years? How much suffering was that?

"Paige!?" I said in a yell, reaching for the leather straps and then stopping myself, emotions conflicted. This was the woman who'd tried to murder me and caused me to lose our baby. She was the woman who'd almost killed Jericho and had murdered his wife and countless others. But to look at her now, the disbelief disturbingly strong, I thought I had to be hallucinating and asked, "Paige Kotes?"

"Casey," she mumbled through the loose tape in a voice that was barely registering. "Help me."

"Casey?" Tracy bumped my arm, her expression haunted. "The setup, it's like what Riddle did."

"You're right," I answered, having seen this before. Tracy had too. It was the MO of a serial killer by the name of Riddle. And like before, there was a needle burrowed in Paige's arm, the bruising around it a storm of repetition, the track marks indicating this had been going on for weeks or more.

I followed the plastic tubing to beneath the gurney where a large pan was filled with blood, collecting it one sickening drop at a time. It was one of the steps the serial killer used to mummify his victims, slowly draining them of their blood, keeping them alive for extended periods, starving them, the torture unrelenting as their bodies ate themselves alive.

"Scott Moore?" I asked when I returned, holstering my gun. She half nodded, made weak by the forced bloodletting. I looked deep into her terrified eyes, realizing the scorpion had become the frog. Paige was the victim now and I suspected that her death was imminent. A tear trickled down the side of her face while I eased the loose tape from her mouth. She stared deep into my eyes and said, "Casey, help me!"

TWENTY-SEVEN

Blue lights continued to flash repeatedly, the rhythm playing out across the garage walls and on Paige's face. There was no knowing how much blood she'd lost. Or how much weight had been shed. I ran a finger over one of the straps, deciding to unbuckle it. I stopped when it pulled on her skin, Paige letting out a groan. Large sores swelled around the leather, skin folding over the sharp edge. Other bed sores were worse and smelling of deep infections. She was here too long to have possibly been involved in any of the murders.

"Her heart rate is thready and weak," a paramedic said, arriving soon after Paige lost consciousness. Her mouth had dropped open, and her breath turned shallow. She'd stopped blinking too, her gaze fixed on the garage ceiling. She looked at Jericho once more and closed them, the sight filling me with a foreboding sense of what was coming.

Jericho stood closer to me as Paige's breathing shifted subtly. We said nothing while at Paige's side in what became her final moments of life. There was one last gasp and then nothing. The paramedic checked her vitals again, turning to us and said, "She's gone. I'm sorry."

"Sorry?" I replied sharply, breath sticking as though it were a passing family member I'd mourn. But it wasn't. It was fucking Paige Kotes and there was no love lost. Yet, a small ember burned, sparking emotion from somewhere deep in me that I couldn't understand. Paige wasn't a family or an old friend. So why did I feel anything at all? "Oh shit."

"I know. I feel it too," Jericho confessed, his large hand pressed warmly against my back. I leaned into him briefly, feeling the moment before having to pivot to the police procedures that needed to be followed. "She took more from me than any person should ever experience. Casey, she took from us."

"She did," I mumbled, blue lights strobing dizzyingly, the flashes skipping off the tools and old license plates hanging on the garage walls. "I think we feel it because she was the victim here. That's all."

"This feels weird. Like I should be singing the 'Witch is Dead' song or something," Tracy said, going to the other side of the gurney. She slipped a fresh pair of latex over her fingers to start the investigation, softly humming the song's tempo, the melody catching.

"It *is* strange," I said, agreeing and emphasizing the moment. "But we've still got a killer on the loose and more answers than questions."

Tracy stopped humming and returned to stand next to me. She bumped my arm with a touch of affection and took Jericho's arm as well. "I can't imagine how this must feel for you guys."

"It's over. Let's get to work." Jericho nodded, cold air rushing over where his hand had been. He looked to the paramedic. "We're going to need the space, and the body."

"Sir?" the paramedic asked, removing his hands from the gurney. A young man, maybe a year into the service, his focus shifted to Jericho's badge. When he looked up, he asked, "I don't understand."

"This is a crime scene now," I answered. I raised my voice

then, loud enough for all to hear. "We'll need everyone not involved in processing the scene to exit the garage."

"Whose blood was that?" Tracy asked, easing the pail from beneath the gurney. She looked up at us, "If Paige was here, then whose blood was on Scott Moore's boat?"

"We don't know," Emanuel warned. "But Samantha and Derek finished and are on their way here."

"Maybe it was all a ruse?" I asked, thinking Scott Moore was alive and behind this. And that all of this was connected to Paige murdering Moore's daughter. He mirrored the murders, adding his daughter's initials, TF, to each victim, personalizing it. But why? I motioned to the bucket, tapping the side, rings vibrating across the surface like a rock tossed into a still pond. "This could be an elaborate plan. Revenge for his daughter and wife."

"Revenge?" Tracy said, asking while working the scene. "Including the blood?"

"All of it," I answered. "That visit to the boat when we met Hiccup, we were close. That could be why he staged his murder?"

"Possible," Jericho said but looked unconvinced. "I wouldn't rule out that Scott Moore is dead, his body carried away by the ocean's tide. We may never find him."

"You still believe Scott Moore is dead?" I asked. He shook his head with uncertainty, hanging onto the original idea. "It wasn't Paige Kotes. Couldn't have been her—"

"Scott Moore? He was a victim," Jericho interrupted, frustrated. "It's got to be someone else who was working with Paige and turned on her. It's like before. She's doing it again the way she brainwashed Barnes, my deputy, to murder my wife and Moore's daughter!"

"Casey? I think I've got something here," Emanuel yelled, his voice echoing slightly. He was at the workbench, flipping

through case files, copies taken from the station. "The collections case. The Jill Carter murder."

"Collections!" Tracy exclaimed. "Another victim?"

"Today," Emanuel answered, holding a calendar. We gathered closer, the dates circled, each of them identifying with a
murder, including the day of the car bomb. The date of the 'I
am Mudborn' poem was on there too, the date it was delivered to the station. A sinking feeling hit me when I saw
today's date circled, Paige's name crossed out in blood-red ink.
Every minute of the case had been orchestrated, each of us a
puppet.

"The last line on today. It says 'junkyard', 'Amanda Rolly'
and a time," I said, checking the time against the nearby clock.
"It's another victim."

The junkyard loomed ahead, the same that had been the center
of a recent case. It hadn't changed at all, the wasteland of
twisted metal and broken glass bathed in the dying light of
dusk. It smelled of rust, oil, and damp earth—a place where
things were abandoned, forgotten, and left to decay. The
skeletal remains of old cars were piled high, their stripped
frames jutting out like bones from the earth, walls erected that
edged the property.

Emanuel took the final turn hard, gravel spitting under the
tires as we sped through the open gates. The chain-link fence on
either side rattled in protest. The lot was a maze of wreckage,
battered vehicles stacked on top of one another, their corroded
edges gleaming faintly under the orange glow of an oil drum fire
at the center of it all.

And standing there, like a specter from a nightmare, was
Scott Moore. He looked worse than before, impossibly aged as
though this was to be a conclusion, an end to a plan. A cigarette
hung from his lips, the smoke curling lazily around his weath-

ered face. His tattered fishing cap was pulled low over his cold, calculating eyes. But it was his arm that drew my attention.

A thick, hastily wrapped bandage covered much of his forearm, blood seeping through in dark patches. I knew, in that instant, that we had been right about the possible ruse. That this was the source of the blood we'd found on his boat. He'd tried to make it look like Paige Kotes had killed him.

But now, here he was, alive. Dangerous. Armed. And standing over a child. Her name was Amanda Rolly, and Alice confirmed for us that the child's parents filed a missing person report less than two hours earlier. Amanda lay at Moore's feet, her tiny body curled in on itself like she was trying to disappear into the dirt.

Her pale skin had lost all color, and her wild, red-rimmed eyes darted between us and Moore, pleading silently. My blood turned to ice when her eyes found mine. The gag in her mouth muffled any sound she might have made, but her breathing was rapid and erratic. She was bleeding.

Flames reflected on the blade from the knife Moore held in his right hand, fresh blood clinging to the steel. The wound on Amanda's side looked superficial and had me wondering if Moore maybe hesitated, maybe he'd wanted to kill her but couldn't. Maybe he'd been having second thoughts. But that didn't matter. We were out of time.

"Moore!" Jericho was the first to step forward, his voice cold as steel. "Let her go."

"Why?" Moore replied, eyes shifting to Jericho. For a moment, something like amusement crossed his face. He took a long drag of his cigarette before flicking it aside, the embers dying as it hit the gravel. "She's already dead."

I followed Jericho, taking a step forward, my hand twitching toward my gun. "She's not dead, Moore. But if you kill her, you don't come back from that."

He let out a hissing chuckle and shook his head. "You think

I care about coming back?" He lifted the knife slightly, pointing it at Jericho. "You should know what this feels like, Sheriff."

"Moore!" Jericho said, fists clenched at his sides, his jaw tightening. "You don't want to do this."

Moore's lip curled. "You still don't get it, do you?" His voice was low, venomous. "This isn't about what I want. This is about what you and your wife Jessie. And what you two let happen to my girl."

The family portrait from Moore's home flashed in my mind. This *was* about his daughter and wife. I took another slow step forward, my voice measured. "Moore—"

"Shut the fuck up!" His voice cracked like a whip, eyes locking onto me now.

"You don't get to stand there, Detective White, and tell me what I should or shouldn't do. You! You had her—" he jabbed the knife toward me— "that makes you just as guilty as he is."

Jericho's stance shifted slightly. "Moore, we were victims too."

Moore barked another humorless laugh. "Victims? You call yourselves victims?" His face darkened, his grip tightening on the knife. "You let Paige Kotes run free. You had a chance to stop her, but you let her kill my daughter."

His voice was hoarse now, thick with pain. His eyes dipped toward Amanda, and I could see it. I could see the conflict battling inside him. It was the struggle between what the man who had once been a father was, and the monster that grief had turned him into. In that moment, I saw our chance.

"Scott, what would your daughter say?" My voice cut through the tension like a blade. "And your wife? What would they both say if they saw you about to murder a little girl?"

He twitched, his gaze jumping around. "Don't talk about them."

"Why not?" I took another step. "This isn't justice. This is you becoming the thing that destroyed them."

"It's not!" he yelled. His breathing hitched. The knife in his hand wavered. Jericho saw it too. "It's justice!"

"She took my wife from me too," Jericho said suddenly, his voice quieter now, rough. "Paige Kotes." He swallowed hard. "She killed my wife the day she killed your daughter."

The words hung in the air, as heavy as the rusted cars surrounding us.

Moore hesitated.

Jericho took a step closer. "She killed Casey's unborn child."

Moore blinked, his features softened. A second passed and his fingers twitched on the knife's handle.

"Look at Amanda," I demanded, knowing the look. Doubt. Conflict. I pointed down at the girl at his feet. "Look at her, Moore. You're about to take someone else's daughter. Someone else's family."

For a moment, just a moment, his face crumbled. "She has to die," he whispered, the madness too deep. His knuckles went white around the handle. "You all have to die."

Jericho moved first. He moved fast, lunging. At once, the world exploded into motion. Moore barely had time to react before Jericho slammed into him like a battering ram, the sound a concussive force of bodies crashing to the ground. The knife flashed while I dove for Amanda, grabbing her and rolling away just as Moore swung wildly.

Tracy was there, hands shaking as she worked to free Amanda's bindings. Emanuel grabbed for Moore's arms, wrestling him into the dirt, their fighting against the desperate thrashing of a man with nothing left to lose.

Amanda was safely behind us, Tracy's eyes wild as she sturdily braced for Moore if he broke free. I leaped between Amanda and the struggle which had turned brutal. Fists swung with a blur, punches landing with yells and guttural grunts, Moore howling, his rage spilling out of him in sharp, animalistic wails. But Emanuel and Jericho were stronger, the cuffs snapping into place around Moore's wrists with a metallic click. It was over.

Or so I thought. A shiver ran across my body when I saw the blood, when I saw Jericho staggering back, swaying slightly, his breath hitched. It was the knife. And it was buried in his side, just below the ribs. The world stopped. My heart froze.

TWENTY-EIGHT

"Jericho?" I asked. "Babe?"

"Huh?" he muttered. He blinked down at the wound, annoyed, like he hadn't even noticed it. Then he let out a soft chuckle. "Well, shit. That's gonna need a few stitches."

"Stitches!?" I wanted to shake him, to yell at him, to make him sit down. But instead, he reached down, picked up his sheriff's hat from where it had fallen, dusted it off, and placed it back on his head.

Bleeding, a dark patch running down his shirt and leg, Jericho began to Mirandize Moore. His voice was as steady as ever. "Scott Moore, you have the right to remain silent—"

"Jericho," I said, reaching him. He continued, the knife buried in his side, his breath coming in slow, measured pulls as if he'd will himself not to bleed. The damn fool was pretending everything was fine.

He glanced once at me and in true Jericho Flynn fashion, he kept talking. "Anything you say can and will…" He exhaled, his jaw clenching against the pain as he continued to Mirandize Moore. I wanted to shake him, force him to sit the hell down, but I knew better. Jericho wouldn't stop, not until Moore was secured and locked away.

"I got you," Moore spat with a sneer, blood dribbling down his split lip. He was still on the ground beneath Emanuel's weight and let out a hoarse laugh. His sun-beaten face was contorted in something between amusement and fury. "Look at you now! Bleeding out for what? Some damn justice?"

"... be used against you in the court of law..."

"Justice died when Paige Kotes got to my little girl," Moore continued to say, his laugh becoming cries.

Jericho didn't even acknowledge him. "You have the right to an attorney..." He was pale now, a sickly sheen clinging to his skin. My stomach twisted in knots, my hands on his back and assessing the wound.

"How is he?" Tracy asked, her hands still gripping Amanda. The child still hadn't spoken, her body trembling against Tracy's chest, fingers wound so tightly into the fabric of her jacket that her knuckles had gone white. Amanda should have been home in bed, safe, wrapped up in the warmth of her blankets, a child with nothing to fear but the dark. Instead, she was here, in this graveyard of broken things, staring wide-eyed at a bloodstained sheriff who refused to fall.

"Sit down!" I demanded. I pressed a hand against Jericho's arm, forcing him to acknowledge me. "You need to sit down."

He finally turned his head toward me, blinking like he was just now registering the weight of the knife in his side. "I was almost done," he muttered, sounding more annoyed than anything. "If you cannot afford an attorney..."

"Jericho, you're losing too much blood."

He gave me that damn lazy smirk. "I've lost worse."

Moore chuckled darkly, shaking his head where he lay in the dirt. "Jesus. You two deserve each other."

I ignored him, looking toward Emanuel. "Get him out of here."

Emanuel nodded, grabbing Moore by the cuffs and hauling him up like a sack of garbage. Moore cried out, staggering under the weight of his own exhaustion, but I didn't care. I had more important things to deal with.

"Babe?" Jericho started to tilt.

I barely caught him in time, my arms coming around him as his weight slumped against me. Tears stung and emotion swelled. "That's enough cowboy crap for one night."

"Huh?" Jericho let out a pained chuckle, his head dipping toward my shoulder. It was shock, the adrenaline wearing. His voice was slurred, thick with exhaustion. "Did we get him?"

I tightened my grip on him. "Yeah. We got him."

"Good." His knees buckled, and I sank with him, guiding him down onto the hood of Emanuel's car as carefully as I could. "Hell of a night, huh?"

"Officer down!" I yelled into my radio. I wanted to be mad and yell, but the blood was flowing like the tears running down my face. Instead, I pressed hard against his side, trying to slow it down. "I need a medic at Patsy's Junkyard!"

Jericho grimaced. "Not down."

I glared at him. "Jericho—"

"Just... sitting." His smirk faltered as his eyes fluttered.

"Yeah? Well, you're gonna stay sitting," I snapped. "Or so help me, I will tape you to this damn car until the ambulance gets here."

Tracy was suddenly at my side, Amanda still clinging to her.

"How bad is it?" she asked, her voice tight with worry.

"Deep," I said, hating to admit it. "Blood is bright. I don't know if that's good or bad. And he's too damn stubborn to notice he's hurt."

Jericho snorted weakly. "Flattery will get you nowhere."

Tracy let out a shaky breath, looking down at Amanda.

"She needs medical attention too. The wounds aren't deep, but she's—" She swallowed hard. "She's in shock."

I looked at Amanda, really looked at her. Her dark, tear-streaked eyes were locked on Jericho's wound, on the blood pulsing through my fingers, on the way the sheriff sagged against the car like a broken puppet. That's what we'd become to Moore, broken puppets. Amanda didn't blink, didn't move. It was like she wasn't there anymore.

I softened my tone, reaching out. "Amanda?" She flinched. I pulled back, my heart aching. "You're safe now."

"She's been through too much," Tracy whispered. "We need to get her out of here."

"Soon," I promised. "First, let's get—"

The distant whine of sirens cut through the air, flashing lights reflecting off the rusted metal around us. The paramedics were here.

Finally.

They rushed toward us, dust kicking. I barely had time to step back before they swarmed Jericho, pushing me aside to start checking his vitals. One of them hissed under their breath as they examined the knife. "Jesus," the other muttered. "You should be unconscious right now."

Jericho exhaled, eyes fluttering again. "I get that a lot."

I crossed my arms, watching as they worked, keeping one eye on Jericho, the other on Amanda. Moore was gone now, shoved into the back of a patrol car, his fate sealed. He would rot in a prison cell, left with nothing but his grief and his hatred.

But Amanda? The girl was his last victim and would have to live with this. She'd carry this night with her for the rest of her life. That was something that couldn't be fixed. A weight settled in my chest.

A second ambulance arrived, paramedics attending to Amanda, custody transferring from Tracy, her saying, "You got her?"

"We have her," the paramedic answered. "Hon, can you tell us your name."

Amanda remained silent, Tracy by my side, squeezing my arm gently. She tried to sound assuring, "Jericho will be fine. Amanda too."

I nodded. But deep down, I wondered if that would ever be enough.

"Need to Mirandize him," Jericho groaned as the paramedics finally lifted him onto a stretcher. "It's important."

One of the paramedics gave him a pointed look. "You should be in a lot more pain right now."

Jericho grunted, shifting against the gurney. "I'll feel it in the morning."

"You'll feel it now," I shot back, my voice shaking despite the steel I tried to force into it. "And you're going to the hospital. No arguments."

His lips twitched, a ghost of his usual cocky smirk, but even that was weak. He tipped his hat at me with fingers that barely held strength. "Yes, ma'am," he murmured.

I rolled my eyes, half convinced that maybe, just maybe, he wasn't as bad off as I feared. The paramedics lifted the gurney. That's when his eyes slid shut. His jaw slackened. And his chest! His chest wasn't moving.

"Wait!" The word ripped from my throat as I lunged forward and grabbed his hand. His fingers were cold. They were never cold. The feel of them turned my stomach inside out.

"Sheriff?" the paramedic said, driving and wiggling a knuckle into Jericho's chest bone.

"No. No, no, no. You don't get to do this, Jericho. Not today. Not ever." I clutched his hand tighter, like I could force life back into him through sheer will.

The paramedic's voice sliced through my head. "Pulse is weak."

Weak? I heard. Tears blurred my vision. I swallowed hard, trying to keep my voice steady, trying to keep him here. "Babe —" I choked, my breath stuttering. I forced a smile, even as tears dripped onto Jericho's face. He needed hope. He needed me. "We're getting married, remember?"

"Casey?" I heard Tracy in my ear, felt her tugging on my arm. "Casey?"

"Jericho!" my voice cracked, but I kept going, because if I stopped, if I let go, I'd lose him. "You have to stay. You have to. Okay? You promised."

Jericho didn't respond. He didn't squeeze my hand back. He stayed limp as they rushed him into the ambulance, doors slamming like gunfire behind them. The junkyard around me felt impossibly silent, the wind humming through rusted-out cars like a funeral song. Then the ambulance sirens wailed to life, slicing through the night, rattling my bones.

Amanda Rolly was safe. Scott Moore was in custody.

But Jericho?

Jericho had to live. He had to.

For now, that fragile and desperate hope was all I had left.

As evening settled over the Outer Banks and Jericho was wheeled into surgery, the events of the day lingered with me and Tracy and Emanuel. It had left a mark on all of us, including Hiccup who Tracy eagerly took home to watch over. But it hit Jericho the worst. I sat, unmoving and saying little as people from all over stopped to say a few words. I'd nod hospitably, even forcing a faint smile when tone and body language dictated it. But mostly, I stared at the floor tiles and the busy shuffle of shoes passing. The chairs and the room filled and emptied, a tide of uniforms coming from stations across the barrier islands, some staying with us. Now, we waited.

I regarded the events that led to this moment, ultimately

blaming Paige Kotes again. Had she not been in our lives, none of this would have happened. Even Scott Moore's path in life would look dramatically different, if lifelines hadn't intersected, crossing with terrible consequences. He'd once been a man like any other. A fisherman, a husband, and a father. A man who worked hard. Who loved his family. And who had likely never imagined himself standing over a bleeding child with a knife in his hand.

But grief had hollowed him out. Loss had twisted him into something unrecognizable and caused him to live a quiet life of violence—a product of his remorse and resentments. He wasn't just a killer. He was the aftermath of a tragedy. A man so broken by what had been taken from him that he no longer resembled who he once was.

That was the real tragedy, wasn't it? That a man who had lived for his family had become a monster in their name.

TWENTY-NINE

The day began with a funeral. The world was safe from Scott Moore, Emanuel having escorted the man to the station jail where he was a guest of the Outer Banks police department. He was already scheduled for a transfer to the mainland and to a state-run facility where we anticipated he'd remain the rest of his life. He talked. He talked a lot, the district attorney and assigned defense attorney acting like scribes as new charges were announced almost daily, sometimes twice and three times.

Some of what Scott Moore had done lay a few feet from us. It was a casket, the ground around it soft enough for me to lean onto my toes. But no matter what, steadying myself alone would be impossible. I needed Tracy's arm to hold onto. Across from the casket, Emanuel stood with his wife, arms looped, their faces somber. Derek attended the funeral with his wife too, along with Samantha and her partner.

The mayor and district attorneys were there, both life-long friends of Jericho. And there were many from the station, including Alice, her hair big and poofed, the wind bending it sideways. Tracy wove her arm with mine, hands clasped. She was dressed in black like me, including the shoes.

Sunlight beamed from between the clouds, rays shining bright on Jericho's face as he stood beside the casket, his son Ryan by his side. He placed his hand on the rosy wood where the shine was bright, his wife's remains inside. He was dressed in a black suit and was clean-shaven, his face smooth and making him look boyishly charming. When he glanced over the casket, a grimace showed briefly, sutures straining from the surgery.

A pastor stood on the opposite side, Bible in hand, the wind turning the thin pages for him. He motioned to Jericho and faced us, the time coming for us to return Jessie Flynn's remains to where they belonged, and undo Scott Moore's attempt to unnerve us all. It was more than an attempt. He'd succeeded. And though Moore never discussed the exhumation, we all suspected Paige may have been behind the idea, regardless of her state.

Birds flitted along the trees that lined the cemetery. The motion took Jericho's attention a moment as a pair of cardinals landed on a nearby headstone. Red and gold, the brighter of the two beamed in the sunshine, food in its beak, it offered it to the other. He'd told me once how Jessie and his son were avid birdwatchers and I'm sure he believed in some way the nearby cardinals were a sign from her, telling him she was okay. The moment was fleeting, the pair leaving a second later when the pastor began the short ceremony. He spoke longer than expected, the ground turning softer, Tracy and I leaning on one another.

"Thank you, Pastor," Jericho said when it was over. He stepped up to Jessie's casket, a single flower in hand, the only one brought today. "I'd never imagined standing here with Jessie again. Not like this."

"He sounds sad?" Tracy whispered in my ear.

"Mm-hmm," I answered softly.

"I am, Tracy," Jericho said, surprising us, his hearing impressive.

"Sorry," she replied.

He shook his head and announced, "Tracy said that I sounded sad. And I am. But in a way, I am happy too. I've been given another opportunity to say goodbye." Jericho had to stop, eyes wet. He fought the emotion, voice breaking as he continued, "Grief stole my first goodbyes. It stole a lot of things. And sadly, I never returned here to say it properly."

"You're here now, it's okay, Jericho," Emanuel said supportively. He wiped at an errant tear, adding, "Jessie knew."

Jericho turned once more to face the casket and placed his hand atop it, the image so striking that I felt it in my heart. He still loved her. Grieved her. And perhaps he always would. "Goodbye, Jessie."

Like I said, the day began with a funeral. But it ended with a wedding. A few hours later, I'd traded my black dress for a white one. White shoes too, only there were no heels needed. Not where we were going. With the sand beneath our feet, it was sandals for most of us and a few of us choosing to go barefoot. I wore a delicate anklet too, which was something borrowed and blue. My hair was pinned and folded and rolled every which way I thought possible, the stylist changing it a few times to get it right. I'd glanced at the mirror, checking the progress and measuring it against a picture torn from a magazine that Tracy had brought with her. There were golden highlights I didn't even know I had, along with a few gray strands that the stylist had done her best to hide. For this bride, it was close enough and I'd be happy to get out of the chair. For now, the stylist worked it some more while Tracy directed.

"You look amazing!" Tracy said, champagne flute in hand, bubbles clinging to a strawberry at the bottom. A hiccup rode on a burp, the pair abruptly cut off with a laugh. She held up her glass, saying, "I better watch it with these."

"Yes, at least until the reception," I told her, sipping my water.

"Hmmm." Her eyes narrowed like a cat's, eyeing the water bottle. "Nothing last night either."

"It's my wedding day," I explained. Not that I felt I needed an explanation, I just wasn't ready to tell her everything.

Another giggle, Tracy finished her glass, adding, "Don't you just want to feel a little sloppy?"

"I think you'll be sloppy enough for the both of us," I told her and handed over my water. "Drink some."

Reluctantly, she took the water, a comical pout on her face while returning to the magazine page. She didn't notice I was staring. But I was. She was gorgeous. I didn't just mean that because she was my daughter. Or maybe I did and just didn't care. Tracy was a beautiful woman. From one of the other magazines, she'd picked the bridesmaids' dresses, a sleeveless lavender dress with a thin shawl around her bare shoulders, they were formal enough for a wedding and also perfect for the beach. Tracy was a stunner. I turned back to the mirror while the last of the makeup was touched up around my eyes, Alice's voice sounding from the door, "I think we're ready. Ladies?"

"They're lining up!" Nichelle Wilkinson said, rushing toward us and wearing the same dress as Tracy. Her eyes were big and beautiful as she stared at me through the mirror. She'd made the drive from Philadelphia to be here, a former member of our team who'd gone on to work for the FBI and who I'd gotten close enough to consider like a daughter. Her lips shined with gloss, the same deep red that I'd applied to mine. And her bronze skin glowed in the window's sunlight while her hair stood tall and was as beautiful as ever. She'd surely turn a few heads today. Hopping up and down, eyelids peeled and eyes beaming like lights. "Are you excited!"

"Of course," I said, but my words were a lie. I was suddenly terribly nervous, my legs wobbly like rubber and my ass cheeks seemingly glued to the chair. I faced the mirror, pinching my lips on a napkin, blotting the lipstick, the color a little too strong for my complexion. It looked great on Nichelle and Tracy, but I thought it made me look like the walking dead. Samantha knelt next to me, looking at me through the mirror, the usual presence of her dark bangs missing. She'd pinned back her hair to show all her face. She was as beautiful as I wanted to be and wanted to feel. They all were. "Have I mentioned that you guys look so amazing!"

Sensing the disappointment, Samantha assured me, "Casey, you're the bride. You're the most beautiful person here today!"

"I think I'm having a minor crisis of confidence," I said, the three of them dismissing it. I forced myself to stand, music from a string quartet reaching us with the first song. I knew it from the list me and Jericho worked, my heart sinking, "Shit, it's time. That's our cue."

"Girls, line up," Alice said, clapping softly. At some point, she'd become our impromptu wedding coordinator, and I was so happy to have her step into the role. There was nobody better than Alice to take on the job.

"Going to the chapel and gonna get married!" Tracy began to sing, voice rising. It was the hundredth time, possibly more, the notes stuck in my brain. When nobody had joined in, she raised her voice, filling the room until Samantha and Nichelle sang.

Even Alice belted a verse, her singing voice off key on nearly every note. "Gonna get married and..." She stood in front of me, taking my hands, her fingers warm. She stopped singing, a motherly look appearing, the sight giving me loving goose-bumps. Her chin quivered, "My dear, you are a beautiful bride."

"Thank you," I said and knelt next to Tabitha who'd been

ready to go since before we arrived. She carried a basket of flower petals, some starting to wilt, her knuckles white in a firm grasp of the wicker handle. I tucked a loose strand of her white hair behind an ear, asking, "Are you ready, baby girl?"

Her mouth twisted, she took some of the petals, asking, "You said to drop these on the *run-ger* thing?"

"The *runner* thing. Un-huh," I answered as the door opened and sounds from the beach flooded the room. Seagulls called and waves broke, we took our places to proceed outside, my sandals sinking just as much as I'd expected they would. For the wedding, I was glad we traded heels for flats—we'd picked the most beautiful ocean front beach in the Outer Banks. I glanced around at the faces, many from my past in Philadelphia and many more from the surprising, unexpected life I'd started in the barrier islands.

I took Tracy's hand and squeezed it, staring deep into her eyes and saying a million things without speaking a word. Where would I have been if I hadn't decided that day to take a chance on a clue that brought me here and brought my daughter back into my life? She'd been missing for so long and everyone had given up.

But I never gave up and now there was an entire life built around that single decision. That life includes Jericho and Thomas and Tabitha. It includes friends and family and a home when all I'd had were a few bags of clothes in the backseat of an old, beat-up car. And it included a new member of the family that nobody, not even Jericho, knew about yet. I'd tell them soon. But not today. I'm sure Tracy would become suspicious soon. It wasn't often I'd pass on a glass of bubbly. My heart filled and walloped hard when the music's tempo changed and everyone stood. "Oh my. Tracy, here we go."

"Mom?" Tracy asked, her voice sounding like the little girl I'd lost years before.

My goosebumps had goosebumps, and I gripped my fingers tightly around hers. I dared a look, trying not to cry.

"I love you."

"I love you too," I answered, smiling broad enough to hurt. In a whisper, I started to sing, "Gonna get married..."

The silly song was stuck in my head. It turned distant when I looked for Jericho. I needed to see him. I needed to see his face, and then I'd know everything was okay. I found Emanuel first, standing at the front, waiting. He was our officiant and held a book in his large hands, sunlight bright on his smiling face. Faces of friends and family blocked Jericho.

This was our wedding day, which had eluded us until now. We'd exchanged vows privately once before while drifting alone in the ocean, floating on waves. But now we were making it real, formal and in front of everyone. I eased up onto my toes and searched past the smiles until I saw him, saw that handsome ruggedness I'd fallen in love with when we first met in a hospital waiting room.

His eyes were glistening, the corners creased from a smile that was fixed from ear to ear. He dipped his chin ever so slightly, speaking to me without saying anything. I took a step, the first toward a new life, Tracy by my side, walking me down the aisle.

I was connected to this place, connected to the people and to Jericho. The ocean roared nearby, its waves crashing and the sun setting behind us. It was our wedding day, and it was perfect.

"I'm good now, Tracy. I'm ready."

A LETTER FROM B.R. SPANGLER

Dear reader,

I want to say a huge thank you for choosing to read *Shadow on Her Grave*. If you did enjoy it, and want to keep up to date with all my latest releases, just sign up at the following link. Your email address will never be shared and you can unsubscribe at any time.

www.bookouture.com/br-spangler

I hope you loved *Shadow on Her Grave* and if you did I would be very grateful if you could write a review. I'd love to hear what you think, and it makes such a difference helping new readers to discover one of my books for the first time.

I love hearing from my readers – you can get in touch through social media or my website.

Thanks,

B.R. Spangler

KEEP IN TOUCH WITH B.R. SPANGLER

www.brspangler.com

facebook.com/authorbrianspangler

x.com/BR_Spangler

instagram.com/brspangler

PUBLISHING TEAM

Turning a manuscript into a book requires the efforts of many people. The publishing team at Bookouture would like to acknowledge everyone who contributed to this publication.

Audio
Alba Proko
Sinead O'Connor
Melissa Tran

Commercial
Lauren Morrissette
Hannah Richmond
Imogen Allport

Data and analysis
Mark Alder
Mohamed Bussuri

Cover design
Head Design Ltd.

Editorial
Kelsie Marsden
Nadia Michael

RAISING READERS

Books Build Bright Futures

Dear Reader,

We'd love your attention for one more page to tell you about the crisis in children's reading, and what we can all do.

Studies have shown that reading for fun is the **single biggest predictor of a child's future life chances** – more than family circumstance, parents' educational background or income. It improves academic results, mental health, wealth, communication skills, ambition and happiness.

The number of children reading for fun is in rapid decline. Young people have a lot of competition for their time, and a worryingly high number do not have a single book at home.

Hachette works extensively with schools, libraries and literacy charities, but here are some ways we can all raise more readers:

- Reading to children for just 10 minutes a day makes a difference
- Don't give up if children aren't regular readers – there will be books for them!

- Visit bookshops and libraries to get recommendations
- Encourage them to listen to audiobooks
- Support school libraries
- Give books as gifts

There's a lot more information about how to encourage children to read on our websites: **www.RaisingReaders.co.uk** and **www.JoinRaisingReaders.com**.

Thank you for reading.

hachette
UK

Printed in Dunstable, United Kingdom